A one-man
weapon
of mass
destruction…

continued . . .

THE CARDINAL OF THE KREMLIN
The superpowers race for the ultimate Star Wars
missile defense system . . .

"*CARDINAL* EXCITES, ILLUMINATES . . . A REAL
PAGE-TURNER."   —*Los Angeles Daily News*

CLEAR AND PRESENT DANGER
The killing of three U.S. officials in Colombia ignites the
American government's explosive, and top secret, response . . .

"A CRACKLING GOOD YARN." —*The Washington Post*

THE SUM OF ALL FEARS
The disappearance of an Israeli nuclear weapon threatens the
balance of power in the Middle East—and around the world . . .

"CLANCY AT HIS BEST . . . NOT TO BE MISSED."
—*The Dallas Morning News*

WITHOUT REMORSE
His code name is Mr. Clark. And his work for the CIA
is brilliant, cold-blooded, and efficient . . . but who is he really?

"HIGHLY ENTERTAINING."   —*The Wall Street Journal*

Tom Clancy's

SPLINTER CELL®

FALLOUT

WRITTEN BY

DAVID MICHAELS

BERKLEY BOOKS, NEW YORK

THE BERKLEY PUBLISHING GROUP
Published by the Penguin Group
Penguin Group (USA) Inc.
375 Hudson Street, New York, New York 10014, USA
Penguin Group (Canada), 90 Eglinton Avenue East, Suite 700, Toronto, Ontario M4P 2Y3, Canada
(a division of Pearson Penguin Canada Inc.)
Penguin Books Ltd., 80 Strand, London WC2R 0RL, England
Penguin Group Ireland, 25 St. Stephen's Green, Dublin 2, Ireland (a division of Penguin Books Ltd.)
Penguin Group (Australia), 250 Camberwell Road, Camberwell, Victoria 3124, Australia
(a division of Pearson Australia Group Pty. Ltd.)
Penguin Books India Pvt. Ltd., 11 Community Centre, Panchsheel Park, New Delhi—110 017, India
Penguin Group (NZ), 67 Apollo Drive, Rosedale, North Shore 0632, New Zealand
(a division of Pearson New Zealand Ltd.)
Penguin Books (South Africa) (Pty.) Ltd., 24 Sturdee Avenue, Rosebank, Johannesburg 2196,
South Africa

Penguin Books Ltd., Registered Offices: 80 Strand, London WC2R 0RL, England

This is a work of fiction. Names, characters, places, and incidents either are the product of the author's imagination or are used fictitiously, and any resemblance to actual persons, living or dead, business establishments, events, or locales is entirely coincidental.

TOM CLANCY'S SPLINTER CELL®: FALLOUT

A Berkley Book / published by arrangement with Rubicon, Inc.

PRINTING HISTORY
Berkley edition / November 2007

Copyright © 2007 by Rubicon, Inc.
Splinter Cell, Sam Fisher, Ubisoft, and the Ubisoft logo are trademarks of Ubisoft in the U.S. and other countries. Tom Clancy's Splinter Cell copyright © 2004 by Ubisoft Entertainment S.A.
Front cover illustration by axb group/Greg Horn. Stepback art by Greg Horn.
Cover design by Rita Frangie.
Interior text design by Kristin del Rosario.

ISBN: 978-0-425-21824-2

BERKLEY®
Berkley Books are published by The Berkley Publishing Group,
a division of Penguin Group (USA) Inc.,
375 Hudson Street, New York, New York 10014.
BERKLEY® is a registered trademark of Penguin Group (USA) Inc.
The "B" design is a trademark belonging to Penguin Group (USA) Inc.

PRINTED IN THE UNITED STATES OF AMERICA

10 9 8 7 6 5 4 3 2 1

To all the loyal "Fisherists" skulking about out there.

ACKNOWLEDGMENTS

While I've said it before, it bears repeating: The author is but the "face" of a book. The heart, muscles, and oftentimes the brains of a book work behind the scenes, unseen, and too often unacknowledged.

Thanks to the following for helping make *Tom Clancy's Splinter Cell: Fallout* the great book it is:

Tom Colgan, Sandy Harding, and everyone else at The Berkley Publishing Group. Thanks for making me look good.

Michael Ovitz and Chris George. Thanks for your confidence.

From Ubisoft: Joshua Meyer, Richard Dansky, Alexis Nolent, Olivier Henriot, Ubisoft Legal Department, and everyone else who has a hand in producing *Splinter Cell*. (All of whom I forgot to recognize in the last book. My apologies.)

Pam Ahearn. Thanks for your support and dedication. You're the best, Pam.

Tom Clancy, without whom *Splinter Cell* wouldn't exist.

And, of course, my wife. I'm glad you're in my life.

1

FISHER knew he was being followed. He knew it by the obvious signs, of course, but he also felt it in his gut. What he didn't know was how many there were and when they would make their move. He'd already picked up the package right under their noses, so they certainly weren't going to let him reach the drop-off. But how close would they let him get?

He stopped before the window of a watch shop and stood admiring the newest Tissots on display. From the corner of his eye, he saw the man he'd named Tail 6.1 (one watcher on his six o'clock position) also stop before a window to study the merchandise. The man was good; as Fisher watched, the man pulled out his cell phone, dialed, then said after a moment, "No, I'm looking at it right now . . . yeah, the exact one you've been looking for . . ."

A good tail personalizes his or her cover, Fisher reminded himself. Without that, a watcher tends to carry a "pursuit aura" that anyone with even the most rudimentary counter-surveillance training would pick up on.

". . . no, the one on Franklin Street . . . right. Okay, bye."

Walking fifty feet behind Tail 6.1, Tail 6.2.2 (two watchers together, a man and woman walking arm in arm, second position behind the first tail), passed their compatriot at the shop window and kept walking, passing Fisher a few seconds later and continuing down the sidewalk. Fisher mentally switched their designation to Tail 12.2—they were now in the lead tail position.

He'd been keeping this imaginary clock face in his head for the past two hours, moving the various pawns around as they changed positions and proximity to him. They were all very good, moving seamlessly as they kept a blanket of surveillance over him, all the while changing clothes and partners and demeanors in hopes of remaining invisible to him. It hadn't worked, but neither had he been able to lose them with the routine dry-cleaning tactics. The other factor: Did they know he'd made them? Probably not; if they did, they would've already taken him.

It would have been ridiculous—all these do-they-know-I-know machinations—if it hadn't been so deadly serious. They'd already come close to catching him in the act two weeks earlier; if it happened this time, he was done.

Fisher checked his watch. Another ten minutes was all he needed.

Ten minutes and one last attempt to lose them.

He turned from the shop window and continued down the sidewalk, but at a slower pace, letting the couple ahead of him gain some distance. The sidewalk and streets were moist with fog from the bay, and the mist swirled around the streetlights, rainbow-hued halos that seemed to shift and pulse as Fisher's path took him closer or farther from each one. In the distance he could hear the mournful gong of navigation buoys.

Ahead he could see the entrance to the alley, a darkened rectangle between two buildings. He'd chosen it the night before for a number of reasons: It sat equidistant between two streetlamps; its end was blocked by a tall hurricane fence topped with barbed wire; and, if he timed it correctly, his lead tails would round the corner ahead before he reached the alley entrance. And, once inside, to keep him in sight, one or more of the watchers would have to follow him in— probably the lone man on his tail. *So, ten seconds for him to reach the entrance, thirty more waiting to see if his target reemerged*, Fisher thought. With luck, he'd have forty seconds to do what he needed to do.

Keeping his eyes fixed on the couple ahead and his ears tuned to the click of heels on the sidewalk behind him, Fisher adjusted his pace, waiting, waiting . . . T he couple ahead rounded the corner. Fisher drew even with the alley's entrance and continued for three more paces, then abruptly wheeled left and strode into the shadowed alley. Feeling the darkness envelop him, Fisher felt a wave of relief. For most of his career, he'd worked strictly in the shadows, and he'd come to think of them as his closest ally. Conversely, this cloak-and-dagger business was done mostly in plain sight.

It was a different kind of game altogether. It had taken some getting used to.

On flat feet he sprinted halfway down the alley until he reached the darkened doorway to his left, then ducked into it. Just as he'd left it, the tin garbage can lid was propped against the brick wall. He snatched it up, tucked it between his legs, then reached above his head and snagged the lowermost rung of the building's fire escape. He chinned himself onto the grated catwalk above and then crab-walked to the right until he reached the first stairway and started upward. At the next landing, he grasped the garbage can lid like a Frisbee in his right hand, leaned over the railing, took aim, and hurled the lid. It sailed true, arcing down the alley. It slammed into the hurricane fence at the far end, bounced off the fencing with a twanging rattle, and crashed into the garbage cans against the wall.

Fisher was already moving, bounding silently up the fire escape ladder two steps at a time. He stopped, pressed his body against the wall, and listened. Below him he could hear heels clicking in the alley. He looked down. His lone tail, having heard the commotion, recognizing it for what it was, and assuming his target was making a run for it, had taken the bait.

The final piece of Fisher's ploy—a homeless man he'd paid $100 to wait in the alley on the other side of the fence until he got his cue—now played his part and shuffled down the alley toward its opposite entrance.

Fisher heard a muttered "Damn," then saw his tail lift his jacket cuff to his lips: "Target on run . . . heading east toward Auburn . . ." The tail turned and sprinted from the alley.

Attaboy, Fisher thought and started a new timer in his head. *Two minutes. No more.*

Ten seconds after the tail disappeared around the corner, a blue van with a red and yellow Johnson & Sons Plumbing placard on its side raced past the alley's entrance and squealed around the corner. Fisher gave the van five more seconds, waiting until he no longer heard the engine, then climbed the final few steps to the fire escape's uppermost platform, then boosted himself onto the roof. It was gravel-covered, flat, and mostly featureless save for a few rusted ventilation chimneys and a lone, phone booth–sized access door in its center. In the distance he could see the twinkling lights of San Francisco's business district and beyond that, the navigation lights of cargo ships moving in the harbor.

Careful to not disturb the gravel, Fisher walked west across the roof, paralleling the sidewalk below until he reached the far edge. As had been the garbage can lid, the aluminum maintenance ladder he'd found here the day before was still in place, lying on its side, tucked against the eaves trough. Quietly he picked up the ladder and, holding it vertically before him, braced the clawed feet on the eaves, then grasped the pulley rope and began extending the ladder upward.

The rung supports clanged against the ladder's aluminum braces, echoing through the alley and the street below. Fisher winced inwardly but kept pulling. There was nothing to be done about the noise; it was necessary. Once the ladder had reached its full height, Fisher leaned backward for leverage and began lowering it across the gap to the next building. As the ladder passed the forty-five-degree angle, gravity took hold. Fisher strained to keep the ladder's twenty-four-foot length steady. Hand over hand, inches at a time, he continued until finally the aluminum supports banged against the opposite roof.

To his north he heard the squealing of tires followed by echoed shouts: "Stop right there! Don't move, don't move . . ."

Then silence. Thirty seconds passed. An engine revved again. Tires squealed.

Fisher allowed himself another smile. *They're on to you, Sam.*

Another half minute passed, and then Fisher heard what he assumed was the plumbing van race around the corner and slide to a stop before his escape alley. Fisher bent over, lifted the end of the ladder, and let it drop with a clang back onto the eaves. He then turned on his heel, walked to the roof's access door, and opened it an inch, leaving it ajar. Finally, he walked to the northern edge of the roof and dropped onto the fire escape below. As he reached the third-floor landing, he heard the rapid crunch of footsteps on the roof gravel.

"Here, here . . . that ladder . . ." a voice called.

Then a second voice: "Got an open door here . . ."

The crackle of radio static, then a third voice: "Units . . . command . . . regroup, back to the street . . ."

Fisher waited until he heard the footsteps running back over the gravel, then braced himself against the brick wall, took two quick steps, and leaped across the gap to the opposite building's balcony. He crouched down, slid open the window, crawled through into the empty apartment, and closed the window behind him.

Two minutes later he was out the building's front door and headed north.

HALF an hour later, he was sitting on a bench in Embarcadero Plaza overlooking the bay, eating a chunk of sourdough bread, and sipping coffee when the Johnson & Sons Plumbing van pulled to a stop at the curb. The side door slid open, revealing four shadowed figures and a bank of monitors and communications equipment. A figure climbed down from the van, walked to Fisher, and stopped before him.

The woman Fisher knew as Jackie Fiest was wearing a blue sweatshirt embossed with a circa 1960s red female symbol. She smiled ruefully at him and shook her head. "You're an SOB, Fisher."

Fisher smiled back. "I assume that means I passed?"

"Passed? Sweetie, you just got done running a dozen of my best watchers in circles for the past two hours. What d'you think? Come on, get in, let's debrief."

_2_

THE warlords and their troops had been instructed to as-
semble in full battle gear shortly before dusk in the camp,
a narrow mountain canyon surrounded by craggy, snowcapped peaks. Straddling the border as it did, the camp had
for the last two years been the main headquarters for the resistance fighters. The puppet government in Bishkek had
neither the resources nor the stomach to venture into the
mountains and had resigned itself to trying to block the
various passes the resistance fighters used to sneak into
the lowlands and wreak their havoc.

The war had been going on for six years, most of which
had seen these men and their thousands of followers living
like animals in the rugged mountain ranges that bisected
the northern third of the country, just south of the capital,

Bishkek. In the post-9/11 domino effect, Kyrgyzstan had been declared by the West to be a hotbed of Muslim extremist terrorism in Central Asia, and with the acquiescence of its neighbors to the south, Tajikistan and Afghanistan, a U.S.-led coalition, using precision air strikes and special operations troops, had toppled the Muslim government and put into power the more moderate minority factions.

The ousted government and its army, having seen the handwriting on the wall, had for months before the invasion been covertly evacuating supplies and equipment from the capital into the mountains to the south. Led by Bolot Omurbai, the country's radical president for the last three years as well as the commander of the newly named Kyrgyz Republic Liberation Army, or KRLA, they had abandoned the capital just hours before the laser-guided bombs had begun to fall. Omurbai, already revered by the Kyrgyz as the father of modern Kyrgyzstan, quickly became a godlike figure as he commanded and fought beside his KRLA partisans, harassing the U.S.-sponsored government forces and chipping away at whatever small gains they were able to make outside the major cities.

A year into the war, Washington decided it was time to behead the snake. A bounty was put on Omurbai's head. From lowly privates in the new government army to musket-wielding peasants who had suffered under Omurbai, the populace took to the countryside, acting as beaters for specially tasked American special forces teams who, after three months of hunting, found Omurbai hiding in a cave along the Kazak border. Omurbai was turned over to government forces.

The Bishkek government made short work of Omurbai,

trying and finding him guilty forty-one days after his capture. The sentence, death by firing squad, was carried out the next day, filmed live before dozens of television cameras from every corner of the globe. Bolot Omurbai, the Joseph Stalin of Kyrgyzstan, was then unceremoniously stuffed into an unmarked wooden casket and buried in a secret location without so much as a stone cairn to mark his grave.

For three weeks after Omurbai's execution, Bishkek and the surrounding countryside was quiet, free from the ambushes, mortar attacks, and small-arms skirmishes that had daily plagued Kyrgyzstan for the past fifteen months.

And then, as if on a cue from a starter's pistol, on the first day of spring, the KRLA returned in force with a coordinated attack that drove the majority of the government forces back into the plains surrounding Bishkek, where the army regrouped, dug in, and repelled the attack, forcing the partisans once again into the mountains.

For the next five years the war raged on, sometimes tipping in favor of the resistance, other times in favor of the government, until a balance of sorts was found—the "Seesaw War," it was dubbed by the media. The U.S. government and its coalition partners, already bogged down in Afghanistan and the Middle East, were able to offer only a minimum of resources and cash to the Kyrgyz government, while the resistance, now commanded by Omurbai's former field commanders, received a steady stream of cash, and old but still-effective Soviet bloc weapons from Indonesia and Iran.

Tonight, however, was not about strategy, the warlords had been told about news—good news that would turn the tide against their enemies. What would be revealed here would both shock and elate them.

As the sun dropped behind the western peaks and the meadow was shrouded in darkness, the three hundred assembled fighters gathered themselves before the platform, a natural tier in the canyon wall. Generator-powered klieg lights glowed to life on either side of the platform, illuminating the six members of the war council sitting cross-legged in a semicircle. Standing before them was Samet, Omurbai's oldest friend and ally and the de facto leader of the KRLA.

"Welcome, brothers, and thank you for coming. Many of you have traveled far to get here and undertaken great risk. Rest assured, your time and effort will be rewarded.

"As you know, we fight as much for a memory as we do our country and for Allah. He who was taken from us was the flame in the night that drew us together, that bonded and hardened us."

A cheer rose from the assembled soldiers. AK-47s and RPGs were raised, and pistols fired into the air.

Samet waited for the tumult to subside, then continued. "Since his loss, we've fought on in his name and for Allah's will. I'm sure you will agree the years have been grueling. Even the strongest among us have been beset by doubts and fatigue. Well, no more, brothers. Tonight, we are reborn."

As if on cue, from the eastern reaches of the canyon there came the thumping of helicopter rotors. The fighters, having learned as their Afghan brothers had learned during the Soviet occupation to fear this, began shouting and pushing, hoping to find either cover or firing positions for RPGs.

"Calm yourselves, brothers, there is nothing to fear," Samet called over the PA speaker. "This is expected. Stand fast."

The crowd slowly calmed and went quiet as all eyes turned eastward. For a full minute the beat of the rotors increased until a pair of flashing wingtip navigation lights emerged from the darkness of the neighboring canyon. The helicopter—an old Soviet Mi-8 HIP complete with 12.7mm nose cannon and 80mm rocket outrider pods— roared overhead, passing thirty feet over the crowd before wheeling right and stopping in a hover over the clearing beside the motor pool. In a blast of rotor wash the HIP touched down on its tripod wheels. After a few seconds, the engine turned off, and the rotors spooled down, first to a dull whine and then to complete silence. For nearly a full minute, nothing moved. The crowd stood in rapt silence, watching the helicopter for signs of movement. Some of the men, their martial instincts so finely tuned, shifted nervously, weapons clutched tightly across chests. The HIP's navigation strobes, still active, flashed blue and white against the canyon walls.

Finally the door slid open, revealing a rectangle of darkness. From above the speaker's platform, a scaffold-mounted spotlight glowed to life and bathed the side of the helicopter in a circle of stark white light. Still nothing moved.

And then a lone figure emerged from the darkness of the helicopter's doorway. Clearly a man, the figure stood well over six feet tall, with broad shoulders and squat, powerful legs. A hood covered his head.

Murmured voices rose from the crowd.

The man raised his hands to shoulder height, palms out, and the crowd settled.

The man reached up and drew back the hood.

The crowd gave a collective gasp. The face they saw was familiar: strong chin, hawkish nose, thick, black mustache . . .

"Greetings, brothers. I have returned, and in that I offer you your country back," said Bolot Omurbai. "I ask you: Who will fight at my side?"

3

THOUGH Jackie had introduced her team—first names only—as soon as they'd regrouped at the safe house, Fisher was still in countersurveillance mode, so it took him a few minutes to stop thinking of them as dots on his mental clock face. Tail 6.1—the man who had for the final hour of the exercise stayed so doggedly on Fisher's six— was named Frederick, and Tail 6.2.2—the arm-in-arm couple that had passed him right before his dash into the alley—were named Reginald and Judy. Most of the other eight faces were familiar, but a few were not, and Fisher absently wondered if he'd somehow missed them. As much as he hoped not, he knew the reality. *For every rat you see, there's . . .*

"Okay, people, I think it's safe to say Sam taught us a few

tricks tonight. So, despite the sting to our egos, let's raise a toast to our rabbit . . ."

As one, the group raised glasses of wine, beer, or hard liquor in a silent salute to Fisher. Fisher smiled, nodded, and raised his own bottle of Coors. The toast was heartfelt and the atmosphere easy, but for most of Fisher's career he had worked alone, and so, like dozens of other surprises this turn in his career had given him, the camaraderie took some getting used to.

After Jackie had pulled up in the Johnson & Sons van and admitted defeat, she, Fisher, and the team had regrouped at a CIA safe house in Sausalito, across the bay from Angel Island State Park, for a postmortem of the exercise. Of those assembled, only Fisher and Jackie knew tonight's exercise had been Fisher's final exam before graduation.

Much of his training over the past three months had been familiar stuff—weapons, unarmed combat, covert communications, surveillance—so Fisher had had little trouble adapting his own background to the material. What had taken some time to get used to was that many of the tradecraft tricks were often done in broad daylight and under close surveillance. Passing someone a message in a darkened alley was one thing; doing so on a busy city street during noon rush hour with dozens of watchers studying your every move was an altogether different matter.

Still, Fisher was unsurprised to find that he was enjoying himself. The challenge of playing and winning the espionage chess game with only your wits and guile was intoxicating.

Tonight's tour through San Francisco's foggy streets had been the culmination of a weeklong "live fire" exercise designed to test his ability to slip into an unfamiliar city, establish and run a network of agents, and then cleanly exfiltrate himself after securing "the key," a crucial piece of information from a notional enemy ministry of defense. The final test had been straightforward if not easy: service a dead drop where one of his agents had placed "the key" and then transport it to his handler on the other side of town, all under the watchful eyes of Jackie's secret police team.

Now friends again, the group sat at a round poker table under a cluster of pendant lights that cast soft halogen pools on the baize surface.

"So tell me this, Sam," said Reginald. "That thing with the ladder on the roof . . . Did you bang it on the edge that last time just to make sure we heard it?" Fisher nodded, and Reginald grinned and shook his head. "Nice touch."

"How about the apartment?" Judy asked, sipping a glass of Chardonnay. "Did you just spot it empty, or what?"

"Checked the newspaper ads two days ago."

"Where?"

"During breakfast. The coffee shop on Sloan. The ad was brand-new, so it was a safe bet it hadn't been rented yet."

"But you didn't circle anything, did you, you crafty bastard," Jackie said. "We picked up that paper, checked it."

"Hell, I don't even carry a pen anymore."

There were chuckles around the table. Fisher knew nothing about these people beyond their first names, but he assumed each of them worked as case officers in the CIA's Directorate of Operations—the real-ife, boots-on-the-ground, secret-stealing, shadow-skulking operatives of film and book.

Each one, like Fisher, would know the rules of working and living as a professional paranoid. In this case, pens were often considered instruments of betrayal, something that can leave a trace of your presence or intentions or even passing interest. The CIA's informal history, passed down from generation to generation of operatives, is full of stories of otherwise smart men and women who'd died from a case of ink poisoning. In this business, memorization and recall was not a luxury but rather a requisite for a long life.

Fisher said, "That homeless guy I paid off . . . Did you—"

"Rough him up?" said Jackie. "No. But Frederick did tug on his beard to see if it was a fake."

More laughter.

"What I meant was, did you let him keep the hundred bucks?"

This brought more gales of laughter. When they subsided, Jackie said, "Yeah, yeah, we let him keep it. We're not barbarians, Sam. The poor guy had peed his pants. I wasn't going to rob him on top of it."

The dissection of the exercise continued for another half hour until finally Jackie asked, "Any feedback from your side of things, Sam? How'd we do?"

Fisher shrugged, took a sip of his beer.

"Come on, man," said Reginald. "Let's hear it."

Fisher glanced at Jackie, who gave him a nod.

"Okay. Frederick, you were on my six most of the night."

"Right."

"Almost flawless, but when you stopped at that shop window and made your fake call, you only punched four numbers—too few for a real number and too many for a speed dial. Reginald and Judy: Reginald, you never changed your shoes. Same pair of Nikes with the black scuff on the toe. Jackie, your command van: It's a 2005 model. The day I first noticed you, I checked the Johnson & Sons fleet. None of them are newer than 2001, and all have painted logos— not magnetic." Fisher paused for a moment, scratched his head. "That's about it, I think."

Collectively, the faces around the table were staring openmouthed at him. Finally, Jackie broke the silence: "Well, I guess we're gonna call that a passing grade for you."

"Come on, man, you noticed how many numbers I punched into my phone?" Frederick said.

Fisher shrugged.

"Seriously?"

Fisher nodded. "Seriously."

As much as Fisher preferred being on his own, now that the program was coming to a close, he couldn't help but wonder if he was going to miss this camaraderie.

The experimental three-month program that had brought Fisher here—a joint venture between the CIA's Directorate of Operations and Third Echelon—had been code-named CROSSCUT and was designed to teach Third Echelon's lone Splinter Cell operatives the ways of "open water" espionage tradecraft—in essence, to teach Fisher and others like him how to do what they do in broad daylight, without the benefit of shadows, stealthy tactical suits, and noise-suppressed weapons.

Fisher's boss, Colonel Irving Lambert, had chosen Fisher as a guinea pig. If Fisher survived the program—which it seems he had—and then was able to put what he learned to work in the field—which was yet to be seen—Irving would send other Splinter Cells through the program.

Truth be told, Fisher didn't need a real-world field test to tell him what he'd learned in CROSSCUT would be invaluable. He would always prefer to work alone, and he'd always prefer shadows to sunlight, but this business rarely conformed itself to one's preferences. The world of covert operations was a roller-coaster ride of balance: chaos versus order; well-laid plans versus inevitable disasters, both large and small. Of course, whether or not Third Echelon continued to participate in CROSSCUT would be Lambert's decision, but Fisher knew what his recommendation was going to be.

Jackie's cell phone trilled. She flipped it open and walked a few steps away from the table. She listened for a few moments, then disconnected and said to Fisher, "Call home."

Fisher turned around in his chair, retrieved his cell phone from his coat pocket, powered it on, then dialed. After two rings, a female voice answered, "Extension forty-two twelve."

"It's me," Fisher replied. Though the woman who answered knew his voice, she followed protocol and paused a moment to let the voice-print analyzer confirm his identity. "Hold a moment, Sam," said Anna Grimsdottir. "I've got the colonel for you."

Lambert came on the line a few seconds later. "Sam, I've got a Gulfstream headed to the Coast Guard Air Station. Get on it and come home."

"Miss me that much, Colonel?"

"No, I just got a message from the State Department. A man admitted to Johns Hopkins asked to see someone from the CIA. It's Peter, Sam. He's in a bad way. You need to get here."

Fisher felt his heart flutter in his chest. *Peter* . . .

"I'm on my way."

4

FISHER pulled to a stop at the guard shack, rolled down his window, and handed his driver's license to the guard, who checked his name against a clipboard. It was a crisp autumn day with a slight breeze; the scent of burning leaves wafted into the car.

The guard scrutinized Fisher's face, then nodded and handed back the license. "Straight ahead to Administration. Long white building with a brick entry. You'll be met."

Fisher nodded and pulled through the gate. The administrative building was a short fifty-yard drive away. Fisher pulled into the awning-covered turnaround and climbed out. An army private appeared at his door. "I'll park it for you, sir. Your party's waiting inside."

"Thanks."

Fisher found Lambert waiting in the lobby. The decor was done in vintage army: pale pus-yellow linoleum tile and walls painted mint green on the upper half and paneled in dark wood on the lower. The tangy odor of Pine-Sol hung in the air. A lone nurse sat behind the reception counter; she looked up as Fisher entered and gave him a curt nod.

Fisher shook Lambert's extended hand. "What's going on, Colonel?"

Just minutes before Fisher's Gulfstream had touched down at Andrews Air Force Base, Grimsdottir had called Fisher with a change of plans. Peter was being moved to the army's Chemical Casualty Care Division at Aberdeen. The CCCD is a division of the army's Medical Research Institute of Chemical Defense. Fisher had had his own dealings with the CCCD over the years, most recently a few months ago as a patient after the *Trego* incident.

Why Peter had been moved Grimsdottir didn't know or couldn't say, but either way, Fisher knew it wasn't good news. Peter's admitting hospital, Johns Hopkins, was top-notch; the possibility that Peter's condition was beyond its abilities worried Fisher.

"The doctors are with him right now," said Lambert. "The chief attending ER doc at Johns Hopkins took one look at him, then got on the phone with the CCCD. They're not talking so far, but if he's here . . ."

"I know." Fisher paced away, stopped, and pressed the bridge of his nose with his thumb and forefinger. He turned back to Lambert. "So we wait."

"Yeah."

The lobby was empty, so they took a pair of orange

Naugahyde chairs near the counter. On the arm of Fisher's chair, scrawled in faded ballpoint pen, were the words, *The Army way: Hurry up and wait*.

Fisher chuckled.

"What's funny?"

"Remember Frank Styles, back at Fort Bragg?" Fisher asked.

He and Lambert had history dating back to their Army Special Forces days and then later as they were selected to participate in an experimental program that took special operators from the army, navy, air force, and marines, and transferred them to another branch of the special forces community. In Fisher's and Lambert's case, they had gone from the Army's Delta Force to the navy's SEAL (Sea, Air, Land) teams.

Lambert, who had early on shown a head for organization and logistics, had later been tapped to head Third Echelon's Field Operations slot, including all its Splinter Cell operatives. At Lambert's urging, Fisher had resigned his commission in the army and joined Third Echelon.

Lambert said, "Stylin' Frankie. Yeah, I remember."

"He always used to joke when he got out he was going to start a Nauga ranch and sell their hides to the army for all these damned chairs."

Lambert smiled. "And dentists' offices."

"Yeah." Fisher leaned forward, rested his elbows on his knees, and stretched his neck. After a moment he asked Lambert, "Did you see him?"

"Peter? Only briefly as they were packing him into the ambulance." Lambert paused, cleared his throat.

"What?" Fisher asked.

"They had him in a tent, Sam."

This made sense. The CCCD dealt with biological, chemical, and radioactive infectious processes. Until they had a diagnosis or could proclaim him noninfectious, the army would handle Peter with Level 4 containment procedures, complete with biohazard suits and positive ventilation plastic barriers. Unless he was unconscious or sedated, Peter had to be terrified watching those space-suited doctors and nurses milling around him.

"Where'd they find him?"

Lambert cleared his throat, hesitated.

"Colonel?"

"We're still working on all the details, but from what I gather, a fishing boat found him floating in a life raft in the Labrador Sea, off the coast of Greenland. He was suffering from hypothermia, barely hanging on. He was taken first to Nuuk, then to the States."

"Greenland," Fisher whispered. *How had this happened?* he wondered. *Had he fallen overboard or gone over of his own accord, and if so, why?* "Did any ships file a missing persons report?"

"No," Lambert said. "I've got Grim digging, but as of an hour ago, nothing."

It seemed unlikely such a disappearance would go unnoticed. What did that mean? There seemed to be only two explanations, then: Peter had either been a stowaway, or he'd been thrown overboard.

AN hour passed, then two, and finally a doctor in dark green scrubs and square, thick-rimmed black glasses pushed through the swinging doors beside the counter. He walked over to them. His hair was plastered with sweat.

"Dr. Seltkins. You're here for—?"

Fisher nodded. "How is he?"

"Well, we've got him stabilized, but I don't know how long that'll last."

"What's wrong with him?" Lambert asked.

"We don't know yet. We're running tests. It's an infectious agent, but of what type we don't know. I'm inclined to rule out biological; his symptoms are . . . unique—too unique for fungal, viral, or bacteriological. My guess is we're looking at some kind of chemical or radiological exposure—or both."

"I want to see him," Fisher said.

"We've got him in Level 4—"

"I know that. Suit me up. I want to see him."

Dr. Seltkins sighed, then looked down at his feet.

Lambert said, "Doctor, if you need authorization—"

"No, you're both cleared," Seltkins said, then looked hard at Fisher. "His condition is . . . It's not pretty. Are you sure you want to—"

"Suit me up," Fisher repeated.

FISHER had been inside Level 4 environments before and had hated each experience for the typical reasons. He was neither claustrophobic nor terrified of running out of air due to a suit puncture. What bothered him most was the lack of freedom. He owed his survival over the years to a number of things—relentless training and practice, superb conditioning, quick thinking, dumb luck—but all of them were useless without freedom, the freedom to move quickly and freely. The ability to react in the blink of an eye had saved his life more times than he could remember. With a Level 4 suit on, its bulbous helmet, oversized boots, and bulky gloves left him feeling as vulnerable as a newborn infant. It was born of rote instinct, he knew, this irrational aversion, but it was ingrained in his mental circuitry.

Led by a pair of nurses, Fisher was taken first to a locker room, where he changed into one-piece surgical scrubs with bootied feet, then on to the first Plexiglas airlock alcove where he was helped into a Level 4 biohazard suit. The nurses checked him from head to foot for proper fit and, satisfied there were no gaps or tears, hooked him into the oxygen system, a series of hoses that hung from swivel tracks in the ceiling. Fisher heard the gush of air rushing into his suit, felt it fill his headpiece. The oxygen, so cold on his skin he felt goose bumps rise on his neck, had a slightly metallic taste.

One of the nurses checked the gauge on his arm, said, "Positive vent," and then they guided him to the second airlock. Beyond the Plexiglas wall, under the cold glare of fluorescent lighting, he could see a single bed with a figure in it. Peter's face was turned away; all Fisher could see was his ear, the curve of his jaw, the clear nasal cannula tube snaking over his cheek toward his nostrils.

Another biohazard-suited figure—a nurse or doctor, Fisher assumed—stood beside the bed, reading a vitals monitor and making notations on a clipboard.

Fisher felt a pat on his shoulder. "You're set," the nurse said. "When the airlock door closes behind you, the next one will open. There's a panic button on your wrist cuff."

Fisher looked down, saw the square, stamp-size red button beneath a hinged clear plastic cover.

"If you run into trouble, just push it, and we'll get to you within sixty seconds. Do you understand?"

Fisher nodded.

"The airlocks are operated from outside. When you're ready to come out, walk to the airlock and give us the thumbs-up. We'll process you out. *Do not* try to force your way out. If you do, we'll have to pump a sedative into your oxygen supply. Do you understand?"

Fisher nodded again. He felt another pat on his shoulder followed moments later by the sucking *swish* of the airlock door closing behind him. He heard the muffled surge of the air movers bringing the airlock back up to full positive ventilation.

The door before him slid open.

Stepping carefully, Fisher shuffled toward the bed. Above his head he heard a metallic rasping, and it took a moment for him to place it: the oxygen hose's track, sliding along behind him. As he neared the bed, the other suited figure came around to his side.

"Sir, we've got him on a fairly high dose of pain meds," the woman said, her voice muffled by her headpiece. "He's mostly lucid right now, but don't be surprised if that changes. He comes and goes."

"He's in pain," Fisher said. "How much?"

She hesitated. "It's hard to quantify it, but we believe it's a significant level."

A significant level. Though his business was rife with them, Fisher had never liked euphemisms; they blurred reality and fostered illusion.

"Please don't touch any of the equipment, the IV lines, or EKG leads."

"Okay."

"I'll be nearby if you need me."

Fisher saw her slip from his peripheral vision. Her hose track rasped along for a few seconds, then went quiet. Fisher stepped closer to the bed until he felt his thighs touch the mattress. Peter lay on his back with both hands curled in loose fists on his chest. The index finger on his right hand twitched in a steady but erratic rhythm, as though tapping out a Morse code message. His fingernails were dark blue.

"Peter, it's me," Fisher said. "It's Sam. Peter, can you hear me?"

Peter groaned. His chest heaved, and from somewhere deep in his lungs came a wet rattling sound. A line of pinkish sputum leaked from the corner of Peter's mouth, rolled down his chin, and dropped onto his chest.

Ah, God . . . Peter, what happened to you?

"Peter, it's Sam. Come on you, *mudack,* wake up." *Mudack*—roughly translated as "dumb ass"—was Peter's favorite nickname for those who tried his patience, and Fisher had over the years done just that, albeit most often intentionally.

Peter's eyes fluttered open, and his tongue, swollen and gray, darted out to lick his cracked lips. With what looked like painful effort, he turned his head to face Fisher.

It took everything Fisher had not to react, and at that moment he knew regardless of whatever diagnosis Seltkins came up with, Peter was a dead man.

Peter's hair, once thick and black, had fallen out in

clumps, leaving behind a jigsaw puzzle of pale, blue-veined skull. What little hair remained looked brittle and had turned yellow white. His face was shrunken, and the skin, paper-thin and nearly translucent, clung to his cheek and jawbones as though his face had been shrink-wrapped. His eyes, once a deep blue, had been leached of all color save a tracery of ruptured, bloody capillaries. His pupils were black pinpricks. The tendons and veins and arteries bulged from the flesh of his neck; it looked like a pair of skeletal hands had encircled his throat and were precariously holding his head in place. No Hollywood special effects wizard could have created what Peter's face had become.

Peter's eyes stared vacantly at Fisher for a long five seconds before Fisher saw even the barest flicker of recognition. Peter opened his mouth, revealing blackened gums, and whispered something. Fisher knelt beside the bed, took Peter's hand and gave it a squeeze, and leaned in closer to hear. Peter's fingertips were scraped raw, the nails on several of them torn away.

"What, Peter? Say it again."

". . . to see you again, *mudack*."

FISHER spent ten more minutes with Peter before he drifted into unconsciousness. Fisher signaled that he was ready to come out, and the same nurses processed him through the airlocks, helped him out of the biohazard suit, then left him to change in the locker room. Five minutes later he was back with Lambert and Dr. Seltkins.

"How long has he got?" Fisher asked.

"Difficult to say."

"Try," Fisher said with a little steel in his voice.

Seltkins spread his hands. "Days. Three at most. What-ever diagnosis we come up with won't matter. He's already in advanced multiple organ failure; we're past the point of no return there. The best we can do is keep him comfort-able."

"Do that," Fisher said. "I'll be back."

Fisher and Lambert turned to leave, but Seltkins stopped them with a question. "If you don't mind . . . I saw you holding his hand. Are you family or a friend?"

Fisher paused a few moments, looking at the floor. "A little of both, I guess. He's my brother."

5

OMURBAI spoke to the troops for a full hour, whipping them into a frenzy for what he proclaimed would be a "new day for the Kyrgyz people, for Islam, and for the ways of their forefathers," then dismissed them to celebrate.

With AK-47s and chants for both their resurrected leader and for Allah, Omurbai retired to a tent with Samet and the three most powerful warlords that together represented the thirty-two *sanjira*, or tribes, in Kyrgyzstan. These men, along with Samet, had kept the KRLA alive in Omurbai's absence. The tent was long and rectangular, its walls lined with heavy tapestries and piled high with trunks and ammunition cases, the floor covered in thick, overlapping rugs of various sizes. At the center of the tent was a scarred mahogany table surrounded by five chairs, and aligned above the table, three hissing kerosene lanterns. Charcoal braziers stood burning in each corner of the tent to ward off the chilled mountain air.

Omurbai took his seat at the head of the table and gestured for the others to sit. As was his place, Samet took the chair to Omurbai's immediate right. Servants entered the tent and placed before each man a ceramic mug and a steaming carafe of warm *chalap*.

Omurbai smiled and gestured for them to drink.

These four men represented not only the bulk of the KRLA's fighting force but also, as Omurbai had drummed into them, the heart of the Kyrgyz people—the true Kyrgyz people—the Sary Bagysh, the Solto, the Bugu, the Adygene, the Dungan, the Uygur—those of pure blood, those who had resisted the "Soviet infection" and resisted still the "insidious disease of Western materialism and modernity that poisons our land." These were favorite topics of Omurbai's, but they were more than simply rallying slogans. They were, he promised, the greatest enemy to the future of the Kyrgyz homeland and of Islam itself.

Omurbai waited until each man at the table had drunk from his cup; then he spoke.

"Brothers, it is good to be home. Good to see your faces again and feel the air of our homeland in my lungs once again. We have much to discuss, but I assume you have questions for me, so let us address those now."

There was silence around the table for a few seconds, and then one of the warlords, the leader of the combined southern, or Ich Kylyk, tribes, spoke up. "My khan, forgive me, but how is it you are alive? We watched you die."

Omurbai smiled. "A worthy question to begin with. You

saw an illusion, my old friend. I had long foreseen the betrayal that led to my capture and was prepared for it. The man you saw die was a loyal son of Kyrgyzstan who volunteered for martyrdom." Omurbai chuckled softly. "The fact that he shared my fine and handsome features was the will of Allah."

There were returning chuckles from around the table.

Another warlord spoke up. "Where have you been? Could you not have trusted us with your secret?"

"As for your first question, the friends of the Kyrgyz people are legion. And to your second question, trust was never the issue, my friend. In fact, it was quite the opposite. I knew our homeland would remain safe in your hands—all of your hands—until I returned. Silence was a necessary evil, and soon you'll see why.

"The new future of the Kyrgyz people begins today, with my return and with your continued loyalty. In a matter of weeks, by the grace of Allah, our homeland will be returned to us and set back on the one true course."

"And what is this course?" the other warlord asked.

"The ways of old," Omurbai replied. "The ways of *Manas*, before our land was polluted by immorality and technology and Western thought. I've watched from afar, my old friends. I've seen the disease spreading across our country, starting in the cities with billboards and flashing signs and dancing. Our people have lost their way, but I tell you this: With my return I bring the cure."

"And this is?"

Omurbai waggled a finger at him as though admonishing a child. "Patience. All will soon be made clear." Omurbai sat back in his chair and silently stared at each man in turn, then suddenly slapped both palms on the table. One of the *chalap* carafes tipped over, spilling its contents on the tablecloth.

"To other business," Omurbai announced. He stood up and began walking around the table, placing a hand on each warlord's shoulder in turn, finally stopping behind Samet. "As you know, Samet here has faithfully stood in my place since my departure. You've followed him loyally, and for that I thank you. The Kyrgyz people—those from the Land of Forty Tribes, thank you. However, I am disappointed in you."

Omurbai had stopped behind Samet's chair with both hands resting on his shoulders.

"Why, my khan?" asked the *Ich Kylyk* warlord.

"As I told you now and I've told you before, the disease that infects our country is insidious. No one is immune. Not you, not me, not the most hardened and loyal soldier. Even Samet here, loyal Kyrgyz that he is, has faltered. Isn't that true, Samet?"

Samet craned his neck to look up at Omurbai. "I don't understand, my khan. How have I failed you?"

"In word, Samet. You have failed me in word. I have it on trusted authority you have been seen in Bishkek—that you have been heard answering to your old Soviet name, Satybaldiyev."

"No, my khan, this is not true—"

From the folds of his jacket Omurbai produced a long, curved knife. In one smooth motion, he reached across Samet's throat, inserted the tip of the knife below his ear, and drew it cleanly across his larynx. Eyes bulging, Samet opened his mouth to speak, but no sound came. Blood gushed from the wound and sprayed across the tablecloth. His head, nearly severed, lolled to one side, and he toppled forward, his forehead cracking against the mahogany. His body spasmed and bucked in its chair for another ten seconds, then went still.

Omurbai jammed the tip of the knife into the tabletop and then looked around the table. "The disease of which I speak, my friends . . . It knows no bounds."

He returned to his chair, sat down, poured himself more *chulap*, and took a sip.

"Now," he said, "to business."

_6_

FISHER hadn't known Peter's true name or origin until he was twenty-one, when his mother and father had sat him down to tell him. Peter, his adopted brother, was in fact Pyotr Limonovich, the only son of a now-dead friend of Sam's father. It wasn't until Peter turned eighteen that their father, now retired from the U.S. Department of State, told them the whole story.

Peter was the son of a man named Ivan, a major in the former Soviet Union's KGB, their equivalent to the United States's CIA; and Fisher's father, a career diplomat, was not a diplomat at all but a twenty-five-year veteran case officer in the CIA.

It had all happened when Fisher was barely old enough to remember his father being gone for an extended period.

A specialist in agent handling and defection, his father had been dispatched to Moscow. This was 1968, the height of the Cold War, his father explained, the years of North Korea's capture of the USS *Pueblo*, the Soviet army's brutal crush of the Czechoslovakian revolt, and the space race— events that for young Sam were only vague headline memories.

A major named Ivan Limonovich had made contact with the CIA's deputy chief of station and over the next few weeks made clear his intention to spy for the United States. The "bride price" as it was known in the tradecraft lexicon, would be that Ivan and his newly born son, Pyotr (Ivan's wife had died in childbirth), would be smuggled out of Russia after two years. The CIA agreed, and Fisher's father was dispatched to be Ivan's primary controller. Over the next two years, Ivan fed the United States invaluable information, including information that led to the release of the *Pueblo*'s crew and details of the Soviet nuclear arsenal that later became essential to the signing of SALT I, the first series of Strategic Arms Limitation Talks between the United States and the Soviet Union. As often happened in the world of espionage, Fisher's father and Ivan became friends.

At the end of the agreed-upon two years, Fisher's father made arrangements to smuggle Ivan and his son from the country, only to see the plans go awry at the last minute. In a running gun battle at the Finnish border, Ivan Limonovich was killed, and with Soviet border troops at his heels, Fisher's father managed to slip across the border with young Pyotr.

Once home, the Fishers did the only thing that seemed right and adopted Pyotr as their own and raised him along with their son Sam. Pyotr, too young to have learned any Russian or gain an accent and too young to have anything but the fuzziest of memories of his father, quickly grew into a typical American boy.

THIRD ECHELON

Dr. Seltkins was as good as his word. Two days after arriving at the army's Chemical Casualty Care Division, Peter died. Fisher, who had spent as much time as they would allow him at Peter's bedside in the airlocked hospital room, had gone to the cafeteria to catch a quick breakfast when the crash code was called. He returned to find Seltkins emerging from the airlock and a trio of nurses at Peter's bed removing the IVs and monitor leads from his now-lifeless body.

Still lacking a diagnosis, the army erred on the side of caution and flew Peter's body to the Umatilla Chemical Agent Disposal Facility in Oregon, where it was cremated in a closed incinerator, then stored in the bowels of the facility inside a specially designed lead/ceramic composite container.

FISHER swiped his ID badge through the reader outside Third Echelon's situation room. There was a muted beep, and the reader's LED turned green. Fisher pushed through the door.

Decorated in earth tones and lit by soft halogen track lighting, the situation room was dominated by a long, diamond-shaped teak conference table. The walls were lined by forty-two-inch, high-definition LCD status boards and monitors that could be calibrated to display a variety of information ranging from weather, local and foreign news broadcasts, radar feeds—virtually anything that could be digitized and transmitted. Four computer workstations, each with enough processing power to control the electrical grids of a small country, were built into each of the long sides of the table.

Fisher had called Third Echelon his professional home for more years than he could recall. A top secret offshoot of the National Security Agency, or NSA, Third Echelon and its small collection of lone Splinter Cell operatives was a bridge of sorts: a bridge between the world of intelligence gathering and covert operations.

Splinter Cell operatives were recruited from the special warfare communities of the navy, army, marine corps, and air force, and then remolded into the ultimate covert soldiers able to survive and thrive in the most hostile of environments. The informal credo for Third Echelon was "no footprints." Third Echelon went where no other government agency could go, did what no other agency could do, then disappeared, leaving behind nothing that could be tracked back to the United States.

Itself the most secretive of the government's intelligence organizations, the National Security Agency was located a few miles outside Laurel, Maryland, on an army post named after the Civil War Union general, George Gordon Meade. Once home to both a boot camp and a World War II prisoner-of-war camp, Fort Meade has been the NSA's home since the 1950s.

Charged with the gathering and exploitation of SIGINT, or signals intelligence, the NSA could and did intercept virtually every form of communication on the planet from cell phone signals to microwave emissions and ELF (extremely low frequency) burst transmissions from submarines thousands of feet beneath the surface of the ocean.

Lambert and Anna Grimsdottir were sitting together at one end of the conference table drinking coffee. Three of the monitors on the wall behind them were tuned to the muted broadcasts of MSNBC, CNN, and BBC World.

Fisher grabbed a mug from the nearby coffee kiosk, poured himself a cup, and sat down at the conference table.

"Morning," said Lambert.

"That's debatable," Fisher said, taking a sip. The coffee was hot and almost bitter, with a touch of salt. Lambert must have made it.

"When did you get back?" Grimsdottir asked. As Peter had no other family than Fisher, and his remains would probably forever remain locked deep inside Umatilla, Fisher had, in lieu of a funeral or memorial, accompanied him on the flight to Oregon and stood by as the technicians slid his body into the incinerator.

"A couple hours ago," Fisher replied.

"You didn't have to come in," Lambert said.

"Yeah, I did. Do we know anything? Anything from Seltkins?" Even as Fisher had boarded the plane for Oregon, the CCCD's labs had yet to determine what had killed Peter.

Grimsdottir pulled a manila folder from the stack before her and slid it across the table to Fisher. She said nothing. Fisher stared at her eyes for a few seconds until she looked away. *Very bad news,* Fisher thought.

Grimsdottir's official designation was computer/signals intel technician, but Fisher thought of her as more like a free safety. To operatives in the field she provided tech and information support and she was, at least for Fisher, that constant voice in his ear during missions that represented his lifeline back to Third Echelon and the real world. Fisher had yet to see a computer-related problem too tough for Grimsdottir to crack.

Fisher opened the folder and skimmed the CCCD's report. Finally, he looked up and said, "What in God's name is PuH-19?"

"Plutonium hydride-19," Lambert answered. "It's a negative hydrogen ion that attaches itself to Plutonium-239 that's exposed to pure oxygen. Usually comes in the form of fine particulates—think of flour, but about a thousand times finer."

"Almost a gas," Grimsdottir added. "It's also pyrophoric, which is a fancy way of saying it's an autoigniter. Its flash point is below room temperature; it's also reactive to water or even humid air. In fact, it's so touchy, the only safe way to handle it is in a pure nitrogen or argon atmosphere."

"Sounds lovely," Fisher said. "Contagious?"

"Not once it's inside the body," Grimsdottir replied. "The hydride particles settle in the tissues and organs and begin . . . dissolving them. Sorry, Sam, there's really no other word for it."

"It's okay. Where's PuH-19 come from?"

"Plutonium-based weapons production."

"Which is good news," Lambert said. "It sharply narrows the list of where Peter picked it up."

Where, maybe, but not how, Fisher thought. After ten

years as a Justice Department investigator, Peter had resigned in protest during Gonzales-gate and gone into business for himself as a security consultant. While certain Peter had an inkling of what Fisher did for a living, they'd never discussed it, and neither did they discuss the specifics of Peter's business. Fisher had long suspected the nature of their work was similar.

"What else?" Fisher said.

Grimsdottir said, "It's about a hundred times deadlier than plutonium. A speck of PuH-19 the size of a head of a pencil is enough to kill a room full of people—which is why its production and storage has been banned by all countries of the world save two: Russia and the United States."

Fisher closed the file and slowly slid it back across the table to Grimsdottir. He looked at Lambert and said, "We need to talk."

Anna took the hint and excused herself. When the door clicked shut, Fisher said, "I'm going to need a leave of absence or—"

"Now, Sam, hold on a second—"

"Or, if you'd prefer, I'll have my letter of resignation on your desk by—"

"Not necessary."

"Colonel, I'm going to find whoever did this to Peter."

"I know."

"And break a lot of laws doing it."

"I know that, too."

"And when I find them, I'm going to kill each and every one of them."

Lambert laid a hand on Fisher's forearm. "Stop. Take a breath. I mean it, Sam, take a breath."

Fisher took a breath.

"While you were in the air with Peter's body, I was at Langley," Lambert said. "We've got the green light from both the DCI and the NID." The director of central intelligence at the CIA and the national intelligence director—the president's intelligence czar. "The mission's ours. Find where and how Peter was infected, track it back to its source, and find out if there's more out there. A coffee cup full of PuH-19 could kill every living thing in New York City. Believe me, we've got a free hand on this."

"They know about my connection to Peter?"

"Yep. It took some doing, but I convinced them you could stay objective. Can you?"

"You have to ask?"

"Normally, no, but there's nothing normal about this. We need live, talking bodies, Sam, understood?"

Fisher nodded. "Understood."

"You step outside the rules of engagement, and I'll take you off this mission faster than you can blink."

"I hear you, Colonel."

"Good. Mission briefing in twenty. Anna's got a lead for you." Lambert stood up and started for the door. He stopped and turned around. "Sam?"

"Yeah?"

"I'm sorry about Peter."

7

LA FONTAINE PARK, MONTREAL, CANADA

FISHER refolded his copy of the *Montreal Gazette* to the Arts & Life page and shifted his eyes left, keeping his target in view. The man was a creature of habit, Fisher had found over the last two days. Same park, same bench, same sack lunch containing a baguette sandwich, an apple, and a pint bottle of milk. Keeping such a routine was a dangerous tendency for a private detective, but then again, Jerry Pults's seeming laziness was Fisher's gain.

The park was abuzz with Montrealers flocking to one of the city's many green spaces. With the last patches of snow gone and the tulips in bloom, spring had fully arrived, and the locals were taking advantage of it.

At ninety acres and more than 125 years old, La Fontaine Park was not only one of the city's largest green spaces but also one of its oldest. It reminded Fisher of New York's Central Park, with enough hills, ponds, bike paths, playgrounds, tennis courts, and cafés that it had become one of Montreal's default get-together spots. In the distance, over the tops of the trees, Fisher could see the row of Second Empire–style houses that lined Rue Sherbrooke.

Pults, a former RCMP (Royal Canadian Mounted Police) detective, though ten years past retirement age, looked a lean and fit fifty years old—save one feature: a stiff left leg that he supported with a cane. Even so, Fisher wasn't about to underestimate the man. Grimsdottir had worked her cyber magic and hacked into the RCMP's personnel bureau database. Pults had had a long and distinguished career and had spent the last three years of it at the RCMP Academy in Regina, Saskatchewan, after a crackhead's bullet had shattered his hip. He was thrice decorated for bravery, an expert marksman, and had for five years been the lead unarmed combat instructor at RCMP Toronto. On the personal side, Grimsdottir had found nothing damning; in fact, Pults and his wife, Mary, his high school sweetheart, had been married for thirty-seven years. Three children, a boy and two girls, all upstanding citizens without so much as a parking ticket.

Unless Pults was hiding some deep secret they'd yet to uncover, he looked as clean as they come. Even so, the man's detective agency was either failing or going through a slump. Over the past two days, Fisher had seen Pults meet with no one, nor did he leave the office for anything but lunch in the park and to go home at night. Grim's probe into the agency's financials showed little activity, and Pults's personal accounts were exactly what you'd expect from a retired cop.

The lead Grimsdottir had found for Fisher involved Peter's last credit card purchase a week earlier at Brulerie St-Denis, a café off Chemin Rheaume. A discreet canvass of the café with Peter's picture led to Jerry Pults, a regular customer.

The question was, what was Pults's connection with Peter, and had it contributed to his death?

AFTER a five-minute head start, Fisher followed Pults back to his office, which was sandwiched between a Vietnamese restaurant and a Thai restaurant/Internet café in a four-story building on Rue St. Andre. Fisher popped into a gift shop across the street and browsed their selection of snow globes and watched Pults's building until he saw Pults's secretary, a mid-forties redhead wearing CD-sized gold hoop earrings, come out the front door and head down the street. Another creature of habit, Fisher had found. She and Pults staggered their lunch hours, same time every day.

Fisher crossed the street, pushed through the building's door, and took the stairs to the third floor. Pults's office was the first door on the right; the silver-painted plastic plaque beside it read PULTS INVESTIGATIONS. Fisher turned the knob and walked through. In the back, behind a Formica-topped reception desk, a muted bell sounded.

"Be right with ya," Pults called.

Fisher walked past the reception desk, turned at a copy machine/coffee room, and stood in Pults's doorway. Pults was sitting on the edge of his desk, one sock and shoe off, clipping the toenail on his big toe. Behind Pults was a floor-to-ceiling bookcase packed to overflowing. Fisher saw some

Herodotus and Plutarch, dozens of World War II and Civil War history books, Shakespeare's sonnets, and a compendium of *Three Stooges* trivia. Clearly Pults was well-read and had eclectic taste. Beside the bookcase was a five-by-seven picture of a dog, a bichon frise, Fisher guessed. It was wearing a superman costume with the word SNOWBALL emblazoned across the front.

"Hey, hi there," Pults said, looking up. "I'll be right—"

"That's okay," Fisher said. "This won't take long. You had lunch with a man named Peter a couple weeks ago at Brulerie St-Denis. As far as I can tell, you were the last man to see him alive."

Pults squinted at Fisher for a few seconds, slipped his sock and shoe back on, then limped around his desk and plopped down in his chair. "Peter's dead?"

Pults looked genuinely surprised. Fisher nodded.

"And who are you?"

Fisher had already given his approach a lot of thought. Both his gut and Pults's personnel file told Fisher the former RCMP detective was an honest man. If he had anything to do with Peter's death, it was probably unintentional. Plus, Pults, being a cop, had heard a lifetime of crap from criminals trying to get over on him. Fisher's best chance was to simply lay his cards on the table and ask for the man's help.

"My name is Sam. I'm Peter's brother."

"Yeah? Huh. Funny, Peter never mentioned a brother."

"He never mentioned a private detective to me."

"Can you prove it?" Pults asked.

"What'd you have in mind? An old Christmas card?"

"You guys had a cat when you were kids. What was its name?"

Interesting, Fisher thought. Pults's question implied more than a simple business relationship, but a friendship.

"Pod," Fisher said. "Short for Tripod. He lost his right front leg in a raccoon trap in the woods behind our house. Peter found him, ran home with him, and pestered our mom till she gave in and let us keep him."

"And how'd he stop the bleeding?"

"He didn't. I did. Used the rubber tubing off my slingshot."

Pults smiled, showing a gap between his front teeth the width of a nickel's edge. "Man, I always liked that story. Tell me what happened to Peter."

Fisher did. After he finished, Pults was silent for a few seconds. He clasped his hands on top of his desk blotter, dipped his chin, and shook his head. "I should have gone with him. This goddamned hip . . ."

"Gone where?" Fisher asked. "Start at the beginning."

He and Peter were business partners, Pults explained, and had been for nearly two years. He was Peter's link to the RCMP and the Canadian underworld, which Pults knew inside and out after two decades. Peter paid him under the table and kept their relationship off the books.

"He played his cards close to the vest," Pults said.

"Runs in the family."

"Anyway, he had a lot of big clients. When he had something for me, I'd handle it. It wasn't often, but it was enough to keep me in salmon lures and fishing trips."

"Which explains your business's low traffic."

"Yeah. I've got a decent pension, so whatever Peter tossed my way was gravy. This last thing, though, was a different animal."

"How so?"

Pults opened his top desk drawer, withdrew a manila folder, and slipped a newspaper clipping from it. He handed it to Fisher, who scanned the article, which included a picture of a woman. She had long black hair, delicate cheekbones, a nose with an ever-so-slight bump in it, and flashing brown eyes. Fisher read the picture's caption and looked up at Pults in surprise. "Carmen Hayes? You're kidding?"

Pults shook his head. "Price, Carmen's father, hired Peter to find her."

Four months earlier, the twenty-eight-year-old daughter of Price Hayes had disappeared on a trip to Montreal. While Price Hayes was infamous—a colorful and crotchety old-money Texas oil baron with a family name as old as Sam Houston's—his daughter, Carmen, was renowned, but only within her chosen field, hydrogeology, the study of how fluid moves through and affects rock. Since graduating from college, Carmen had worked in the exploration division of her father's company.

According to Price Hayes, his daughter had responded to a corporate headhunter's invitation to meet with the CEO of Akono Oil, a Japanese firm specializing in deepwater petroleum exploration and extraction. The day after arriving in Montreal, Carmen disappeared. Through its general counsel, Akono Oil claimed it never extended such an offer to Carmen, and none of its corporate staff had been in Montreal during that time.

Both the FBI and the RCMP had worked the case with fervor, turning over every rock and every lead, large and small, but to no avail. No sign of Carmen could be found. Her trail ended the moment she stepped out of her hotel that morning. For the first month after her disappearance, the mystery of Carmen Hayes had been a regular on every cable news channel and tabloid show.

"Mr. Hayes had pushed and rousted every government official he could get on the phone on either side of the border," Pults said. "But there was nothing they could do. Before he hired Peter, Price had gone through three other private investigators, some of the biggest and best in the business."

"How long had Peter been on it?"

"About a month."

"And?"

"And I think he had something. He didn't share much with me, and that had me worried. He said it was for my own good. He was looking at a man named Aldric Legard."

"I've heard the name," Fisher said. "Quebec Mafia."

"Right. A brutal son of a bitch. Was the number two man until one night five or six years ago. He and the boss are sitting down to a nice dinner of *potage aux pois chiches*. The boss had a spoonful of it halfway to his mouth when Legard jammed a stiletto into his eye. Boss goes headfirst into the *potage,* Legard keeps eating. Piece of cake."

"That'll put you off your soup," Fisher said.

"And then some. So, Legard moves to number one and starts shaking up the business. The old boss was into contracts, unions, high-end escort services, and so on. Legard ditches all that and starts up with heroin, coke, and white slavery."

"Pardon me?"

"White girls, late teens or early twenties, mostly blondes, shipped over to Indonesia and the Middle East for stripping or sex—or both. Legard has quite a customer base. He even takes requests: height, weight, eye color . . . you know. Legard's also—"

"How many?" Fisher said.

"Girls?" Pults shrugged. "Who can say? Most of them live off the grid. They disappear, and no one notices except their friends—who rarely report anything, given the way they feel about police. If I had to guess at a number, though . . . Well into the hundreds."

"Christ," Fisher said. "What else?"

"Legard's also elbow deep in Ottawa. He's on a first name basis with half the House of Commons. Just a rumor, of course, but it would explain why he's not locked up in some hole somewhere."

"So Peter thought Legard had snatched Carmen Hayes?"

"That's my guess, but she doesn't fit the profile: brunette, closer to thirty than twenty. Most of Legard's acquisitions are runaways or street kids. I think Peter figured Legard had been contracted to snatch Carmen and deliver her somewhere for someone. Not a regular customer. If you want someone kidnapped, why not go to someone who's done it a lot?"

This was an unexpected turn, Fisher thought. He'd never had the slightest inkling Peter had been involved in the Hayes kidnapping. How did an oil baron's missing daughter, a Canadian crime boss, and white slavery tie into PuH-19 and Peter's death?

Fisher said, "Okay, so Peter asked you to do a background check on Legard . . ."

"Yeah, he was looking for a way in—a corner he could peel back. He never told me how he got interested in

Legard, but the theory was that *if* Legard had snatched Carmen, she'd probably gone down the same pipeline Legard uses for his other girls."

"You told me you should have gone with him," Fisher said. "What did you mean? Someplace specific?"

"One of Legard's front companies is called Terrebonne Exports. Fish canning and export. He's got a fair-size fleet and warehouses all along the St. Lawrence Seaway and on Nova Scotia. Peter thought Legard was using his ships to smuggle the girls overseas."

This made sense. There was a reason why ships and ports were the preferred venue for smugglers, terrorists, and sundry criminals. Ports were virtually impossible to fully secure, and ships were, by their very nature, a warren of nooks and crannies tailor-made for hiding contraband, inanimate and human alike.

The question was, did he follow what was likely Peter's course and look at Legard's warehouses, or did he go to Legard himself and ask—not so nicely—what had happened to Peter and why?

The truth was, Fisher had made up his mind before he even asked the question.

8

FISHER heard a muted squelch as the subdermal receiver implanted beneath the skin behind his ear came to life. Then, a few seconds later, Grim's voice: "Do you read me, Sam?"

Fisher lowered his binoculars and shimmied backward, deeper into the underbrush. The night was chilly, hovering at fifty degrees Fahrenheit, and a low mist clung to the ground. Overhead he could hear the occasional pinging screech of bats hunting the darkened treetops for insects.

Before him lay a half-mile stretch of the St. Lawrence River and beyond that, the village of Saint-Sulpice and, on its outskirts, Aldric Legard's estate, a sprawling three hundred thousand square-foot French country mansion set on ten acres of rock elm and white oak.

The approach Fisher had chosen seemed tailor-made for him. This section of the St. Lawrence was bisected by Iles de Boucherville, a series of narrow, tree-covered islands that ran parallel to both shorelines and were uninhabited save the dozens of strobe-topped navigation towers designed to warn off passing ships. Lined with hundreds of tiny coves and inlets, the islands appealed to the SEAL in Fisher as not only the perfect insertion point but also the perfect E&E (escape and evasion) route. If he ran into trouble and had to retreat under pursuit, the islands' geography would work to his advantage.

Fisher said, "Grim, you know I gave up trying to read you long ago. You're an enigma."

"Sweet-talker."

Fisher's communications system, specially made for Third Echelon by DARPA, the Pentagon's version of James Bond's Q division, consisted of two parts: the subdermal receiver, which directly vibrated the set of tiny bones in the ear known as the ossicles, or more colloquially, the hammer, anvil, and stirrup; and the second part, the transmitter, which was a butterfly-shaped adhesive patch known as an SVT, or subvocal transceiver, worn across the throat just above his Adam's apple. This had been the hardest of the two components to master and required a skill Fisher likened to a cross between whispering and ventriloquism. For all that, though, he loved the system; it allowed him to communicate while bad guys stood five feet away.

"I'm loading your OPSAT now," Grimsdottir said, referring to the operational satellite uplink. Fisher had come to think of the OPSAT as his own personal Palm Pilot on steroids. Worn across the forearm, the OPSAT served not only as Fisher's encrypted satellite communications hub, but it also fed him images and data that ranged from a simple weather readout to a real-time satellite feed from a fifteen-ton Lacrosse-class radar-imaging satellite orbiting four hundred miles above the earth's surface. More than that, like Grimsdottir's voice in his ear, the OPSAT had come to represent for him a link back to the real world. Working alone, in places filled with people only too happy and capable of killing him on-site, was challenging enough. With the OPSAT, lifesaving information and a friendly voice were only a few button presses away.

"Data dump complete," Grimsdottir said.

Fisher pressed his thumb to the OPSAT's screen. A red horizontal laser line scrolled down the screen as the biometric reader captured his thumbprint.

// . . . BIOMETRIC SCAN ENGAGED . . .
. . . SCANNING FINGERPRINT . . .
. . . IDENTITY CONFIRMED . . . //

The OPSAT booted up, showing a transreflective screen in black, green, and amber. Fisher pressed a few buttons, checked the database and uplink, then said, "Good to go."

Lambert's voice came on the line. "Sam, the ROE are tight on this; you're on allied soil."

In this case, Fisher's rules of engagement were straight from the manual, and he knew the words by heart: *Avoid all contact. Leave no trace of presence. Less-than-lethal force authorized if contact unavoidable. Lethal force authorized only to maintain mission and/or operative integrity.* Translation: Don't be seen and don't kill anyone unless the mission will otherwise go to hell in a handbasket. Fisher had always enjoyed the line, "operative integrity." This was yet another euphemism: Getting captured or killed was the same thing as a failed mission.

"Got it. No war with Canada," Fisher replied. "I'm on the move. Call you on the other side."

FISHER'S choice to go directly to the source—Montreal's godfather, Aldric Legard—had been an easy one. Not only was Legard his best chance of finding out what had happened to Peter, and why, but also of finding Carmen Hayes. While the mystery of her disappearance had piqued Fisher's curiosity, his first concern was of a more practical nature. Regardless of whether his visit to Legard provided him a lead, he knew one thing: It seemed clear that Peter's pursuit of Carmen's disappearance had gotten him killed, and so, logically, if he could retrace Peter's steps he would eventually run squarely into the people who had not only killed Peter but also whoever had the PuH-19.

Fisher slipped the face mask over his eyes and slithered belly first down the embankment and into the water. He coiled his legs and shoved off the muddy bank, propelling himself into the channel. The current caught him, and his weight belt slowly drew him beneath the surface. He fitted the microrebreather, which was roughly the size and shape of a five-pound hand weight, into his mouth and took a sharp breath to activate the chemical gas scrubber; he was greeted by a slight hiss and the cool, metallic taste of oxygen flowing into his mouth.

As his body descended through the water, he felt its chill

envelop him. After a few seconds his tac suit quickly absorbed and redistributed the cold.

Fisher was biased, he knew, since the thing had saved his life more times than he could count, but as far as he was concerned, his tac suit—officially, the Mark V tactical operations suit—was as close to magic as DARPA had ever come. A one-piece black coverall festooned with the various pouches, pockets, and harness attachments needed to carry all his equipment, the tac suit's interior was fitted with the latest generation Gore-Tex while its exterior was made up of Kevlar and Dragon Skin, the world's first "move when you move" body armor. Dragon Skin could stop shrapnel and any bullet short of a sniper's high-powered penetrator round. The Gore-Tex was designed to maintain Fisher's core body temperature and could do so down to ten degrees and as high as one hundred ten.

The truly magical part was the camouflage system. The outer Kevlar layer was impregnated with a substance codenamed Cygnus, after the first officially identified black hole. The liquid polymer fiber was matte-black and microroughened so as to trap and diffuse—if only for a fraction of a second—light particles. It wasn't invisibility per se, but Fisher had found that shadows seemed much deeper while he was wearing the tac suit. Completing the camouflage was the use of disruptive patterning through the odd placement of his pouches and pockets, all of which were of different sizes and shapes. In low-light conditions, the human eye was drawn to movement, color difference, and geometric form. Of the three, form was the most challenging problem, but by rearranging and resizing the pouches, the outline of the body becomes fuzzy.

He reached up and touched a button on his face mask. Two halogen lights, one built into each side of his mask, came to life, emitting a pair of pencil-thin red beams. As designed, they converged directly ahead of him, at arm's reach. He lifted the OPSAT to his face and studied the screen. His course to the opposite shore, marked as a green parabolic line, took into account the river's current and would, barring any miscalculation, bring him to the surface within ten feet of the outer stone wall of Legard's estate.

He slipped on his webbed swimming gloves and started swimming.

9

WHEN the parabolic course line on the OPSAT screen shortened to a few millimeters, Fisher turned off his mask lamp, stopped stroking, and let his momentum carry him forward. He let his arms hang down until he felt his fingertips scraping the soft mud bottom. He jammed his fingertips into the muck until he had purchase, pulled himself down until his belly touched the mud, then began easing himself forward, inch by inch, until the upper rim of his face mask broke the surface. He waited a moment for the water to drain away from the glass, then removed the rebreather and looked around.

He froze.

Standing on the bank, not five feet before him, was a figure, silhouetted by moonlight. Fisher's breath caught in his throat. Slowly the man raised his arm up across his body, then stopped. The orange tip of a cigarette glowed to life, then went dark. Fisher scanned the man's outline until he found what he was looking for: Jutting from shadows at the man's right hip was the stubbed nose and raised triangular sight of a compact submachine gun—a Heckler & Koch SL8-6, by the looks of it. The SL8-6 was the civilian version of the German army's G36 assault rifle.

The guard's presence here answered one of Fisher's questions; Grim's research into Legard's home had turned up the presence of twelve to fifteen full-time, live-in guards, but what she couldn't tell was how far their patrols went. Now Fisher knew their patrols extended beyond the walls to the rest of Legard's estate.

Fisher remained still, barely breathing, until the guard finally finished his smoke break. He tossed the cigarette butt into the water, where it hissed out, then turned and started back up the tree-lined embankment toward the wall.

Fisher counted another sixty seconds in his head and then, with exaggerated slowness, dipped his face back beneath the surface, removed his mask, and clipped it to his harness. From a pouch on his chest, he withdrew his op goggles and settled them over his head. He pressed a button, and goggles powered up, emitting a barely perceptible whirring hum followed by a soft click that told him they were fully operational. He flipped to NV, or night vision, and the darkness turned to a field of gray green before his eyes. Instead of simply clumps of indistinguishable foliage, he could make out individual shrubs, could even count leaves on the end of a nearby branch.

Gotta love technology, Fisher thought. *But only to a point.*

He was and always would be, old-school. Gizmos and gadgets were useful, but without trained hands and experienced brains to apply them, they were worthless. There was no substitute for eyeballs and boots on the ground.

He flipped the goggles through the other two available modes: infrared, or IR, for thermal; and EM, or electromagnetic, for electrical signals that could range from a radio beacon to invisible electrical barriers. He paused in each mode, scanning the ground before and around him, then up the embankment to the wall. He saw nothing.

He looked left, downstream, then right, upstream. About a hundred yards up the shore, he could see Legard's private dock, a canopy-covered structure that jutted thirty feet into the river. Tied to slips on either side of the dock were four blue-on-white Baja 26 Outlaw speedboats with what looked like MerCruiser engines—600 horsepower, Fisher guessed. Each boat also came with its own radar antenna jutting from the stern air foil.

He belly-crawled from the mud and into the tall grass along the shore until he reached heavier foliage, where he rose to his knees. Weapons check. His loadout for this mission was standard: a 5.72mm/anesthetic dart pistol with a twenty-round magazine and muzzle noise/flash suppressor; fragmentation and disruption grenades; a genuine Fairbairn-Sykes fighting knife; and finally the 5.56mm SC-20K AR assault rifle, another gift from DARPA.

The SC-20, chambered for a 5.56mm bullpup round, was a marvel of versatility and compactness. Equipped with a flash/sound suppresser with a 97 percent effective acoustic dampener, when fired, the SC-20 emitted a sound no louder than a tennis ball being thrown into a down pillow. What truly made the SC-20 special, however, was its modular design. With its subbarrel-mounted launcher, Fisher had access to a variety of weapons and sensors including ring air foil projectiles, adhesive cameras and microphones, and shock projectiles—each appropriately nicknamed the Sticky Cam, the Sticky Ear, and the Sticky Shocker—and gas grenades of varying potency.

All told, Fisher's gear, which weighed over forty pounds, allowed him to see, hear, move, kill, and incapacitate better than any covert soldier on the planet.

Now he went through each item, checking its operation, securing pouches, and tightening harness points until satisfied all was in order. He took one more scan of the surrounding forest, then rose to a crouch and sprinted toward the wall.

He stopped and dropped to a crouch beneath the drooping boughs of a hemlock tree. Ten feet ahead lay the wall, a patchwork of mortared black, gray, and brown fieldstone. The top of the wall, ten feet from the ground, was rounded and topped with jagged triangles of clear glass, like staggered rows of sharks' teeth glinting in the moonlight. It was well-designed, Fisher had to admit. There were neither jutting edges for handholds nor crevices for grapnel points.

Would a man like Legard, having the enemies he'd made to reach the top, be satisfied with just a ten-foot, shard-topped wall? Fisher doubted it. As an old SEAL buddy used to say, "Better safe than sorry *and* dead."

Fisher sidestepped behind the trunk, then grabbed the lowermost limb above his head, swung his left leg up, hooked his heel on the limb, and pulled his body up. In a crouch, he sidestepped down the limb until he could see the top of the wall through the leaves. He switched his goggles to EM mode. The image before his eyes was a swirling mass of barely perceptible dark blue amoeba-like shapes and wispy gray lines. Fisher scanned the top of the wall.

Reading EM was more an art than a science, much like a doctor deciphering an X-ray or ultrasound image. The modern world was a sea of electromagnetic pulses: power lines, telephone and television cables, satellite Internet transmissions, and cell phone signals. Over time, Fisher had mastered the art, but still it took him a full thirty seconds to spot what he was looking for.

Running parallel to the top of the wall, clusters of pin-prick dots appeared and disappeared at regular intervals. They were barely there, just a split-second flash, but it was enough to tell Fisher he was seeing a passive pressure sensor embedded in the top of the wall. The pinpricks were faint electrical impulses traveling down the sensor cable in search of breaches. Cut the cable, the pulses detect it and alert the monitoring station. Put any pressure on the cable, same reaction. Fisher scanned the other side of the wall and searched for signs of cameras or sensors. He saw nothing.

He switched back to NV. Over the treetops, perhaps four miles away, he could make out the peaked roofline and dormered windows of Legard's house. Closer in, just on the other side of the wall, Fisher saw something else: a winding path cutting through the groundcover; the foliage, however, was untouched. *Dogs,* Fisher thought. While Grimsdottir had confirmed Legard kept bullmastiffs on the property, she didn't know whether they were loose or paired with handlers. This "game trail" through the undergrowth told Fisher the dogs were loose—perhaps all the time, but most likely only at night. Left to their own devices, dogs on patrol will follow regular paths through their territory.

"Dogs," Fisher muttered. "Why'd it have to be dogs?"

Fisher loved dogs—would have owned a couple if not for his erratic schedule and long absences—but he also hated dogs, especially the kind that can run twice as fast as a man, can tackle with the ferocity of an all-star NFL linebacker, and had fangs sharp and strong enough to pulverize bone. Bullmastiffs were especially dangerous, not only for their size, which can range to two hundred pounds, but also because they worked in complete silence. No barking, no growling. Also, dogs on the run are nearly impossible to shoot until they're almost upon you. Fisher's choice had always been to give them a wide berth, both for his sake and for theirs. With luck, he would do so tonight.

As for the pressure sensor array in the wall, Fisher was unconcerned. Such sensors were only effective for intruders unaware of their presence. From his perch in the tree he panned along the wall until he found the location he needed, about fifty yards to the left. He hopped down and picked his way through the trees to the spot and then crouched flat against the wall. From one of his pouches he withdrew the Monkey Claw, a miniature football-shaped grapnel made of reinforced Grivory, a hardened fiberglass resin copolymer with enough tensile strength to support six hundred pounds. This was a distinctly low-tech tool he rarely got a chance to use.

Working from memory, he backed away from the wall until he could see the treetop he'd mentally tagged, then cocked his arm and threw. Inside the grapnel, a microaccelerometer sensed the velocity change and set off a series of squibs. Just as the grapnel disappeared over the wall trailing the kite's tail of pencil-thin wire, Fisher saw the grapnel's arms spring out and lock into position. He heard the muffled crackling of branches, then silence. He backed into the undergrowth and waited for two minutes to see if the noise had drawn any attention. Nothing happened.

Now he would find out if he'd been spending enough time in the gym. The grapnel's wire, knotted at intervals of two feet, was too light by itself to set off the sensor cable. He gathered up the slack in a loose loop, then carefully lifted the wire free of the wall and gave it a tug. It held firm. Next he braced his right foot flat against the wall, the left behind him for leverage, then, with the cable clutched in both fists, he raised his arms directly above his head and leaned backward. With the cable drawn taut, he lifted his left foot off the ground and placed it against the wall beside his right so he was hanging from the wall at a forty-five-degree angle. Immediately his shoulders began to tremble with the tension. The wire, quivering under Fisher's weight, hung suspended a few inches above the wall's shards.

Arms held vertically above him, elbows locked tight, Fisher lifted his right foot ever so slightly and slid it upward a few inches, then did the same with his left. One step at a time, his arms burning with the strain, he climbed upward until the tips of his boots were even with the top of the wall and resting against the shards. Now he began reeling himself in, hand over hand, until his body was nearly vertical, his toes balanced on the edge of the wall.

Now to see if you've spent enough time practicing breakfalls, Sam old boy.

He took a breath, slid his right hand as far forward on

the cable as he could, and tightened his grip. He flexed his ankles and bunched his calf muscles. In one explosive move, he jerked on the wire and pushed off with his toes. His body vaulted forward. He tucked his head to his chest, curled into a ball, and glanced through his armpit in time to see the ground rushing toward him. He turned his body, rolling his shoulder just as the impact came. He somersaulted once, came up in a crouch, and crab-walked into the undergrowth.

He sat still for half a minute to catch his breath, then keyed his SVT and said, "I'm in."

Grimsdottir replied, "In one piece?"

"Oh, Grim, that hurts."

"Status?"

"Clean."

As did all special operations troops, Splinter Cells used a mixture of standardized radio protocol and a language all their own to communicate. In this case, *clean* meant no complications of any kind. A *sleeper* was a lethal casualty, enemy combatant; a *napper* was a nonlethal casualty, enemy combatant. *Wildfire* meant a Splinter Cell was engaged in an open gun battle, and *breakline* meant he or she had been compromised, and the mission was in jeopardy. *Skyfall* meant the operative was now in E&E (escape and evasion) mode. Fisher had yet to call a breakline, but he knew operatives—friends—who had, and having broken the number one rule—leave no traceable footprints—they'd been summarily detached from Third Echelon.

"I've updated your OPSAT," Grimsdottir said. "Got some tighter terrain imagery of your next waypoint. Exactly how much money does this guy have?"

Fisher didn't know, and he didn't care. If Aldric Legard wanted his own private indoor/outdoor white-water kayak course, so be it. Fisher was only too happy to use the indulgence to his own advantage.

"Heading to waypoint two," Fisher said.

_10_

WITH no time restrictions except the coming dawn, which was still eight hours away, Fisher took his time picking his way through the forest surrounding Legard's house. Wherever he crossed one of the bullmastiffs' patrol trails, he planted a Sticky Ears on a nearby tree, then noted its location on his OPSAT map. Once he had planted a dozen Ears, he climbed a nearby tree and made himself comfortable. The dogs were eerily quiet, but with concentration Fisher was able to pick up their signature, a faint huffing as they moved down the trail, the crunch of pads on undergrowth or the click of claws on protruding roots, even the wet snuffling as one would stop to take in an interesting scent. Luckily, bullmastiffs were poor scent dogs, so Fisher had little worry about being tracked to his hiding perch.

Even so, twice a dog passed beneath his tree, and Fisher would watch, breath held, until the massive creature would wander off and disappear. These were no ordinary bull-mastiffs, he realized. Each weighed at least two hundred pounds, a solid mass of muscle with a head the size of a basketball.

Good doggies, Fisher thought.

For now, the guards didn't concern him. Using his NV binoculars, he'd counted eight guards patrolling the grounds around the mansion, but none of their routes took them farther out than two hundred yards from the house proper.

AFTER an hour of listening and watching, he was able to discern a pattern in the dogs' movements as they patrolled the grounds. Using his stylus, he marked the routes and times on the OPSAT's touch screen. Now the dogs appeared on his screen as orange triangles moving along the green lines of their paths. The guards' movements, however, were much more erratic, so Fisher could only inscribe a rough circle around the mansion in which the guards seemed to stay.

So far Fisher had found no other sensors. No cameras, no laser grids, no motion detectors. Nothing. He was unsurprised. Men of Legard's stature tend to believe their own press: *Who would dare intrude on my territory, much less attack me? No one would be so foolish. All the better,* Fisher thought. Like his kayak course, Legard's arrogance and delusions of grandeur were weaknesses Fisher was only too happy to exploit.

He waited for the next dog to make his orbit near Fisher's tree, then climbed down and started moving.

IN Grimsdottir's probe of Legard, she had been able to, as she put it, "digitally liberate" the blueprints for Legard's custom-made French Country style mansion. While this alone would be invaluable to Fisher once he penetrated the house, it was the architectural nod to the crime lord's hobby—kayaking—that most interested Fisher now. According to the architect's landscaping blueprints, the man-made kayak course, complete with boulders, waterfalls, and switchbacks, carved a meandering, three-mile descending loop through the trees surrounding the mansion, starting and ending at an enclosed tunnel connected to a glass-domed, twenty thousand square-foot pool/arboretum. Powered by massive pumps and pneumatically driven incline planes that could adjust the current and force of the water, Legard's course could, at the touch of a button, change from a sedate Class I stream, to raging Class V white-water rapids.

Fisher took his time moving from his tree perch to what he'd dubbed the "red zone," the outer perimeter of the guards' patrol ring. Three times he had to stop and go still as a dog neared his position. Frozen in place, barely breathing, Fisher was unable to check the OPSAT, so he had to simply listen for the telltale sign of a dog approaching: a random huff of breath or the crunch of a twig.

After an hour of picking his way through the trees and shadows, he reached the banks of Legard's kayak course, which was currently set at stream speed. If he hadn't known better and had this part of the course not been marked with slalom flags every twenty feet, Fisher wouldn't have guessed he was looking at a man-made stream.

He crab-walked down the embankment to the stream, which lay three to four feet below ground level, then stepped into the waist-deep water and started paddling upstream. After twenty minutes and fifty yards, Fisher saw the first glimmer of the mansion's floodlights through the tall grass that lined the stream's banks. Now he would start seeing guards. He removed the SC-20 from its back sling, then moved to the opposite bank—the mansion-side bank, he'd dubbed it—and belly-crawled up it until his head touched the grass, then inched forward until he could see the grounds.

The mansion lay a hundred yards away. The mansion's rear exterior was done in traditional French Country white stucco and brown, rough-hewn vertical beaming. Affixed to the apex of each of the eight peaks of the roof was a halogen spotlight that shone down on either the lawn or the paving-stone patio that ran the length of the house to the kayak course's dome. Lit from within by amber lighting dulled by tinted glass, the dome rose from the mansion's right side like a Disney World attraction. Fisher zoomed in on its base until he could make out the dark circle that marked the kayak course's exit from the dome. Somewhere on the back side would be a corresponding entrance, where the course emptied into the dome's pool.

Fisher switched his goggles to NV and then, through squinted eyes to obscure the glare, zoomed in on one of the spotlights. By touch he adjusted the controls on the side of the goggles, moving an eclipse ring over the bright dot of the spotlight. He zoomed in again and focused below the spotlight. *There you are* . . . A camera. He scanned the rest

of the lawn and patio, counting three guards moving along
the rear of the house.

The camera and spotlight were both rotatable and slaved
to one another, Fisher assumed. Where the spotlight went,
the camera followed. *One more hunch to indulge,* Fisher
thought. He shimmied back down the bank to the water,
found a squash ball–size stone, then crawled back up to the
grass. He waited until the nearest guard closed to within
thirty yards of him, then hurled the stone. It landed with a
thud in a patch of darkness between spotlights. The guard
turned at the sound. He pulled what looked like a portable
radio off his belt, brought it to his lips for a few seconds,
then reached into his pocket and retrieved a thumb-size rectangular object, which he pointed toward the nearest spotlight. The spotlight began rotating, the beam skimming
across the grass until it reached the stone's landing point,
where it stopped. The beam shifted several times, gliding up
and back, left and right, until the guard, seemingly satisfied
nothing was amiss, pointed the remote control back at the
spotlight, which rotated back to its original position.

Fisher sat still for five more minutes, then brought the
SC-20 to his shoulder, thumbed the selector to STICKY CAM,
then focused the scope on a tree along the bank about fifty
feet upstream. He fired. With a soft *whoosh-pop* of compressed air, the Sticky Cam arced out and planted itself
against the tree's trunk about twenty feet off the ground,
just below the lowermost branches. Using the OPSAT's
touch screen, Fisher panned the camera left and right to
make sure he'd placed it correctly. He had. At full extension, the camera could scan the entire length of the mansion's backyard. He set the Sticky Cam to slow auto pan,

then crawled back down the bank, reholstered the SC-20, and started upstream again.

Each step upstream brought him not only closer to the mansion but closer to the guards, so Fisher took care, stopping every dozen steps to crouch down and study the OPSAT's screen, which he'd programmed to give him a real-time feed of the Sticky Cam's pan. The guards were still accounted for, each either standing in place near one of the mansion's doors or walking across the lawn or patio.

Now the stream started to gain elevation. With every step closer to the dome, the grade increased, first from a gentle twenty degrees, then to a steep forty-five degrees, until Fisher was climbing through the water from boulder to boulder. The watercourse, now propelled by gravity, splashed around him, tossing up clouds of spray and froth. Occasionally Fisher's hand, groping for a hold, would land on one of the mechanical incline planes or the rim of one of the water conduits.

Ten feet from the dome, Fisher was climbing vertically through what was essentially a waterfall sluicing from the tunnel entrance. Careful to stay behind the curtain of water, he worked mostly by feel until at last his right hand found the curved lower rim of the tunnel. He paused to catch his breath, then placed his left hand next to his right and chinned himself up until his sternum was level with the rim. He raised his knee, hooked it over the edge, then braced his foot against the tunnel's side and pushed hard, rolling himself into the tunnel.

Immediately his body became a dam. He felt the current roiling against his back and shoulders, shoving him back toward the edge. He braced both palms against one side of the tunnel wall, his feet on the other, and arched his back, letting the water flow out below him. Hand over hand, foot over foot, back still bowed over the water, he walked himself up the tunnel until he reached the mouth, which rested half submerged in the dome's pool. With a groan of relief, Fisher let himself slide headfirst into the water. He resurfaced and looked around.

The interior dome could indeed pass for a Disney World attraction. Landscaped to a picture-perfect replica of a jungle oasis, the dome was its own ecosystem, complete with shoreline littered with boulders, ferns, and miniature waterfalls lit from beneath by amber spotlights, which cast undulating shadows on the bushy stands of bamboo that curved over the pool all the way to the smoked glass ceiling, some thirty feet above Fisher's head. Somewhere in the canopy came the squawking of night birds; Fisher couldn't tell whether the sounds were real or recorded. Either way, true to form, Legard had spared no expense on his hobby.

The pool itself, which measured roughly two hundred feet by two hundred feet, was kidney-shaped, with six to eight Jacuzzi-size coves built into the sides at irregular intervals. Each cove featured its own waterfall, which splashed onto the surface and sluiced through a narrow opening and into the pool proper. At the far end, under an arch of ferns, he could see a flagstone walkway bordered by green miniature spotlights. *An exit,* Fisher thought.

He sound-keyed his SVT, then said, "At waypoint four."

"Roger," Grimsdottir responded. "Is it everything you'd hoped for?"

"Like Canada's answer to Disney. I'm moving on."

11

HUNCHED over, Fisher padded down the flagstone walk-way, disabling the spotlights as he went with the SC pistol's EM scrambling function, until he reached the exit door, a black walnut, ten-paneled monster with massive, black wrought-iron butterfly hinges.

Lacking the time for a detailed pre-mission surveillance or a pair of human eyes on the inside to feed him information, Fisher knew he would have to play much of the penetration by ear. He knew Legard was home but little else. The mansion had eight bedrooms large and lavish enough to serve as a master suite, and another twelve rooms that served as loung-ing or entertainment or recreation spaces. Legard was a noto-rious insomniac, according to Grimsdottir's research, so there was no telling where Fisher would find the man.

He slipped his flexicam under the door's bottom edge; the OSPAT's screen showed a long hall done in brown travertine tile and Moroccan carpet runners, both lit by tulip-shaped Tiffany wall sconces. He switched to NV, then to IR, and saw no movement, so he switched finally to EM and scanned the corridor for signs of sensors or cameras. He saw nothing.

He withdrew the flexicam, then tried the doorknob. It was locked but, despite the door's imposing appearance, the lock was easy, clicking open under his picks after only twenty seconds.

He eased the door open a few inches and peeked through. All clear. He stepped in, swung the door shut behind him, and started down the corridor, which appeared to be lined on only one side with rooms, four of them; the other wall contained three narrow doors—closets, Fisher surmised. The wall sconces were dimly lit and spaced at twenty-foot intervals; Fisher left them alone. Too many bad bulbs would alert any security guard worth his or her salt.

The first room, a lounging space complete with sectional leather sofas, a round, open-hearth fireplace, and a wet bar, was empty, as was the second, a game room complete with two poker tables and a billiard table, its baize surface glowing beneath a Craftsman-style billiard lamp.

As Fisher approached the last room, where the corridor ended and turned left, he could hear strains of a television playing—an *American Idol* rerun, it sounded like, along with the voices of two or three men.

To his right Fisher heard footsteps padding down stairs. Fisher stepped left, opened the closet door, stepped inside, and pulled it shut behind him. He pulled out the flexicam and slipped it under the door in time to see a pair of booted feet pass the closet and disappear into the TV room. The TV went mute.

Fisher cracked the door an inch.

". . . the boss, anyway?" one voice said.

"Couldn't sleep again. He's upstairs, playing d'Artagnan with his sparring dummies," came the reply from who Fisher assumed was the newcomer. "Bruno's watching over him."

"Lucky Bruno . . ."

So Legard had another hobby: fencing.

"I'm going outside for a smoke."

Fisher eased the door shut again. The feet passed by the door and disappeared around the corner. Fisher waited until he heard a door slam somewhere in the distance.

He slipped out of the closet and started up the stairs.

A quick search of the second floor, which ran only half the length of the house, revealed only bedrooms and bathrooms, so Fisher continued to the third floor. The first three rooms were for recreational purposes: a handball court, an archery course, and a gym complete with elliptical machines, treadmills, vertical climbers, and a battery of Cybex weight-lifting machines.

As he moved toward the fourth room, he heard the clanging of steel on hardwood, followed by a shout, like a martial artist's "Kee-yah." Fisher bypassed the fourth room and crouched at the fifth door. He slipped his flexicam under the door and was greeted by a long, high-ceilinged white room lit by recessed halogen lighting. Floor-to-ceiling mirrors lined both the long walls, and between them a polished maple wood floor. Staggered down the center of the room were six to eight fencing dummies, like padded scarecrows with hardwood arms and legs and a round head made of black, vulcanized rubber.

Fisher panned the flexicam up toward the vaulted ceiling. At the junction of the wall and the curve of the ceiling was a long bank of windows running the length of the space. Fisher panned back down, angling the camera back and forth until he saw at the far end of the room a man in a black-and-white mesh mask and a white metallic-filament jumpsuit lunging and thrusting at one of the dummies. Also at the far end was a single guard, seated beside a door with his HK SL8-6 lying across his knees. The man looked bored, his shoulders slumped as he alternately watched the fencer and studied his fingernails.

Fisher withdrew the flexicam and retreated to the room he'd bypassed, which he found was a locker room: four shower stalls along one wall, a small dry sauna and cedar lounging benches on the other. Fisher turned off the lights, walked to the window, checked it for alarms and found none, then slipped the latch and swung both panes inward. The cool night air washed over him, sending a shiver up his arms and down his back. Over the treetops, he could see the moon had just passed its apogee and was now on its downward arc. He checked his watch. Still a good six hours before sunrise.

Outside the window was a stone ledge not more than six inches wide. Fisher climbed onto the sill and then, in a crouch, stepped out onto the ledge and closed the windows behind him. Carefully, slowly, he stood up, balanced forward on the balls of his feet so he was pressed against the wall. He could feel the reassuring solidity of the stone through the chest of his tac suit. He slid his hand along the wall until his fingertips found a gap in the stone; he wedged his fingers knuckle-deep into the crevice, then stepped right once, then again, then again. To his right and above, less than three feet away, he could see the roof's drainpipe slope upward to meet the eaves trough of the vaulted fencing room.

Three more steps brought him even with the angled pipe. With his left hand, he reached up, grabbed the trough, and began to slowly put weight onto it. When he had almost half his body weight on it, the pipe gave a faint creak but held steady. It was bolted firmly into the stone, not simply screwed or wired into place. *God bless a sturdy eaves trough,* Fisher thought.

He got a firm grip on the pipe with his left hand, then extricated his right hand from the crevice, stretched up, and hooked his right hand higher on the pipe. His legs swung off the ledge, now dangling in space. He repeated this move twice more, sliding his left hand forward, reaching higher with his right, until finally his fingertips found the open edge of the fencing room's eaves trough. On the forward third of his fingertips, he chinned himself up to the roofline, then hooked a foot onto the trough and levered himself up. He dropped flat on the cedar shingles and lay still for a few moments.

Grimsdottir's voice came into his ear: "Fisher, I've managed to untangle Legard's wireless Internet signal. They had some decent firewalls up; took me more time than I'd anticipated."

"And?"

"And every computer but one looks like a dedicated security workstation. Personal computer on the fourth floor, last room in the northeast corner. My guess: It's either Legard's bedroom or office. You get me a hard link to it, and I'll hack in."

"Consider it done. I'll get back to you."

Fisher pushed himself up into a crouch and crab-walked to the windows. The windows, which from below had appeared vertical, were actually sloped inward. Fisher slipped the latch of the nearest window and opened it an inch.

Twenty feet below, under the glare of the halogen lights, he could see Legard, now without his face mask, moving down the line of dummies, thrusting, lunging, and spinning, dispatching each with a death blow before moving on to the next.

Legard was a handsome man, with long, flowing black hair, chiseled cheekbones, and a lantern jaw. He looked ten years younger than his actual age of fifty. After he'd dispatched the last dummy with a lunging strike to the throat, Legard strolled back through the gauntlet, his foil tucked under his arm, a broad grin on his face.

"What do you say, Bruno, eh? Am I not a joy to watch?"

The guard, now sitting up straight, said, "Yes, boss, amazing stuff."

Still smiling, Legard removed his gauntlets and tossed them at Bruno. "Someday you'll see the beauty in it, my friend. Your senses have been blunted by our product, yes? All those fresh, pretty things . . . hard to concentrate on what really counts in life."

"True, boss."

"How's our guest getting along?"

"Full of complaints, that one."

Guest? Fisher thought. *Carmen Hayes?*

"He's a pampered scientist, Bruno, a lab rat. What do you expect?"

Not Carmen.

"It would be nice if he stopped whining. I called Baie Comeau. They're loading him aboard in a few minutes. He's been curled up in a corner, whimpering all night."

Baie Comeau, Fisher thought. Grimsdottir's briefing had listed Baie Comeau, one of Legard's port warehouses along the St. Lawrence. Clearly they were loading someone aboard one of Legard's ships. But bound for where, and to whom?

"We'll be rid of him soon enough. Go get me some water, will you?"

Bruno got up and stepped through the door.

Fisher didn't hesitate. He drew his pistol, set the selector to DART 1, then opened the window another two inches. Legard was standing at the far wall, practicing his fencing poses before the mirror. Fisher took aim and fired. The dart struck true, plunging into the nape of Legard's neck. He gave a faint gasp, staggered forward a couple steps, arms flailing as he looked for something to latch on to, then crumpled, sliding down the mirror to the floor.

Fisher holstered the pistol, swung the window all the way open, hooked the Monkey Claw on the sill, then let the wire drop to the floor and followed it. With a quick whip of the wire he freed the Monkey Claw, then wrapped it up, restored it, and sprinted to the mirrored wall where Legard lay. The switch panel beside the door controlled the lights, he assumed. He flipped all four switches. The room went black. He pressed himself to the wall, flipped down his goggles, and switched to NV. He drew a lead-and-leather sap from his belt and waited, eyes on the door.

Ten seconds later, he heard the knob turn. The door swung open, casting a skewed rectangle of yellow light on the maple floor. Bruno's shadow moved forward, followed by Bruno himself as he crossed the threshold.

"Boss? Hey, boss, are you—"

Fisher was up and moving. Right arm cocked, he took two quick steps toward Bruno, then flicked his wrist. The lead and leather sap impacted just below Bruno's ear with a dull *thud*. Bruno collapsed, and the water bottle he'd brought for Legard rolled across the floor. Fisher caught Bruno's body, dragged him out of the light, and laid him down. He drew the pistol and waited. Five seconds, ten, then thirty. No shouts of alarm. Fisher crept to the door and peeked around it; the hall was clear. He swung the door shut and locked it.

He holstered his pistol and turned back to Legard.

Time to have a chat with our white slaver.

12

FISHER'S SC pistol had a variety of dart selections, ranging from low to high in anesthetic dosage. Level three would keep a 180-pound man unconscious for ninety minutes; level two, half that; level one, fifteen to twenty minutes. Legard, whom Fisher assumed weighed nearly two hundred pounds, would take around ten minutes.

He was two minutes off. Eight minutes after Fisher darted him, Legard groaned, lifted his head from his chest, and shook it. He blinked his eyes a few times, then opened them and looked around. Fisher had propped him against the mirror with one of the padded dummies behind his back, his hands bound behind his back by a plastic flexicuff. Bruno, who had gotten a level two dart after he went down, was similarly bound, save one addition: a gag made of his own socks.

Now, crouched a few feet away from Legard, Fisher studied the crime lord in the gray-green glow of his NV goggles. The room was pitch-black, except for what little pale moonlight made its way through the upper windows. The rest of Legard's training dummies stood like frozen sentinels down the center of the room, multiplied by the mirrors on both walls.

Legard cleared his throat, then spoke: "What's . . . what's going on? Bruno, are you there? Bruno!"

"Keep your voice down," Fisher whispered. "Raise it again, and I'll put a bullet in your knee. Nod if you understand."

Legard nodded.

"Bruno's taking a nap. You and I need to have a chat."

"Who the hell are you? Don't you—"

"Know who you are? Of course I know who you are, Mr. Legard." People like Legard were predictable. First the indignation, then the threats, then the propositioning. "And just to save time, yes, I know what a mistake this is, invading your home; and yes, I know what you'll do to me if you catch me; and, no, I don't want any money to let you go. Did I miss anything?"

"You're a dead man."

"We've already been through that," Fisher whispered. "Time to move on."

"You can go fu—"

Fisher jammed the barrel of the pistol against the sole of Legard's foot. "Be nice, or you'll be fondling your foil from a wheelchair. Understood?"

"Yes, I understand."

"Okay, here's how it's going to work: I'm going to ask you some questions. I'm a decent judge of character. Now, just because I'm also a nice guy, I'm going to give you two free lies. After that, I'm going to start hurting you. Are you ready?"

"Yeah . . ." Legard grumbled, clearly not yet a believer.

"Tell me about a woman named Carmen Hayes."

"Who?"

"Brunette, late thirties, scientific type. Not the typical blond-haired runaway you sell. She was snatched off the streets of Montreal four months ago."

Legard chewed his lower lip as though giving the question careful thought. "Sorry. Don't know her."

"That's one lie. Okay, we'll come back to her later. The man you were talking about with Bruno—your ill-mannered guest. Who is he, and where's he going?"

Legard shook his head. "There's no one here. I have no guests."

"You're sure?"

"Yes."

"Turn your head to the side."

"What?"

"Turn your head to the side. *Now.*" Legard did so. Fisher said, "Lift your chin a little . . ."

Legard did so. Fisher fired a shot into the training dummy just below Legard's chin. Legard recoiled, nearly tipping on his side. Fisher propped him upright.

Legard blurted, "You're crazy, Jesus Christ, you're crazy."

"It's a distinct possibility," Fisher replied. "I'm going to ask you one more time, and then I won't ask again until you're bleeding and crippled. So answer carefully. Tell me about Carmen Hayes and your mystery guest at Baie Comeau."

Legard started talking.

FISHER'S pistol had in fact four dart settings: one through three, and then level four, which was yet another bit of magic from the shadowed halls and devious minds at DARPA. Fisher had read the scientific name for the dart's contents once and its tongue-torturing complexity made him glad they'd given it a code name, *Spigot,* which, he assumed was meant to describe what the chemical did to a person's short-term memory—namely, it opened a notional valve on his or her brain and let twenty to thirty minutes of short-term memory leak out.

There are two kinds of memory, short-term and long-term; the former stored by the frontal and parietal lobes, the latter stored weblike throughout different portions of the brain. The bridge between the two, the part of the brain that converts short-term memory into long-term memory, is governed by the hippocampus, which is where Spigot worked its magic. By partially dissolving the chemical glue that holds the hippocampus bridge together, Spigot created a mild version of retrograde amnesia that turned the target's previous thirty minutes of memory into dreamlike recollections that faded within minutes of regaining consciousness.

So, despite his first instinct, the truth was, Fisher had had no intention of killing Legard. As much as the man deserved to be gone from the planet—and Fisher was giving serious thought to paying him another visit after all this was over— his death would stir up a hornet's nest of trouble, especially if he was in contact with whoever he'd delivered Carmen Hayes to and whoever was about to deliver his latest prisoner, the man Legard had identified as Calvin Stewart.

If Fisher was going to follow the trail of clues that appeared to have gotten Peter killed, he needed this pipeline to remain open. Of course, Fisher was painfully aware that by maintaining the pipeline's integrity, he was allowing Legard to send who knew how many kidnapped girls to their overseas buyers. *Another time,* Fisher thought, *another late-night visit.*

In quick order, he hit Legard with a level three dart and a level four, then unbound him. He did the same to Bruno, then returned the training dummy to its stand and turned the lights back on. While both men would awake confused, neither would remember anything of the last half hour. Legard was fencing; Bruno watching. And then . . . nothing until they awoke. And if Fisher did his job right, leaving no trace of his presence, and nothing was found missing or out of place following the inevitable security sweep Legard would order, their minds would find a way to write off the experience.

In the end, Fisher felt certain Legard had told him the whole truth. He had in fact kidnapped Carmen Hayes, but the request had come to him anonymously through a series of cutouts, one of whom he trusted. The price had been right—US$500,000—so Legard had taken the job. Calvin Stewart's kidnapping had been the same story: kidnapped off the street after being lured to Montreal by a bogus job offer. Legard knew little about either Hayes or Stewart, except that they were both "science types of some kind," nor did he know where they were ultimately bound. Legard's latest victim, Stewart, was to be initially delivered to the same place he'd sent Carmen Hayes: a waterfront warehouse in Halifax, Nova Scotia. A group of masked men had met Legard's own crew and taken custody of Carmen—as they would, Fisher assumed, take custody of Stewart.

But why? Who was collecting scientists, and why? And what did either of them have to do with Peter's death? *Too many questions,* Fisher thought, *and not enough answers.* Perhaps his next stop would remedy that.

Fisher keyed his SVT and said, "Grim, I've got a name for you: Calvin Stewart. Somewhere I think you'll find a missing persons report on him. I need everything you can dig up."

"Got it. Anything else?"

"A warehouse in Halifax." Fisher gave her the particulars. "They're loading Stewart onto a ship in Baie Comeau. That's my next stop. Where's Bird?"

"Idling on the tarmac at St-Mathieu-de-Beloeil. ETA to evac point Charlie is ten minutes."

"Radio him for me, tell him to put on his flying hat. I'll be calling."

Fisher signed off, then slipped out the fencing room door and padded down the hall to the last door on the east side, the one Grimsdottir suspected contained the only personal computer in the house. The door was unlocked. Inside he found what looked like a private study. The lights were off save a single spotlight in the ceiling that cast a dim pool of light on the hardwood walnut floor. He found the

PC—a high-end Alienware—on a rolltop desk in the corner and plugged the OPSAT's USB into the PC's port.

"Hooked up," Fisher told Grimsdottir.

"Roger. Scanning . . . Nice firewall . . . nice, but not nice enough. There, I'm in. Downloading now." Thirty seconds passed, then, "Done, Sam."

Fisher disconnected the USB. "I'm ex-filtrating."

TWENTY minutes later he was sliding out the pool's exit chute and climbing down the rocks into the kayak course. He looked east and could see on the horizon the barest hint of reddish pink under a fringe of leaden clouds. This was false dawn, he knew. The true sunrise was at least four hours away. *Red skies at night, sailor's delight,* Fisher thought. *Red skies at dawn, sailors take warn.* It was an old nautical saying that he'd found to be more often accurate than not. In fact, he could smell the tang of ozone in the air. Rain was coming.

Having already trail-blazed his infiltration route through the forest surrounding Legard's mansion, he simply followed the course in reverse order, moving more quickly this time and pausing only to avoid the guards and dogs. An hour later he was at the wall. He crouched down and checked the OPSAT to ensure his spot was still dog-friendly, then called up the OPSAT's communication screen, tapped the airplane icon, then selected from the drop-down menu the commands, CALL TO followed by EVAC POINT C. Five seconds passed, then Fisher heard in his ear, "Roger. En route. ETA ten. Out."

Fisher scaled the wall and headed for the water.

13

FISHER lay belly down, his face mask awash in the shallows of the river, for four minutes, gauging the current and watching the rain clouds gather over the treetops, then pushed off, stroked a hundred yards into the channel, and stopped. The current immediately took hold of him, dragging him downstream. Three minutes later he was a half mile away from Legard's estate when he heard the faint thrumming of a plane's engines, followed a few seconds later by the sight of the flat-bottomed, rounded nose cone of a V-22 Osprey emerging from the fog along the southern shoreline.

The Osprey dropped to twenty feet, swooped over Fisher, then banked, its engine nacelles rotating from horizontal to vertical as it slowed to a hover and then began drifting backward until its tail was directly above Fisher.

The tail ramp lowered, and a coiled rope rolled out and dropped into the water beside him. Fisher looped his arm into the thick rubber horse collar and gave a thumbs-up at the ramp, where he knew a high-resolution night-vision camera was focused on him.

The Osprey lifted upward, and the winch began reeling him in.

FIVE minutes later, dried off, coffee cup in hand, and changed into a pair of blue coveralls, Fisher sat down in the empty engineer's seat in the rear of the cockpit and said, "So, how's everyone's morning so far?"

The pilot, an easygoing southern boy nicknamed Bird, said, "Peachy, Sam, and you?"

Fisher shrugged. "The usual. Hi, Sandy."

Sandy, Bird's copilot, one of the first women to break into the male-dominated special operations community, nodded back at Fisher. "Sam." Where Bird was a carefree soul, Sandy was the polar opposite: taciturn and all business. Fisher liked Sandy, but he could count on one hand the number of times he'd seen her smile. Together, Bird and Sandy formed a balanced pair.

The newest edition to Bird's crew, the Osprey's engineer/navigator/loadmaster, was an Annapolis wunderkind graduate named Franklin. Fisher wasn't sure if Franklin was his first name or last, but Bird had dubbed him Franco, so Franco it was. He had a quick, easy smile and could do black-belt-level sudoku, in pen, with one half of his brain while calculating glide paths with the other.

Fisher was very much at home aboard the Osprey, which

Bird had dubbed *Lulu*, per his prerogative as the captain, and had spent almost as much time flying aboard it as he had driving his own car. Billed as both a VTOL (vertical takeoff and landing) and STOL (short takeoff and landing) craft, the Osprey was not only Third Echelon's workhorse, used for dicey insertion and extraction missions in "denied areas," but had over the years been Fisher's lifesaver many times.

"Morning, Franco," Fisher said.

"Morning, sir," Franco said with a nervous smile. Though both Bird and Sandy denied it, Fisher suspected they'd been telling their new crewman tall tales about him—that Fisher ate live ducklings for breakfast and he'd been responsible for the *Hindenburg* disaster in 1937.

"Bird, how far to Baie Comeau?" Fisher asked.

"Two hundred miles. Should have you there in forty."

Too long, Fisher thought. If Bruno's prediction was right, Stewart might have already been loaded aboard whichever of Legard's ships would be carrying the scientist to Halifax. They'd have to catch the ship at sea.

Fisher grabbed a headset on the bulkhead, settled it on his head, and swiveled the microphone to his mouth. Bird said, "Sit room on button two." Fisher punched the button and said, "You there, Grim?"

"Here."

"Any luck?"

"Some. Calvin Stewart's boss reported him missing two weeks ago. Stewart is a particle physicist at University of Toronto. He's working on a grant from the U.S. Department of Energy; I'm trying to get the specifics, but the DOE is being cagey.

"As for the ship, the only one in Legard's fleet that's filed departure with the Baie Comeau harbormaster is a dry cargo hauler called *Gosselin*. She left port twenty minutes ago, heading for the Gaspé Passage. She should be passing Pointe-des-Monts right about now."

Fisher did a quick mental calculation. By the time he was feet-down on the *Gosselin*'s deck, it would be four a.m., the darkest part of the night, but it would leave him only a couple of hours before the day watch began. He'd have to move quickly.

"You get that, guys?" Fisher asked.

"Roger," replied Sandy. Franco, sitting across the aisle from Fisher, was already bent over his folding desk, tapping keys on his navigation computer's keyboard.

Grimsdottir said, "I'm updating your OPSAT with blueprints and specs for the *Gosselin* now. What I can't tell you is where they're keeping Stewart."

"I have an idea how we can find out," Fisher replied, then explained his plan. "Once I'm aboard and in place, we'll use it to shake the tree. Bird, you got any ideas about getting me aboard?"

"I can drop you in the drink ahead of her—"

"Not enough time."

"Or I can . . ." Bird trailed off, hesitant.

"What?" Fisher asked.

"Or we can test out a little trick Sandy and I've been practicing awhile."

"And just how much testing have you and Sandy done?"

Sandy replied, "Enough that we're reasonably confident we won't kill you."

"Oh, well, if you're *reasonably* confident . . . Okay, let's hear it."

Bird outlined the plan, then said, "You game?" When Fisher didn't immediately reply, Bird mock-slapped his own forehead. "Sorry, I forgot who I was talking to. Go get a few winks, Sam. I'll call you when we're twenty out."

Fisher walked back into the cabin and folded down one of the bulkhead cots and stretched out. He closed his eyes to sleep but almost immediately knew sleep wouldn't be coming, so he lay still, listening to the hum of the Osprey's engines, and thought.

Peter's dead. Until now, until he'd allowed himself to slow down and open his mind, the truth of the statement had been missing for him. He'd boxed it up and gone through the motions: holding Peter's lifeless and tepid hand, the autopsy report, the cremation and the memorial. He'd detached himself from all of it—yet another skill essential to this business. Learn how to attenuate or shut off altogether any emotion that steals focus from the job at hand. Fisher felt a twinge of guilt that he had, albeit unknowingly, treated Peter's death in the same way. Using his mission mind to deal with something as personal as this felt disrespectful and disingenuous.

And what about his promise to Lambert? His first instinct had been to take a leave of absence from Third Echelon and track down Peter's killers himself, and while that urge still lingered in the back of his head, Fisher also knew there were more important things at stake here. Peter had died of PuH-19, plutonium hydride-19, a substance so deadly most of the earth's First World countries—even the ones incapable of nuclear weapons or energy production—had banned its storage. Where had Peter picked up the poison? Grimsdottir had said there'd been a week gap between

Peter's last credit card purchase in Halifax and when he was fished from the Labrador Sea. So far, Grimsdottir's monitoring of the North American and European medical networks had turned up no cases of poisoning similar to Peter's. It appeared as if Peter had been the only one exposed to PuH-19, which in turn suggested it had been intentional. There were only two countries that hadn't signed the ban on PuH-19: the United States and Russia. That didn't, however, mean there weren't other nations producing PuH-19. So where did that leave him? Still only one option: Track back Peter's investigation into the disappearance of Carmen Hayes and hope it took him to the source of the PuH-19 and whoever was behind it.

One way or another, wherever the trail led him or however long it took, someone was going to pay.

"RISE and shine, Sam. Got your target on radar. Eighteen minutes out."

Fisher opened his eyes; he hadn't realized he'd dozed off. Unlocking the emotional box into which he'd put Peter's death had evidently helped. "I'm up."

"Franco's coming back to help. No worries, we used him as a guinea pig on this thing. He knows it backward and forward."

Fisher rolled upright and put his stocking feet on the floor; through the chilled, nonskid metal he could feel the thrumming of the Osprey's engines. Franco appeared at the edge of the cot and handed him a cup of coffee and an energy bar wrapped in plain white wrapping with the words, in black, ENERGY SUPPLEMENT, FRENCH VANILLA,

ONE EACH, A/N 468431 stenciled on the side. It was as thick as Fisher's wrist and nearly as long as a paperback book.

Fisher took it and looked at Franco. "Got some heft to it, doesn't it?"

"Another DARPA product. Coming soon, government-issue Kit Kat bars."

Fisher smiled at him. "Franco, was that a joke?"

"Uh, yeah . . . I guess so. Anyway, I've tried them. Not bad. Three of these a day, and you've got all the nutrients and calories you need."

Next they'll come up with dehydrated water, Fisher thought with a rueful smile.

"When you're ready," Franco said, "I'll meet you at the ramp."

Fisher downed his coffee, gulped down the energy bar, which was, in fact, palatable if not wholly chewable, then donned his tac suit and web harness and settled the SVT strap around his throat. "Up on SVT," he told Bird and Sandy.

"Four minutes to ramp down," Bird replied.

Fisher walked back to the ramp, where Franco was kneeling at the winch, working.

"Ready?"

"Yes, sir. Same principle as fast-roping except for the altitude."

This was a huge understatement, Fisher knew. A standard fast-rope insertion by a hovering helo or Osprey was done at an altitude of fifty to ninety feet. What Bird and Sandy had been practicing was still in the experimental stages: HADFR (high-altitude dynamic fast-roping)—in other words, fast-roping at four hundred to five hundred feet above a moving target. There were a number of problems with this, primarily wind shear and targeting, which were different sides of the same coin. At five hundred feet, the force of the wind on the unfortunate soul dangling at the end of the fast rope—also called the worm—was considerable and unpredictable, often driving the worm far behind and to the side of the aircraft. The other side of the coin—targeting—was dicey because the flight crew would have either a degraded visual fix on the target or, in the case of bad weather or darkness, no fix at all.

Bird and Sandy had solved these problems with a custom-designed clear Lexan fairing that would hang, affixed, to the rope before the worm. Much like the curved shield carried by riot control police, the fairing cut the wind and decreased the drag to nearly zero. The targeting issue was solved in two parts: First, by a wireless transmitter that would feed real-time video from Fisher's NV goggles straight to an LCD screen mounted between Sandy and Bird; and second, by a miniature LTD (laser target designator) pod strapped to Fisher's wrist and index finger that not only uploaded his desired landing point but also his position relative to it. What Fisher saw, Bird would see; where Fisher pointed his LTD would be where Bird steered the Osprey. Fisher had to only look and point and then unhook himself when he was over the target.

HADFR addressed the primary drawback of standard fast-roping: noise. Helicopters and Ospreys were loud. There was no mistaking either the thunderous chop of rotors approaching your position nor the down blast fifty feet above your head as the craft went into a hover to deploy fast-roping troops. For bad guys the din was as good as an early warning alarm.

The issue that could complicate this particular HADFR was that Legard's ship, the *Gosselin,* had a robust navigation radar with an operable ceiling of seven hundred feet. Bird would have to work some of what Fisher had come to call his "aviational magic," or as Bird himself called it, "sleight of wing."

Franco finished cinching the rig onto Fisher, then patted him on the shoulder.

Bird said in his ear, "Two minutes to ramp down. How're ya feeling, Sam?"

"Like a flying worm."

14

FISHER felt and heard the Osprey's engines slow as Bird throttled back and rotated the nacelles to three-quarters, bleeding off speed for altitude as he dropped the craft into the *Gosselin*'s radar bubble. The Osprey would be directly over the ship now, Fisher knew, but in one of its radar blind spots—the other being a ring approximately three hundred yards in diameter around the ship at wave-top height, where the radar's signal would be lost in sea clutter.

"One minute to ramp down," Sandy called in Fisher's ear. "We're matching up the couplers. Stand by."

Like Pave Low special operations helicopters, this generation of Osprey was equipped with what was called a hover coupler. When engaged, the coupler could lock the craft into either a precise fixed spot over the earth's surface or slave its position to a designated target, in this case the *Gosselin* as it steamed out of the St. Lawrence Seaway and into the Gaspé Passage.

"Not going anywhere," Fisher replied. *Yet*. He felt that familiar and welcome anticipation/adrenaline flutter in his belly. He closed his eyes and slowed his breathing, centering himself. As it always did, the image of his daughter Sarah's face appeared before his eyes. This had become a ritual for Fisher, a good luck touchstone he performed before each mission. He opened his eyes. *Focus, Sam. Time to work.*

Outside, over the roar of the engines, he could hear the hail-like splatter of rain on the fuselage. "Weather report, Sandy?"

"True winds light, three to five from the northwest; relative winds between us and the target's deck, fifteen to seventeen knots; heavy and steady rain; temperature forty-eight degrees Fahrenheit."

"All in all," Bird added, "a downright lovely day."

"I'm sure they've got coffee aboard," Fisher replied. "I'll see if I can scare up a cup."

"Altitude, four hundred ninety-one. Ramp down in thirty seconds. We're slaved to the target. As soon as you're out the door, steering and cable slack on your command."

The cabin lights blinked out, then glowed back to life in night-vision-friendly red.

"Roger," Fisher said, and pulled up the hood on his tac suit and settled his goggles over his eyes. A thought occurred to him. He leaned closer to Franco, who was buckling into a safety rig on the bulkhead, and said, "The fairing—"

"Freshly coated in DARPA's own version of Rain-X. Water should bead up and roll away."

"Right."

"Ramp coming down."

A moment later Fisher heard the whirring of the ramp's motors. Accompanied by a sucking whoosh of cold air, the ramp's lip parted from the curved edge of the fuselage's tail, and a slice of black sky appeared. The ramp continued descending, then stopped, fully open. Outside, Fisher could see skeins of clouds whipping past the opening and, in the breaks between the clouds, the distant twinkling of lights; the ships moving up and down the St. Lawrence showing up as individual specks, the cities and highways along the seaway as threads and clusters.

Franco patted him on the shoulder again and called into his ear, "Whenever you're ready."

Fisher nodded, performed a final check of his rigging, then turned around so he was facing forward, then backstepped up to the edge of the ramp until his heels were dangling in space, then coiled his legs and launched himself backward.

Per the plan, Franco let out an immediate four hundred feet of cable, which brought Fisher to a halt a hundred feet above the *Gosselin*'s mainmast, still unseen in the darkness. Though the true wind speed was negligible, Fisher's relative speed through space was almost eighteen miles an hour, which was enough to turn the otherwise vertical rain into a diagonal, slashing deluge that peppered the fairing like blown sand. True to Franco's prediction, however, the water beaded up and sluiced away before it could obscure Fisher's vision. Through his harness he could feel the cable thrumming with the tension, like a plucked guitar string.

"Cable stopped and locked," Bird said in his ear. "On you now, Sam."

"Roger."

Fisher powered up his NV goggles and heard, very faintly in his ear, the familiar hum. His vision went to gray-green. And directly below his feet, not more than a third of a football field away, he could now see the top of the *Gosselin*'s mast and the crescent-shaped dish of the navigation radar making its slow rotation.

Fisher pushed a button on the LTD pod on his wrist and then extended his index finger, aiming it at the ship's afterdeck. He'd chosen this spot for his insertion primarily because of the weather. In this rain, if a stern lookout was posted, he or she would have likely withdrawn to the overhanging awning on the second-level aft superstructure. Same for anyone taking a smoke break. He switched his goggles to IR and scanned the afterdeck and superstructure for human-shaped thermal signatures. He saw none. *God bless bad weather,* he thought and switched back to NV.

"Reading your LTD clearly," Sandy said. "Confirm designated aim point as afterdeck, midline, twenty feet forward of stern."

"Confirmed," Fisher replied. "Give me sixty of cable."

"Sixty feet of cable," Franco repeated. "Spooling now."

Fisher felt himself dropping through the air. He was now aft of the mainmast. The cross-girdered tower, partially obscured by the rain, appeared before his eyes, seemingly rising disembodied from the darkness. He was forty feet above the afterdeck and twenty above the superstructure, almost dead center on the ship's midline.

Fisher felt himself bump to a stop.

"Cable stopped," Franco called.

"Confirm cable stopped," Fisher replied.

Again he scanned the superstructure and afterdeck and again saw neither movement nor heat signatures. He knew better than to do an EM scan; this close to the *Gosselin*'s navigation radar, all he would see is a blinding swirl of electromagnetic waves that would leave him with a three-day headache. He switched back to NV. Down the length of the superstructure he could see the faint yellow glow of light escaping from the pilothouse's port and starboard bridge wing doors—and cast in shadow on either wing a lone figure standing at the railing. Port and starboard lookouts. Not a concern right now. Their attention would be focused forward.

Fisher said, "Give me thirty of—" He stopped. On the afterdeck, a door opened on the superstructure, revealing a rectangle of red light. Standing in the rectangle was a man-shaped shadow. "Disregard my last. Hold cable."

"Holding cable."

The figure stood still for a second, then lifted its cupped hands to its face. Fisher saw the flare of a lighter. The hands dropped away, revealing the glowing tip of a cigarette.

Fisher said, "Stand by. Got a crewman on a smoke break."

Fisher dangled in space, swaying slightly in the wind, which was partially blocked by the ship's superstructure, for another five minutes until finally the crewman finished his cigarette and then leaned forward and swung the door shut.

"Clear," Fisher radioed. "Preparing to deploy."

He heard the double squelch of "Roger" from Franco in his ear.

He scanned the afterdeck for a clean drop zone. There. A patch of open deck bracketed by a barrel-size bollard near the port rail and the raised, glassed-in control cabin for the stern winch. Fisher pointed his LTD at the spot.

"Read distance to deck."

Sandy replied, "Thirty-eight feet. Stand by. Calculating vertical variance."

In the cockpit, Sandy would be using the flight computer to read the rise and fall of the *Gosselin*'s deck on the waves. Nothing got your attention or tended to break ankles like landing on a deck that was bucking up to meet you. It was like stepping off what you thought was the second-to-last step on a stairway only to find one more beneath your foot—only much worse.

"Variance of two feet, Sam."

Four feet in either direction, Fisher thought.

He said, "On my mark, give me a sharp drop—thirty-four feet."

"Roger," Franco said. "Sharp drop of thirty-four on your mark."

Fisher watched the deck heave and drop below his feet. In the corners of his eyes, beyond the port and starboard deck railing, he could see the roiling, curled white edges of the waves. For a fraction of a moment he felt a wave of vertigo; he focused on the deck and blocked out the peripheries.

Wait for it . . . wait . . .

The deck heaved upward, paused, then dropped again.

"Mark."

He felt his belly lurch into his throat as Franco quick-spooled the cable. Half a second later Fisher jerked to a stop. He hit the rig's quick release, felt himself dropping, then hit the deck on the balls of his feet, dropped his shoulder, and rolled right, behind the bollard.

"Down, safe, and clear."

"Retrieving cable."

"Thanks for the ride," Fisher said. "I'll call you when I'm ready to shake the tree."

"At your service, boss," Bird said.

Fisher did a quick NV/IR scan of the deck around him, then sprinted, hunched over, to the superstructure, where he flattened himself against it. Palms pressed against the aluminum bulkhead, he sidestepped until his shoulder was pressed against the jamb of the hatchway in which he'd seen the smoker. He crouched down, then undogged the hatch a half inch and inserted the flexicam. The lens revealed a red-lit passageway, ten feet long, and ending in a split ladder way, one going up and one going down.

According to Grimsdottir, the *Gosselin*'s crew numbered eight: captain, first mate, helmsman, three cargo handlers, and two engineers. It was four twenty. Most of the crew would be asleep, with the first mate and helmsman on the bridge and one engineer on duty in the engine spaces. The big question mark was, who, if anyone, was guarding Calvin Stewart? Had Legard sent a bodyguard or two to mind the prisoner? He would soon find out.

Fisher withdrew the flexicam, then drew his pistol, opened the hatch halfway, stepped through, and pulled it shut behind him. He crouched for a full minute, listening and watching, until he was sure he was alone, then holstered the pistol.

He tapped the OPSAT's touch screen and called up the

Gosselin's blueprint. Drawn in green wireframe on the black screen, the schematic was fully three dimensional, and the OPSAT's stylus let him pan, rotate, and zoom the image. He played with it until he found what he wanted: crew's quarters, second level, forward, just below the pilothouse.

He crept to the ladder and peered down, belowdecks, and saw nothing, so he mounted the ladder and climbed upward until his head was even with the deck above. Another passageway. This one, which had no direct access to the weather decks and therefore had no chance of emitting light other ships might mistake for navigation lights, was lit not by red lamps but by wall sconces, which cast pools of dim light on the overhead and deck.

On cat's feet Fisher climbed the remaining few steps, then started down the passage. He counted doors as he went. There were ten, one for each crew member and two spares. The doors were evenly split down the port and starboard bulkheads, five to each side, with an eleventh door—a janitor's closet—in the middle of the port bulkhead. As Fisher had feared, there were no name placards on the bulkhead, so finding which room held Stewart would take more time than he had. It was time to test his ruse.

He walked to the end of the passage and stopped before the last door, where he crouched. From a pouch on his calf he withdrew a thumb-size cylinder of compressed air topped with an articulated and long-stemmed nozzle like those found on cans of WD-40.

Inside, suspended within the compressed air, were thousands of RFID (radio frequency identification) chips, each the size of a grain of sand—essentially RFID powder.

Miracles of miniaturization, RFID chips had initially been designed for loss prevention in U.S. retail stores. Each product gets an adhesive tag into which RFID powder has been embedded and each chip, or grain, is equipped with 128-bit ROM, or read-only memory, onto which a unique identification number has been engraved by an electron beam. When a chip, or a sprinkling of chips, comes within range of a detector, the ID number is read and verified as purchased or not yet purchased.

For Fisher's purposes, the good folks at DARPA had taken the RFID powder concept one step further, first by coating each chip's surface with a silicate that acted much like a cocklebur that attached itself to anything and everything, and second by affixing to each grain an external antenna—a tiny ribbon of wire half an inch long and barely the width of a human hair—that extended the chip's transmission range to twenty feet.

As usual, of course, Fisher hadn't liked DARPA's official name for the RFID powder, which contained so many letters and numbers it looked like a calculus equation gone wrong, and had renamed it Voodoo Dust.

He pointed the canister at the deck before the door and pressed the nozzle. He heard a faint *pfft*. He backed down the passage, pausing at each door to coat the deck with the powder until he reached the janitor's closet, where he turned around, walked to the opposite end of the passage, and then repeated the process, back-stepping until he'd covered each doorway and returned to the closet. He opened the door, slipped inside, and shut it behind him. On the OPSAT, he zoomed and rotated the *Gosselin*'s blueprint until the passageway filled the screen; there, in the black deck space between two notional bulkheads, were several dozen tiny blue dots, each one pulsing ever so slightly. Each dot, he knew, represented roughly one hundred RFID chips. The dots were spread down the passageway, three or four of them per door.

Into the SVT, he said, "Paint job done. Shake the tree."

"Roger," Sandy replied from the Osprey. "On your button four. Ten seconds."

Fisher tapped the OPSAT's screen, calling up the communications panel, then switched his earpiece to the indicated channel. For five seconds there was nothing but static, and then Sandy's voice: "Cargo vessel *Gosselin*, this is the Canadian Coast Guard patrol ship *Louisbourg*, over."

Silence.

"I say again, cargo vessel *Gosselin*, this is the Canadian Coast Guard patrol ship *Louisbourg*, do you read, over?"

"Yes, *Louisbourg*, this is *Gosselin*, we read you."

"*Gosselin*, I am on your zero-five-one, four nautical miles. Confirm radar contact."

Ten seconds passed and then, "Roger, *Louisbourg*, we see you. How can we be of service?"

There was in fact a Canadian Coast Guard patrol ship named *Louisbourg*, and it was in fact stationed in Gaspé, Quebec, but unbeknownst to the *Gosselin*'s captain, *Louisbourg* was hundreds of miles south, patrolling the coast of New Brunswick. The ship ten miles off the *Gosselin*'s starboard bow was in truth a Japanese cargo ship carrying DVD players and plasma televisions to Montreal.

"*Gosselin*, you are in Canadian territorial waters. You are ordered to heave to and stand by for inspection."

"Uh . . . *Louisbourg*, we are a cargo vessel home ported

in Montreal and bound for Halifax. May I ask the reason for the inspection?"

"*Gosselin*, you are ordered to heave to and stand by for random spot inspection," Sandy repeated, an edge to her voice now. "Confirm compliance, over."

"Understood, *Louisbourg*. Heaving to. *Gosselin* out."

Well played, Sandy, Fisher thought. Now, with the tree-shaking done, it was time to see what, if anything, would fall out. If Stewart were aboard and not already tucked away into one of the ship's nooks and crannies, Sandy's threat of a boarding party would likely scare his keepers into moving him.

Fisher snaked the flexicam out the louvered panel at the bottom of the door and switched to a fish-eye view so he could see both ends of the corridor.

Two minutes passed without any activity. Then he heard it: a pair of feet pounding down a ladder somewhere forward of him and above. The pounding got louder until the footsteps entered the passage outside Fisher's door. A man appeared at the forward end of the passage. Fisher tapped RECORD on the OPSAT's screen, then switched the flexicam's lens to regular view and swiveled it to focus on the man, who was now striding down the passage. The man stopped at the fourth door on the starboard side, slipped a key into the lock, then pushed through the door. Fisher heard muffled voices, then a shout, some scuffling. The figure reappeared, now with a gun in his right hand and the bunched collar of Calvin Stewart in the other. Stewart's hands were duct-taped before him. His captor half dragged, half marched Stewart down the passageway, and then they disappeared from view down the ladder.

Fisher withdrew the flexicam and studied the OPSAT's screen. Most of the blue RFID dots remained in the passageway, but four of them—about four hundred chips— had done their job and clung to the shoes of Stewart's captor. The dots were moving aft and down. *All hail the Voodoo Dust,* Fisher thought.

He rewound the flexicam's video feed to where Stewart's captor entered the passageway, then manipulated the timeline bar, forwarding and rewinding until he had a clear, well-lighted view of the man's face.

"Well, this is unexpected," Fisher whispered.

The face on his screen was Asian—Korean, if he wasn't mistaken.

— 15 —

"I agree," Lambert said in Fisher's ear. "This is unexpected."

Fisher had already compressed the flexicam's video feed and sent it to Third Echelon via encrypted burst transmission. Grimsdottir had quickly isolated the Korean's face, pulled a still frame from the video, and was now running it through the NSA's database—whose reach encompassed the CIA, the FBI, Homeland Security, and Immigration—looking for a match.

"You're tracking them?" Lambert asked.

Fisher checked his OPSAT. "Yeah, hold on . . . They just stopped." As he watched, the cluster of blue dots that represented Stewart and the Korean split in half, one staying in place while the other headed forward, in the direction of the bridge. "Okay, I think they parked him somewhere.

Gotta move. Sandy's going to give me twelve minutes before she hails them again. Don't know if they'll move him again, but I'd better assume so."

"Agreed," Lambert said. "Go."

Zooming and panning the *Gosselin*'s blueprint as he went, Fisher followed Stewart's RFID cluster down three decks, deeper into the bowels of the ship, then finally into the aft cargo area. He found himself at the mouth of a long, dark alleyway bordered on both sides by winch-lifted cargo bins, each the size of a mobile home and fronted by a padlocked ten-foot-by-ten-foot door.

He flipped down his goggles and switched to NV, then tracked the signal to the end of the alley and stopped before the last bin on the port side. On his schematic, the blue cluster was pulsing steadily on the other side of the door.

Fisher knelt before the door and went to work. The padlock was tough, resisting his picks for a full two minutes before popping open with a muted *snick*. He hooked the padlock on his belt, then unholstered his pistol and flattened himself against the bin, opposite the hinges. Using his foot, he swung open the door and peeked around the corner.

There, lying in the fetal position on the floor of the bin, was Stewart. He looked asleep, but as Fisher stepped through the door, Stewart gave a whimper and curled himself into a tighter ball, forehead touching his knees. He started rocking.

"Please, please, please . . ." he muttered. "Leave me alone . . ."

Good Christ, Fisher thought.

He swung the door shut, then knelt down and flipped

up his goggles. He touched a button on his web harness, and an LED light came out, casting the still-balled-up Stewart in a pool of light.

"Mr. Stewart."

"Please, please, please . . ."

"Mr. Stewart," Fisher repeated, this time more firmly. "I'm here to help you."

Stewart stopped rocking. He cracked an eyelid and squinted at Fisher. "What?"

"I'm here to help you."

"Who are you? What's going on?"

This was going to be a tough conversation, Fisher knew. He needed Stewart to cooperate, and he couldn't risk taking him off the ship. This man was his only link to Carmen Hayes; she his only link to whatever had gotten Peter killed—and in turn the PuH-19 itself. It was a chain he couldn't afford to break.

He briefly considered using Spigot, but Stewart was clearly frazzled, both physically and mentally. Spigot could turn him into a vegetable. So, how to convince Stewart to remain a prisoner, in what was likely his closest imagining of hell, keep his mouth shut, and play the role of human beacon while Fisher tried to put the puzzle together? There was no easy way to do that. He decided to play it straight.

"Mr. Stewart, I need a favor. Can I call you Calvin?"

"What?" Stewart replied. "What, yes, okay, sure. You're going to get me out of here, right? Let's go . . . now, before they come back."

"Calvin, the favor I need from you is this: I need you to stay here, keep your ears and eyes open, and play dumb."

"Huh?"

"The people that kidnapped you also kidnapped a woman a few months ago. She's a scientist, like you."

"I'm sorry about that, really, but I can't—"

"If I take you off this ship, these people will—"

"I don't care what they will or will not do. Get me out of here."

"Keep your voice down, Calvin. You're a physicist, aren't you?"

"Yeah . . ."

"You know what PuH-19 is?"

Stewart's face changed, his eyes and lips narrowing. "Yeah, I know what it is."

"We believe someone connected to the people who took you and this other scientist have some PuH-19. They've already killed one person with it. We don't know how much they have or what they plan to do with it. You take a coffee can full of that stuff, disperse it in a city . . . Well, you know what happens."

"Yeah." Something interesting happened as Fisher watched Stewart's face. The color returned to his skin, and the muscles on both his jaws bunched. He took a deep breath and said, "PuH-19. You're sure?"

Fisher nodded.

"Oh, God," Stewart rasped. "Good God, I was afraid of that."

"If you can hang on for just a little while longer, we can put the pieces together and track these people down. But it only works if you stay here and ride this out. I know it's a crappy deal, and believe me, if I could do it any other way, I would. Can you do it?"

Stewart swallowed hard, hesitated, then nodded. "Yeah, I can do it. One thing, though."

"What?"

"Don't forget to come get me, huh?"

Fisher smiled. "You have my word."

Fisher checked his watch. Time was up. He held up a finger for Stewart to be quiet, then said into his SVT, "Talk to me, Sandy."

"The Japanese cargo ship is two miles off *Gosselin*'s bow. We better do it now before they're close enough for a visual. If that happens, the jig is up."

"Go ahead."

Fisher switched comm channels, turned back to Stewart, and said, "In a few minutes they may come back and take you back to the cabin. If they do, I'll come find you."

"Okay."

"Be right back."

Fisher slipped out of the bin and crept to the end of the alleyway. He planted a Sticky Ear at the entrance, set the OPSAT to STICKY EAR—ALERT ON CLOSE PASSAGE, then returned to the bin. In his ear he heard Sandy's voice:

"Cargo vessel *Gosselin*, this is the Canadian Coast Guard patrol ship *Louisbourg*, over."

"*Louisbourg*, this is *Gosselin*, roger, over."

"Be advised, *Gosselin*, we have been ordered to break off and assist a search and rescue. You're released; continue on course, over."

"Uh . . . roger, *Louisbourg*, continuing on course. *Gosselin* out."

Fisher switched back to the primary channel and said, "Nicely done, Sandy."

"At your service. Standing by for extraction."

Fisher sat down beside Stewart. "I've got an alarm set; if they come back, I'll know."

Stewart nodded.

"What can you tell me, Calvin? Who's the Korean?"

"I don't know."

"When did you first meet him?"

"Just when I got aboard here. They had me locked up somewhere, I don't know where. It sounded close to the water. They had a hood on me."

"Earlier, when I mentioned PuH-19, you said, 'I was afraid of that.' What did you mean?"

"That guy—the Korean, I guess—he's been asking me about PuH-19 . . . about its properties . . . how much experience I've had working with it—that kind of thing."

"And?"

Stewart hesitated. "I don't know if I can . . . you know. Classified stuff. Sorry."

"Okay. I'll find out." *Grimsdottir will find out.* Fisher assumed it was weapons research. "But, suffice it to say, you're an expert on PuH-19?"

"Yeah. I wish I wasn't, but yeah."

An odd couple, Fisher thought. A hydrogeologist and a particle physicist who specializes in what was probably PuH-19-related weapons research. What did the two have in common? At first glance, the *hydro* part of Carmen Hayes's specialty, combined with Stewart's knowledge of PuH-19, suggested someone had plans to introduce PuH-19 into a water supply, but you didn't need a hydrogeologist for that. One of New York City's primary sources of drinking water was the wide-open and largely unguarded Ashokan

Reservoir in the Catskills, and the story was the same for most cities in the United States, large and small. The trick was finding a toxin deadly enough to survive dilution; PuH-19 would certainly do that.

So, again, why these two scientists? What was the overlap in their specialties that had made them targets for kidnapping?

Either way, it sounded like Stewart's Korean interrogator was simply probing Stewart's knowledge level. Stewart showed no signs of physical abuse, which told Fisher that whoever had snagged Stewart needed more than just his knowledge; they needed him alive. They needed his hands-on expertise for something tangible.

Fisher didn't want to think about what that might be.

16

THIRD ECHELON SITUATION ROOM

"GOT a match," Grimsdottir announced, pushing through the situation room's door. She strode to the conference table where Fisher, Lambert, and William Redding, Fisher's occasional advance man and field handler, were sitting. As of late, however, Redding's role had become that of free safety: research, weapons and gear, brainstormer at large. His de facto uniform of the day was a sweater vest, pocket protector, and horn-rimmed glasses that looked as old as Fisher. Though Fisher had never seen it personally, Redding's personal library of books—both contemporary and arcane—was rumored to exceed twenty thousand.

It was eight o'clock at night, and the space was lit only by a cluster of blue-shaded pendant lamps hanging over the table; the monitors and status boards were dark.

Grimsdottir sat down opposite Fisher and triumphantly plopped a manila folder on the table before Lambert. Fisher could see the *Take that!* gleam in her eyes. Nothing pleased Grim more than besting a technical challenge. Evidently, finding a name to match the Korean face Fisher had captured aboard the *Gosselin* had given Grim a run for her money.

Lambert opened the folder and scanned its contents. "Chin-Hwa Pak," he announced. "Ostensibly a North Korean salary man, but the CIA had him pegged as an operative for the RDEI."

The Research Department for External Intelligence was North Korea's primary foreign intelligence collection agency. Along with the Liaison Department, which was tasked with conducting intelligence operations against South Korea and Japan, the RDEI was overseen by the Cabinet General Intelligence Bureau of the Korean Workers' Party Central Committee.

Internal security in North Korea was handled by the Ministry of Public Security (MPS) and the State Security Department (SSD). The latter, which was managed directly by Kim Jong-il himself, specialized in political espionage; the surveillance of citizens, government officials, and visitors alike; and the monitoring of communication systems, including television, radio, and newspapers.

Fisher had been in North Korea five times, and five times he counted himself lucky to get back out.

"So, if North Korea's behind the kidnapping of Hayes and Stewart," Redding said, "we have to assume she's already there and that's where Stewart is headed."

"It would be best if that didn't happen," Fisher said. "If

you're right and Carmen is there, reaching her—let alone getting her out—is going to be tough. Grim, where's the *Gosselin* right now?"

Grimsdottir used a remote control to power up one of the forty-two-inch LCD screens, then tapped a key. The screen resolved into a satellite image of Canada's east coast: Quebec, Nova Scotia, and Newfoundland, including the Gulf of St. Lawrence and the Gaspé Passage, where Fisher had boarded the *Gosselin*. A pulsing red triangle with the annotation GOSSELIN beside it sat in the channel between the Gaspé Peninsula and Anticosti Island.

"Still headed for Halifax, it looks like," Fisher said.

Grimsdottir nodded. "If she stays on course and speed, she should tie up at Legard's warehouse there in twenty-nine hours."

"The beacon Fisher planted on him—still active?" Lambert asked.

Before leaving Stewart, Fisher had planted a long-range beacon on him: a fake, adhesive thumbnail with an embedded chip. The Voodoo Dust had neither the range nor the durability for their purposes.

"Strong and clear. He's still aboard," Grimsdottir answered.

Brave man, Fisher thought, recalling the transformation he'd seen Stewart undergo at the mention of PuH-19. He'd gone from a whimpering mess of a man to a determined mole in the space of ten seconds. Nor had Fisher forgotten his promise to go back for Stewart. What was in doubt was whether he could do that before Chin-Hwa Pak managed to spirit him away to North Korea.

Lambert turned to Fisher. "Sam, go home, get some

sleep, then come back for prep and briefing. We'll want you at Legard's warehouse long before *Gosselin* docks."

Fisher nodded and started to rise. The phone at Lambert's elbow trilled. Lambert picked up, listened for a few moments, then grunted a "Thanks," and hung up. To Grimsdottir, he said, "Give me MSNBC, Grim."

She worked the remote again. The LCD screen beside the satellite image came to life.

". . . now, reports are sketchy," the MSNBC anchor was saying, "but it appears there is military activity taking place in Kyrgyzstan's capital city of Bishkek. According to a BBC correspondent on scene, about an hour ago the city came under what appeared to be mortar bombardment. Do we have video . . . ? Yes, I'm told we have video, courtesy of BBC news . . ."

The screen changed to a daylight scene of what Fisher assumed was Bishkek. The BBC cameraman was on a rooftop, panning across the cityscape, as the correspondent spoke. In dozens of places throughout the city columns of black smoke were visible. Sirens warbled in the distance, and car horns, both from anxious drivers and alarms, blared.

"These are very concentrated strikes," the correspondent was saying. "Not your typical mortar barrage, I would say. I've been in both Afghanistan and Iraq during these types of attacks, so I'm certain what we're seeing is in fact a mortar attack, but the precision is astounding . . ."

The camera continued to pan, then paused and moved back, focusing a half mile down an adjoining street where what looked like an armored personnel carrier sat burning, a geyser of black smoke jetting from its top.

"There . . . there's an APC that's been hit. Johnny, can

you zoom in . . ." The camera zoomed in. "See there, no visible crater near the vehicle. That appears to be a direct hit."

On the screen, a cluster of people, mostly women and children, dashed across the street in front of the APC and disappeared down an adjacent alley. Closer in, an open truck full of soldiers wheeled around the corner, swerved around the burning APC, then turned again out of camera range.

"Government troops are clearly scrambling at this point," the correspondent continued, "but so far we've heard no sounds of small-arms fire, nor seen any close-quarters fighting. However . . ."

"Mute it," Lambert said. Grimsdottir did so. "Here we go again."

Since March 2005, when President Askar Akayev had been forced out of office, Kyrgyzstan had been a political powder keg as various factions, extreme and moderate, religious and secular, had fought for control of the country. As one of the Central Asian "stans" that sat atop what was likely one of the world's greatest untapped oil deposits, Kyrgyzstan's strategic importance to the United States was immeasurable, which was why in late 2005, after signs of the Taliban's resurgence in Afghanistan became undeniable, and a moderate government had finally taken control of the Kyrgyz government, the Bush administration had begun pouring money and resources into Bishkek.

All that changed the following spring with a grassroots rebellion fomented by the Hizb ut-Tahrir, in which an extremist Rasputin-like Uygur warlord named Bolot Omurbai seized power and declared Kyrgyzstan an Islamic republic. Omurbai's rule, which almost immediately returned Kyrgyzstan to a Taliban-style country, lasted less than a year before a moderate rebel army, backed by U.S. and British materials, money, and advisers, toppled Omurbai and sent him and his army running for the mountains. Omurbai was captured three months later, tried, and executed; his army scattered.

"If the BBC guy is right," Redding said, "and that was a mortar barrage, someone needs to hit the panic button. There're only a few ways they—whoever *they* are—could get that accurate: eyeballs on the ground to measure and map target points and/or satellite-linked, computer-controlled mortars."

"Bad news, either way," Grimsdottir agreed.

If rebels had in fact infiltrated the Kyrgyz government so thoroughly they had perfectly pinpointed targets in the capital, the government's underpinnings were already crumbling. Worse still, if Redding was right and the rebels had gotten their hands on sophisticated weaponry, it was likely they had more at their disposal than precision mortars. It meant they had money, resources, and a sponsor interested in seeing the moderate Kyrgyz government gone. And the United States, still deeply entrenched in Iraq and Afghanistan, was in no position to help. The good news was, most of Central Asia's oil reserves had yet to be exploited, so there was little infrastructure with which the Kyrgyz extremists could meddle and no oil flow they could garrote. However, that wasn't true in all the neighboring stans. One of the West's greatest fears was a country like Kyrgyzstan falling to extremists and then setting off a domino effect in the region.

"Well," Lambert said, "right now, that's someone else's bad news to address. For us, PuH-19 is still missing. Sam, let's have you back in here in fourteen hours. You've got a ship to meet."

—17—

WITH time to spare, Fisher took a commercial shuttle flight, the last one of the night, from Boston to Halifax and touched down shortly after midnight at Stanfield International Airport. As he walked off the Jetway, he powered up his cell phone; there was a text message from Grimsdottir: CALL ME. URGENT.

Fisher dialed, and she picked up on the first ring. "Change of plans," she said without preamble. "The *Gosselin* made a sudden stop off Michaud Point—the southern tip of Cape Breton Island."

"And?"

"And they're moving Stewart. Looks like a small boat's taking him ashore."

Damn. As the crow flew, Michaud Point was one hundred

sixty miles north of Halifax; by road, probably another fifty on top of that. "We have any assets there?" Fisher asked.

"One, but he's just an information resource. An old friend, in fact."

"Any airports or strips nearby?"

"Strips, but mostly for puddle jumpers and inland charters. If they're going to get Stewart out, they'd have to do it by boat again or get him to an airport proper. I'm putting both Stewart and Pak on the watch list—observe and report, no apprehension unless directed. If they make for an airport, we'll know it."

"Good."

"How soon can you—"

"Bird and Sandy are en route. There's an airstrip at Enfield, a few miles north up the One oh two. I'm on my way."

GRAND RIVER, CAPE BRETON
ISLAND, NOVA SCOTIA

BY the time Stewart's tracking beacon made it ashore and finally came to rest at what looked like the middle of nowhere on Cape Breton's rugged southern coast, dawn was only a few hours away, so at Fisher's suggestion, Lambert scrubbed the mission. Before Fisher could track down Stewart and Pak and find out what they were up to, he needed to get the lay of the land. According to Fisher's map of Cape Breton, there were no towns or villages to speak of between Grand River and Fourchu, some thirty miles to the north.

Grimsdottir's contact, an old college friend turned history author named Robert A. Robinson—RAT, as Grim called him—lived in Soldiers Cove not far from Grand River with his wife of thirty-five years, Emily.

Robinson, a Middle East policy expert kept on a consultant's retainer by the CIA, was also, despite being Canadian neither by birth nor citizenship, the foremost expert on the obscure subject of Cape Breton Island history.

"He can brief the hell out of you, make a laser out of your cell phone, and recite obscure sci-fi trivia until you bleed from the ears," Grimsdottir had said.

"A jack of strange trades," Fisher said.

"And he knows how to keep his mouth shut. You can trust him."

Fisher's first impulse was to simply follow Stewart's beacon and do his own surveillance, but Stewart and Pak seemed to be going nowhere for the time being and, as Fisher had learned the hard way over the years, the six *P*s were unbreakable laws of nature one didn't taunt: Prior Planning Prevents Piss-Poor Performance. Better to know where he was going before he dove in headfirst.

Fisher found Robinson's home, a three-story Victorian that backed up to horse pastures on two sides and a creek on the other, on the outskirts of Soldiers Cove, population 101. It was eight in the morning, and mist still clung to the grass and low-lying bushes. He pushed through the gate in the white split-rail fence and followed a crushed shell path to the front door. It opened as he mounted the porch steps.

A man in a wheelchair, his lap covered by a red argyle

blanket, wheeled onto the porch. "Don't tell me: You must be Sam of the no last name."

Fisher smiled. "I must be. And you must be Robert the RAT."

"Ha! I see Anna's been telling tales out of school again." Robinson had a genuine smile and booming laugh. "Come in, come in. Coffee's on."

Fisher followed him down a hardwood hallway into a country-style kitchen complete with a wood-burning Napoleon stove. Robinson wheeled through the kitchen and bumped the chair down two short steps into a four-season sunroom. Fisher took the indicated seat.

To the east, the sun was rising, a perfect orange disk suspended over the horse pasture at the rear of Robinson's property. A cluster of horses were standing near the fence, chewing grass, their breath smoking in the air.

"Not a bad way to start the day, is it?"

Fisher took a sip of coffee and shook his head. "Not bad at all."

"**SO**," Robinson began, "Anna told me you were a grim fellow, that I shouldn't for any reason cross you if I value my life."

Fisher stared at him. "No, she didn't."

"No, she didn't—but she told me to say she did."

"She's a card, that Anna."

"She is indeed. To business: You're looking for a man; he's somewhere around between here and Fourchu. Can you show me where, exactly?"

Fisher pulled a Palm Pilot from his pocket, powered it up, and pulled up the map screen. Stewart's beacon was marked as a tiny red circle. He showed it to Robinson, who frowned. "Latitude and longitude, please?"

Fisher tapped the screen with the stylus, changing the map's overlay.

"How precise is this beacon—I mean this *spot*, on the map?" Robinson said with a sly grin.

Doesn't miss much, Fisher thought.

"Give or take three feet."

"Ah, the joys of technology. It's all about physics, you know, all about physics."

"Pardon me?" Fisher said.

But Robinson was no longer listening. He had pulled a Gateway laptop from his chair's saddlebag and was powering it up. Muttering the latitude and longitude coordinates to himself, he called up Google Maps—"The bane of the National Reconnaissance Office, you know," he said to Fisher. "Now everyone can play their game"—then punched in the coordinates and studied the satellite image there.

"Just as I thought," Robinson said.

"What?"

"Your quarry, Sam my new friend, is in Little Bishkek."

Bishkek. Robinson's mention of the word was so unexpected it took Fisher several seconds to process what he was hearing. "Bishkek. As in Kyrgyzstan's capital?"

"Yes, sir. That Bishkek. The same Bishkek that is, as we speak, in the midst of yet another civil war. Are you a big believer in coincidences, Sam?"

"No."

"Me neither. But that's not even the worst news. Your little red circle there—if the coordinates are accurate—is not just in Little Bishkek, it is inside the walls of Ingonish."

"Which is?"

"The home—a castle slash fort, really—to the mayor, general, chief enforcer, and king of Little Bishkek, Tolkun Bakiyev."

"You'd better back up," Fisher said, "And give me a little history."

"Back in the seventies, a group of enterprising Kyrgyz families that specialized in crime of the organized variety, started feeling unwelcome in Bishkek. Back then, before they went into Afghanistan, the Soviets got serious about injecting their proletariat gospel into the stans, including Kyrgyzstan, by helping the Bishkek government crack down on the working-class-unfriendly Mafia. Bosses, henchmen, and sundry thugs began disappearing and dying left and right.

"Knowing they couldn't fight the Soviet bear, and being more interested in profits than in principle, what was left of the Kyrgyz Mafia struck their tents and emigrated for greener pastures. Some went to Europe, some Australia, some America, but one family—the Bakiyev clan—came to Nova Scotia. The other families failed, broke apart, or were otherwise destroyed by local organized crime or law enforcement, but the Bakiyevs played it smart. They found a rundown and mostly uninhabited village on the coast of Cape Breton, moved in, took up the local trade of fishing, and just generally worked at fitting in and making babies for six or seven years, all the while attracting other wandering Kyrgyz.

"Once the elder Bakiyev—Tolkun's father—thought their group had properly assimilated, he quietly turned the town back to its old ways of organized crime. Now they specialize mostly in smuggling black-market goods, from fake iPhones to Gucci knockoffs that they ship into the United States. No one really knows how much influence Tolkun has outside Little Bishkek, but since the town's founding, not a single outside land developer has managed to make any inroads there. It's a tight-knit community, Sam, and they're not the welcoming sort. You've seen those westerns, where a stranger walks into the saloon and the music stops and everyone just stares at him?"

"Yeah."

"That's what it's like driving through Little Bishkek. You stop for a cup of coffee, and you've got a hundred pair of eyes watching you until you hit the town's outskirts again. They're not unfriendly, exactly, but it's pretty clear that if you're not Kyrgyz, you don't want to be shopping for apartments."

"I understand."

"I truly hope so, Sam. If you're planning on getting him out of Little Bishkek, and they're not willing to part with him, the odds are stacked against you."

Fisher, staring at the horses cantering through the pasture, nodded slowly, then turned to Robinson and smiled grimly. "I love a challenge."

18

TWO hours after dusk, as night fully closed in over the coast, Fisher turned south off Cape Breton's main southern coast road, the St. Peters–Fourchu, onto a winding dirt track that took him to the beach. He rolled to a stop in the gravel parking lot in the lee of a sand dune and shut off the headlights and engine. He sat quietly for few minutes, listening to the engine's *tick tick tick* as it cooled and watching the clouds gather over the sea. The rain would be here in less than an hour, and while its coming would present its own challenges for the mission ahead, the rain would dampen sound, deepen the shadows, and the clouds would cover the full moon, which had been his biggest worry.

His cell phone trilled. He checked the caller ID screen,

then tapped the CONNECT button on his Bluetooth headset. "Hi, Grim."

"I've got the colonel on as well, Sam."

"Evening, Colonel."

"I understand you've managed to find yourself a tough nut to crack."

"It's a gift I have."

Between Robinson's own maps and books and firsthand knowledge of the area and Grim's computer research, they had over the last ten hours built an impressive profile on Tolkun Bakiyev's home, the fort known as Ingonish.

Ingonish, named after the city on the northern tip of the island, was built in 1740 by the French and changed hands half a dozen times over the next eighteen years as the French and British fought first the Seven Years' War, then the King George's War. Intended as a siege fort to guard what was now the Grand River Estuary, Ingonish never saw battle and as such never gained a place in the history books, earning in the mid–nineteenth century the nickname, the Forgotten Castle.

Upon leaving Robinson's house, Fisher had immediately called in to report the Kyrgyzstan connection. Like Fisher, Lambert wasn't a believer in coincidences, and he immediately tasked Grimsdottir and Redding with finding a connection—any connection, no matter how slight—that might explain a link between Carmen Hayes, the hydrogeologist; Calvin Stewart, the particle physicist; Chin-Hwa Pak, the North Korean RDEI spy; and the PuH-19 that had killed Peter. All were pieces of what appeared to be the same puzzle, but there was so far not even a hint of what bigger picture they might form.

Right now, though, Fisher had to focus on the task at hand: getting into Ingonish.

"Your OPSAT is fully loaded," Grimsdottir said. "The problem is, the castle hasn't been a tourist attraction for twenty years, since Bakiyev bought it, so we don't have any recent pictures. The good news is, the thing's made mostly of stone, so there's not much remodeling the guy could have done. Between Robert's library and what I've been able to pull off the Net, we put together a partial blueprint of the place. There're going to be gaps, though, so play it by ear."

"One of my specialties," Fisher replied.

"Sam, same ROE as before," Lambert said. "We need to keep this pipeline open, especially if it might eventually lead to Kyrgyzstan."

Bodies tend to clog pipelines, Fisher thought. "Understood. I know you've probably already considered this, Colonel, but that mortar attack on Bishkek . . . T heNorth Koreans have that kind of technology—stolen, of course, but they've got it nonetheless."

"Yeah, I know. And satellite access."

Through front companies, the North Korean RDEI had for years been snatching up space on commercial satellite launches and piggybacking on existing commercial Land-sats (land satellites) in orbit.

Fisher checked his watch, then craned his neck so he had a clearer view through the windshield. The rain clouds were slipping over the coast, and against the lower curve of the moon he could see wisps of rain. "Time to get the show on the road."

"Stay in touch," Lambert said, "and stay invisible."

Fisher did his Superman imitation in the car, slipping out of his street clothes to reveal his tac suit underneath, donned his web harness, belt, and rucksack, then climbed out and started jogging.

Ingonish, situated on the northern edge of Little Bishkek, was a mile up the beach. Fisher covered the distance in six minutes. He stopped in a crouch against the cliff beneath the fort, some two hundred feet above his head. Down at the tide line, the ocean was hissing across the sand and receding, a soothing, rhythmic *swoosh-hiss* broken only by the distant groaning of foghorns. Fisher licked his lips and tasted salt.

Above his head came a screech. He pressed himself against the rock and looked up. Halfway up the cliff, the flapping shadow of a bird wheeled away from the rocks and disappeared in the darkness. Fisher, suspicious now, flipped down his goggles and switched to night-vision mode and scanned the cliffs above.

"You've got to be kidding me . . ." he murmured.

Scattered in nests among the nooks and crannies across the rock face were hundreds, perhaps thousands, of cormorants. *A perfect, self-sustaining organic early warning system,* Fisher thought. He had zero chance of scaling the cliff without setting off an explosion of screeching birds.

Rising from the top of the cliff for a quarter mile to the north he could see the towers and crenellated walls of the fort itself. Scattered across the wall were four stories of arched, inset widows; here and there, some were lit from within. Fisher used the goggles to zoom in but saw no one moving behind the glass.

He said into the SVT, "Penetration route one is out. Switching to PR two."

"Roger," Grimsdottir replied. "Problem?"

"Birds," Fisher replied. "Lots and lots of birds."

PR two had been Fisher's second choice primarily because
to reach it he had to go precisely where he didn't want to go:
through downtown Little Bishkek. Facing a naturally suspicious and xenophobic population, the idea of picking his
way down the main street—at night or not—was unappeal-
ing at best. Robinson had mentioned that yet another of Little Bishkek's quirks was that at night its inhabitants fielded
an unofficial police force, citizens that patrolled the streets
and sidewalks armed with billy clubs, flashlights, and whistles. The clubs and flashlights didn't particularly concern
Fisher, but the whistles did. Little Bishkek's population was
694, and he was beginning to think a single whistle blast
would bring each and every one of them to the streets.

Fisher jogged back to his car, then up the winding track
to the St. Peters-Fourchu, where he crouched down in the
bushes and kept watch for a few minutes to ensure he was
alone. Satisfied, he sprinted, hunched over, two hundred
yards down the road, staying in the undergrowth along the
shoulder until he reached the junction where St. Peters-
Fourchu met Quqon Road, Little Bishkek's main thorough-
fare, which curved again to the south, toward the bluffs.
Another thirty seconds of running brought him within sight
of the village's westernmost building, a small, tin-roofed
post office. He crouched down against the building's hard-
board wall, scooted to the edge, and peeked around the corner. A drizzle was now falling, lightly pattering on the roof
above. The drainpipes gurgled softly with the runoff.

Little Bishkek's layout was straightforward: Businesses and restaurants lined the northern and southern sides of Quqon Road, the latter sitting atop the cliffs overlooking the sea, a mile south of Ingonish. From the road's northern edge, residential streets radiated inland for half a mile. As far as Fisher could see, the village's architecture was comprised mostly of saltbox construction with hard and clapboard siding, dormered windows, and steeply pitched slate roofs. Over the tops of the businesses, each of which was fronted by a raised, continuous boardwalk and a hand-painted sign in both French and Kyrgyz, Fisher could see dozens upon dozens of chimneys—most emitting a curl of smoke—and scattered squares of lighted windows. The storefronts were painted in various shades of pale blue, butter yellow, and mint green. Lining the boardwalk every fifty feet or so was an electric, gaslight-style streetlamp, the globes glowing yellow in the darkness.

Fisher switched to night vision and scanned the street. He saw nothing but a single cat, ghostly in washed-out gray green, dash across the street and disappear down a side street. He switched first to EM—as expected he saw no signs of cameras or sensors—then to infrared to scan for thermal signatures.

Hello there . . .

Two figures, standing together at the corner of a building on this side of the street about a hundred yards away. In IR, they were man-shaped cutouts cast in various temperature shades of red, yellow, green, and blue. As Fisher watched, he could see a long, dark blue cylinder dangling from each man's hand. Billy clubs. The men talked for a few more minutes as one of them smoked, then shook hands and parted company, one crossing the street and heading north, the other mounting the boardwalk and heading in Fisher's direction, tapping the billy club against his thigh as he walked.

Fisher crept back along the building until he reached the rear wall, where he found an open-faced porch. Its outer rail sat three feet from the edge of the cliff, which dropped away into darkness. Far below he could hear the faint rush of the surf, and closer in, seemingly coming from a few feet down the rock face, soft cooing sounds he assumed belonged to the cormorants. Between the porch rail and the cliff's edge was a narrow gravel path. He crouch-stepped around the porch's corner railing onto the path, then down to the building's next corner.

"Arretez!"

The voice, speaking in French, came from Fisher's left. He spun and found himself facing a pair of legs. He looked up in time to see a billy club sweeping down toward his face. He jerked his head backward, felt the club graze his cheekbone and, as he fell backward onto his butt, he drew his pistol and squeezed off a single shot. The bullet entered below the man's chin and exited the top of his skull. His head snapped back, and he toppled forward, his billy club skittering down the path. Fisher rolled out of the way. The man landed with his upper torso over the edge of the cliff, teetered there for a moment, then slid over the edge. There came the distant flapping of wings and scattered squawks, but after five seconds silence returned. Fisher crab-walked down the path, retrieved the guard's fallen billy club, tossed it over the edge, and then crawled beneath the floorboards of the porch and went still.

Close. Too close.

Little Bishkek's citizen cops were armed with more than just clubs and whistles; they also came equipped with some very quiet footsteps.

Fisher waited another five minutes, watching to see if the encounter had drawn any attention, then keyed his SVT and said, "Sleeper; clean."

"Roger," Grimsdottir replied.

Whether his clean report would prove truly accurate or not, only time would tell. In his brief, Robinson had doubted the village's cops were on any check-in schedule or supervision. Fisher checked his watch: still three hours before shift change. Time enough if he moved quickly. Even if the man's body were found tonight, it was unlikely the crash into the rocks below would have left much to identify. Hopefully the trauma would camouflage the bullet wound.

In fact, Fisher thought, a little staging might help the ruse. He crawled back onto the path and used his hands to smooth out the man's erratic footprints near the path. He took another NV/IR scan of the area to ensure he was still alone and then used his boot heel to gently kick away a foot-wide section of dirt along the cliff face. With luck, the indentation would look like a section that had simply given way beneath the man.

Fisher got up and started moving.

19

OVER the next hour Fisher picked his way slowly through the heart of the village. In addition to the other guard he'd seen upon reaching the outskirts, he found three others, each seemingly moving in random patterns, sometimes up and down the residential streets bordering Ququon Road, sometimes on the boardwalks along the storefronts, but always moving aside for occasional stops to chat with a fellow guard. Fisher absently wondered whether this level of patrol was the norm or if it had been prompted by the new arrival at Ingonish. He hoped it was the former; it might mean security measures inside the fort itself had similarly remained unchanged.

Finally, just before midnight, he was within fifty yards of the fort itself. The fort's facade, a stone wall twelve feet tall and, according to Robinson, four feet thick, rose directly from the road and was broken only by a pair of massive, cross-beamed oak doors. It wasn't the wall or the doors that interested Fisher but rather an architectural detail Robinson had mentioned in his brief.

He circled to the rear of the next-door building—an outdoor café with green and white awnings—and crept along the cliff-side path until he was within arm's reach of the fort's wall. Here, running between the café and the wall, was a three-foot gap in the street's cobblestones covered by a rusted iron grating. Through the grating, four feet below, Fisher could see cracked and jagged cobbles.

The canal, which Robinson had called a siege runnel, lay at a slight slant and perpendicular to the main road, and began just inside the front wall with an L-shaped junction. It ended at the edge of the cliff with a funnel-like chute, also covered in iron grating.

Though it had never seen any action, Robinson had said, the siege runnel had been designed as a stationary siege defense system into which cannonballs and boiling pitch could be dropped and then rolled onto invaders on the beach below.

Down the alley Fisher heard footsteps clicking on the cobblestones. He dropped flat on the path, his face pressed into the dirt. At the mouth of the alley, a silhouetted figure had stopped. The man clicked on his flashlight and shined the beam down along the siege runnel. The light played over Fisher's face, paused for a few seconds, then clicked off. The man walked on. His footsteps creaked as he mounted the boardwalk steps, then faded, clicking on wood as he continued down the street. Fisher slowly reached up, toggled his goggles to IR, waited until he could no longer hear the footsteps, then waited another two more minutes until he was certain the man hadn't doubled back.

Still on his belly, he crawled forward until his fingertips touched the edge of the runnel's grating. From his right thigh pouch he withdrew what looked like three twelve-inch strips of heavy filament tape. Each strip was made up of two bonded halves, one half containing a superconcentrated coat of gelled nitric acid, the other half a catalyst, and between the two a thin strip of neutralizing agent. Jutting a few inches from the end of each strip was a nub of knotted cable.

He placed two strips perpendicularly across the grating, about a foot apart, and the third along the grating's far edge where it met the cobbles. Next he reached out his left hand, gripped the center of the grating and then in turn pulled the cable nub from each strip. Five seconds passed, and then Fisher heard a faint hissing, like air escaping a tire's valve stem. The hissing went on for a full sixty seconds, then slowly faded away. The severed grating gave way. He tensed his forearm, taking the grating's weight, then caught it, scooted forward, laid it in the bottom of the runnel, and crawled down.

Five minutes later he had the grating back in place, secured by homemade black baling wire clips he'd fashioned earlier that day.

"At PR two," he radioed. "Moving in."

"Roger," Grimsdottir replied.

Now safely inside the runnel, Fisher had two options for gaining entry into the fort proper: one a sure thing and the other a maybe. Forts of this period, which used this particular type of siege defense, usually, but not always, had two ports into which defenders fed their bombs: a cannonball port, just inside the fort's walls—this would be the L junction Fisher had seen earlier—and a pitch slot, normally located inside the castle near a forge for heating the pitch. This was Fisher's preferred entrance.

He switched his goggles to NV and on hands and knees began crawling up the runnel toward the street.

Suddenly, behind him at the cliff's edge, came the crunch of footsteps on gravel.

Fisher froze, looked around. Ten feet ahead of him he saw a square of darkness set into the side of the runnel. Moving as quickly as he dared without giving himself away, he crawled to the opening, duck-stepped into it under a cobblestone overhang, and went still. He drew his pistol, switched the selector to DART 4, and looked up through the grating. Fisher was under no illusions here. Putting a shot—dart or bullet alike—through the grating was a one-in-a-thousand chance.

For a few seconds nothing moved. All was silent.

And then, like a ghost gliding out of the darkness, a guard crept into Fisher's field of vision. The man, walking on flat feet, had his whistle clamped between his teeth, his billy club clutched in his fist and held before him. Carefully, slowly, Fisher backed himself deeper into the opening until he felt his back press against something hard. His heart pounded in his chest. He felt sweat gathering on the small of his back and his sides.

Keep moving, pal, just keep—

The guard stopped. He clicked on his flashlight and knelt down, playing it beneath the foundation pilings of the café next door, then down along the runnel. He stood up again, then stepped over the grating toward the fort's outer wall.

Checking the rooftops, Fisher thought. He took in a calming breath, let it out slowly.

After another sixty seconds, the guard stepped back over the grating, took one last look around, then headed down the alley toward the street.

FISHER had found his "maybe" entrance. The pitch slot was eighteen inches wide and three feet tall and sealed from the inside by an ancient but solid-looking wooden hatch and a brand-new stainless steel padlock. Someone had given at least passing attention to Ingonish's small security details, but as he'd found at Legard's estate and he often found when dealing with men who lived by ego and ruled by threat of violence, Tolkun Bakiyev probably assumed his reputation alone was security measure enough. The rest—locks, sensors, cameras—were secondary. For men like that, admitting you needed heavy, sophisticated security was to show weakness.

Fisher picked the padlock and opened the hatch an inch, testing the hinges for telltales, but like the padlock, someone had looked after this detail as well; the hinges had a fresh coat of oil on them—WD-40, by the smell of it. He checked the jamb and hinges for wires or sensors; there were none. In the cracks between the cobbles, however, he spotted a gooey black substance. He worked his fingernail into a crack and dug out some of the substance. He sniffed it. Tar. Fisher smiled. Ingonish may have never seen any real warfare, but it appeared someone had at least tested out her defenses. He stared at the tar for a few more moments, strangely fascinated, wondering exactly how old it was. Ingonish was built in 1740; the tar was at least two hundred sixty-eight years old. *Amazing,* Fisher thought.

He slid the flexicam through the crack. On the other side of the hatch was another four feet of cobble-lined runnel that ended in an up-sloping ramp; beyond that, Fisher could see a twenty-foot-by-twenty-foot room with brick walls. Set into the right wall were two windows he assumed overlooked the cliff and between them a wide, open-hearth fireplace. On the nearest wall, just to the left of the flexicam's lens, was a long woodworker's bench backed by a Peg-Board holding a variety of hand tools, from screwdrivers to pliers to hand planes. A workshop. On the bench itself were several birdhouses in various states of construction. On the far wall was a single wooden door, but unlike those he'd encountered outside, this one was modern, a maple six-panel slab with brushed nickel hardware.

He gave the room a thorough scan in all three modes—IR, NV, and electromagnetic—and all looked clear, so he withdrew the flexicam, packed it away, then pushed the hatch all the way open and crawled through. When he reached the slope, he belly-crawled until he was just below the level of the floor, then took a final EM scan of the room. Again, he saw nothing.

He stood up and stretched his limbs, then checked the OPSAT. On the RFID tracking screen, which Grimsdottir had overlaid with her cobbled-together blueprint of Ingonish, Stewart's beacon, now a red diamond, pulsed steadily. Fisher turned in a circle, orienting himself with north, then checked the screen again. He panned and zoomed the blue-print.

Stewart's beacon was three floors above him at the northern end of the fort.

He said into the SVT, "I'm in. Target beacon is steady. Moving on."

"Roger," Grimsdottir replied. "What's your ETE?"

Fisher checked his watch. "Ninety to one-twenty. Something up?"

"More action on the Kyrgyzstan front."

"Understood. I'll keep you posted. Out."

What now? Fisher thought.

20

INGONISH was a trapezoid, with its base running parallel to the cliff and its narrower, truncated top facing inland to the village. Each of the trapezoid's four corners was anchored by a stone watchtower eighty feet tall and topped with a gallery for archers. A fifth tower, twice as wide and forty feet taller than the others, was set between the two cliff-side corners, at the midpoint of the wall, and was topped by an expansive cupola that had once hosted the fort's three eight-inch antiship mortars. According to Fisher's OPSAT blueprint, Ingonish measured roughly three hundred feet, or one football field, to a side and encompassed some ninety thousand square feet. He prayed Stewart's beacon remained in place; if not, he had too much territory to cover and not much time with which to do it.

Fisher knelt before the workshop door and snaked the flexicam underneath. His vision was filled by a massive locomotive's driving wheel, crank, and coupling rod. Fisher tapped the OPSAT screen, changing the resolution and switching to fisheye. He checked again. A toy train, a replica steam locomotive. It didn't seem to be on a track, so Fisher slid the flexicam out a little farther and gave the locomotive a tap. It toppled onto its side, and beyond its plastic wheels Fisher could see the rest of the room.

Both he and Grimsdottir had been wrong. Tolkun Bakiyev had done a lot of remodeling. What lay before Fisher had once been a warren of workshops, storage bunkers, and soldiers' sleeping quarters made of heavy timber and thatch-and-mud brick. The warren would have been surrounded by a stone wall, twenty feet tall and set thirty feet in from the outer wall. Between, the two stone staircases would have risen to the second floor, which would have held the officers' quarters, the armory, and tunnels through which soldiers could access the fort's five battle towers.

All of it, save the stone staircases rising along each of the four walls and an arched stone passageway that joined them, was gone and in its place what Fisher could only describe as a playground. The train he'd seen was part of a set, a railway diorama built into the wall ten feet off the floor. It was complete with villages and towns, way stations, mountain tunnels, gorges, and waterfalls. A full quarter of the floor was dominated by a polished solid wood skateboard park, complete with half-pipes, high banks, stairs, pyramids, and grind rails. Near the far wall Fisher could make out what looked like a three-lane bowling alley, and beside that an inflatable kid's red-and-yellow bouncy fun castle. *Wonderful,* Fisher thought. *BakiyevLand*.

Fisher's brief on Bakiyev had mentioned no children. Either the man just liked to have fun, or he was an idiot-child in a man's body, or his home frequently served as a playground for Little Bishkek's children.

The remainder of the space was taken up with no less than a dozen seating areas sectioned off with hanging rug walls, each containing its own cluster of leather couches, chairs, and a jumbo plasma TV screen. Robinson had guessed and Fisher had agreed that Bakiyev's living spaces were likely in one or all of the watchtowers.

He took a few still shots for the Third Echelon photo album, did a final, full-mode sweep of the room, then withdrew the flexicam and opened the door and set out.

He picked his way down the center of the room, heading for the north stairway, using the skate park's obstacle course as cover. At the halfway point he heard, faintly, the squealing of tires, tinny and cartoon-like, and a voice muttering in Kyrgyz. Ahead and to his left, in one of the seating areas, Fisher could see the flickering of television light behind one of the rugs. He crouched down and crept around a grind rail.

Seated on a red leather couch before a plasma television were two men. Leaning against the couch beside each man Fisher could see the barrel of an AK-47. On the screen, the two men were racing dune buggies down a virtual Caribbean beach. One of the buggies missed a dune jump and tumbled end over end. The man on the left groaned, dropped the controller, and threw up his hands. He snatched up his rifle, said something to his partner that Fisher didn't catch, then walked off in the direction of the bowling alley. The other man leaned back and lit a cigarette, blowing a cloud of blue smoke toward the screen.

Fisher changed course, steering away from the men and around the skate park until he reached the north wall. The bowling alley, which sat at the foot of the stairway, was directly opposite Fisher now. The guard who'd wandered off was now standing beside a lighted popcorn kiosk complete with a red-and-white-striped awning, scooping his hand inside and shoving popcorn in his mouth. His AK sat propped against the kiosk's wheel. Fisher found a dark corner and crouched down to wait. The guard gorged himself for another astonishing ten minutes, then let out a belch, picked up his AK, and wandered back toward his buddy, who had returned to playing the dune buggy game.

In his ear, Fisher heard Grimsdottir's voice: "Sam, we've got activity again."

Since focusing the NSA's electronic attention on Tolkun Bakiyev and Ingonish, she'd picked up several cell phone transmissions from two different cell phone numbers, all of which she was picking apart, and an intermittent satellite Internet signal. The problem was, Bakiyev had installed not one but two servers in the fort, both Hewlett-Packard Pro-Liant DL360 G5s, one acting as his own private web server, the other as what Grimsdottir had called an "anonymizing intercept gateway proxy server," the use of which, Fisher gathered, was a high-tech and expensive way of cloaking your Internet activities.

Grimsdottir was making progress in breaking through the firewalls, but it was slow going. One of Fisher's goals was to find the server room and perform a hard link. There aren't many practical reasons for law-abiding private citizens to own such systems. If there were any skeletons in the closet, those servers might be the door.

"What kind of activity?" Fisher asked.

"Cell phone and server. Somebody's talking and surfing in there."

"Point me."

"South of you, say sixty yards, and up forty feet. Feeding to your OPSAT now."

Fisher checked his screen. "Got it."

HE waited until Orville Redenbacher had resumed the dune buggy race, then slipped along the wall and around the corner to the stairway. The stones were covered by a red, black, and ochre Persian rug runner that Fisher's estimate put at US$10,000.

He was five feet from the top when he heard a door slam somewhere to his right. Hunched over, he padded up the final few steps, then dropped to his belly and peeked around the corner. At the far end of the arched passage, where it curved around the bulge of the tower, a man in a gray velvet track suit was leaning on the railing, looking down at BakiyevLand.

"Hey, you two, what's the racket?" the man said in heavily accented English.

Fisher switched his goggles to NV, zoomed in on the man's face, and snapped a photo.

One of the men—Orville, it sounded like—said, "Sorry, boss, sorry."

On Fisher's OPSAT, the picture he had just taken had

been rotated in three dimensions and the missing features filled in. Beside it was another photo that appeared to be a Canadian immigration shot. Beneath the photos the words MATCH: TOLKUN BAKIYEV flashed.

"Just keep it down," Bakiyev replied. "I'm going to work for another twenty minutes, then I'm going to bed. I want it quiet."

"Sure, boss, no problem."

"And don't eat all my popcorn, damn it."

Bakiyev turned and strode back through the tower door and slammed it behind him. *Twenty minutes to nighty-night,* Fisher thought. He checked his OPSAT; Stewart's beacon lay to his left and above him, inside the north tower.

ONCE through the tower door, Fisher found himself facing a narrow spiral staircase that ascended around a center column of stone and heavy oaken crossbeams. Ten feet above his head he could see floor joists. He mounted the staircase, testing each step with his foot, testing his weight, before moving on.

On the first floor he found the space divided by four rooms, like wedges from a pie. Fisher stopped at each door to scan the interior with the flexicam. All four rooms— sleeping quarters—were empty. He moved to the second floor and again found only empty bedrooms, though only three this time as the tower narrowed with each floor. On the third floor, the final one below the archer's cupola, Fisher found, predictably, only two rooms. The first room, another bedroom, contained what appeared to be a figure under the covers of a single trundle bed. Fisher switched to EM and immediately saw a troubling signature: a tight funnel of swirling gray light in the far corner of the room near the ceiling. Security camera. He switched back to NV, centered the flexicam on the security camera, then tapped the OPSAT screen: CURRENT IMAGE>SLAVE AND TRACK MOTION>SCREEN OVERLAY. The OPSAT processed the request and replied, FINISHED. He switched screens. On the fort's blueprint screen, Stewart's room now showed a partially transparent red cone emanating from the corner in which the security camera lay.

Now, the question was, why did only this room have a security camera? He thought he knew the answer, but it took thirty seconds of panning and zooming to confirm it. *There*. The sleeping figure's right hand was resting outside the covers on the pillow; attached to the wrist was what looked like a handcuff. *Stewart*.

Fisher moved to the final room. Inside, Chin-Hwa Pak was sitting on the edge of his bed in his pajamas using a stylus to tap on a smart phone. On the nightstand, under the glow of a shaded reading lamp, was a semiautomatic pistol.

Fisher checked his watch. Pak looked ready to go to bed; he would wait a few minutes, then check again. He found a corner and crouched down, leaning against the wall.

Something . . . Fisher thought. Something was nagging at his subconscious. Something about one of the other bedrooms . . .

Fisher got up and crept back down the spiral staircase to the first floor, then found the room in question, the first one to the left of the stairs. He gave the room another precautionary EM scan, then picked the lock, slipped inside, and shut the door behind him. He walked to the nightstand beside the bed and turned on the reading lamp.

This room, unlike the others, which were almost spartan in their furnishings, was well-appointed: a queen-size bed with a down comforter, a rolltop desk, a built-in bookshelf across from the bed, artwork on the walls . . . This was no ordinary guest room. Bakiyev hadn't gone to special lengths for his other two guests—even his North Korean spy—so why this room?

Fisher went to work. He took his time, searching every nook and cranny of the room. In the nightstand drawer he found a laminated map of Kyrgyzstan with traces of grease pencil on it. Trapped behind the nightstand and the wall he found a faded envelope. On one corner of the envelope's rear, written in blue ink, was a doodle, some scratched-out added numbers, random lines. The main address and return address were written in English—the clumsy block letters of someone unfamiliar with the language. The return address was Bishkek, Kyrgyzstan; the main address read, "University College London." All were in black ink.

Inside Fisher found a letter, written in Kyrgyz by a feminine hand. The date was March 1967. Fisher's grasp of Kyrgyz was weak, but he was able to piece together and translate the letter's salutation: *My Dear little Soso* . . .

Soso, Fisher thought.

He sat down on the bed, scanned the remainder of the letter for any other recognizable phrases, then thought for a couple minutes. He keyed his SVT. "Grim, you there?"

"Here."

"Steak dinner says I can guess what your Kyrgyzstan news is."

"You're on."

"Bolot Omurbai isn't dead."

There was a solid five seconds of silence, and then she said, "What? What are you talking about?"

"I think I'm sitting in Omurbai's temporary mausoleum."

21

"**YOU'VE** lost me, Sam," Grimsdottir said. "Hold on, let me patch in the colonel . . ."

Lambert came on the line: "What've you got, Sam?"

Fisher repeated what he'd said to Grimsdottir, then added, "If I'm not mistaken, Omurbai's mother used to call him 'little Soso'—after Stalin's childhood nickname."

"Checking," Grimsdottir said. "Yeah, that's right. What about the letter?"

"March 1967, University College London. He would have been . . ."

"Eighteen or nineteen," Grimsdottir answered. Fisher could hear keys tapping in the background; after half a minute, she came back. "Omurbai studied there— economics—for a year before he dropped out."

"Speculate," Lambert ordered.

"Omurbai was there years and years ago," Grimsdottir replied. "Long before he took over the country."

"Or the letter is new, and whoever the Kyrgyz government killed was one of Omurbai's body doubles." He told them about the blue-ink doodle on the back of the envelope. "Plus, this room is untouched—almost a shrine. I doubt it would've been kept like this if Omurbai had visited before his rise to power. He would have been just another fellow Kyrgyz to Bakiyev. And the laminated map—the copyright reads 2007."

"Let's play this out," Lambert said. "Omurbai escapes Kyrgyzstan, leaving a body double in his place and telling his commanders to fight on until he returns. From there, with the help of Tolkun Bakiyev he makes his way to Little Bishkek, where he hides out, licks his wounds, and regroups—"

"And makes friends with the North Koreans," Fisher added.

"Right. And uses their advisers, their weapons, and their money—and Bakiyev's network—to plan his return to power."

"That sounds about right," Fisher replied. "A lot of unanswered questions yet, but it's plausible. The biggest question is: What're the North Koreans getting out of the deal? What does Omurbai have to offer them?"

"Speaking of Omurbai's big comeback," Grimsdottir said, "that's the other news. The latest reports show the Kyrgyz government on the edge of collapse. There's fighting inside Bishkek now; the rebels are pushing in."

"They always had the numbers but not the direction,"

Fisher said. "Without Omurbai they were aimless—a gaggle of warlords that couldn't agree on what kind of tea to serve at meetings, let alone wage a war."

"And now," Lambert said, "maybe they have their rudder back."

—— **22** ——————————————————

THEY talked for a few more minutes, then Fisher signed off and returned to the third floor. He checked in on Pak and found him lying in bed reading, so he moved to Stewart's room, picked the lock, and slipped inside. He stood motionless for a few moments, pressed flat against the door, listening. He started side-sliding along the wall, following the contour of the room, checking the security camera's detection cone on the OPSAT as he went, until he was standing directly beneath the camera itself.

He studied the camera's underbelly. He saw no signs of a microphone, but he did see a manufacturer's name and model number. He relayed them to Grimsdottir. "I need an encode for a loop switch."

While both Fisher's SC pistol and rifle were EM jammer

capable, he used the feature sparingly. His concern wasn't about whether or not the jammer was effective (it was), but rather about the intangible part of the equation; that is, the human part: what a security guard does when one of his or her monitors turns to static for no apparent reason only to resolve itself seconds later. And what do they do when another camera displays the same static, then another. Human judgment is an unpredictable beast. Some guards will write off the interference; some will not. It was those who worried Fisher, so whenever possible he preferred the now-antiquated and admittedly more tedious "loop switch" method.

"No problem. Stand by." She came back ten seconds later. "Got it. Encoding now."

On his OPSAT screen, a series of seemingly random numbers and letters were marching across the screen. They disappeared, and in their place was the word READY. From his web belt Fisher withdrew a loop interrupter switch—a loop switch, for short—a six-inch length of UTP Cat6 cable with a miniature C-clamp on each end. On the inner side of each clamp was a ring of sharp, tiny connector teeth; inside the cable itself, a microprocessor; and jutting from the center of the cable between the clamps, an infrared port.

Fisher aligned the loop switch's IR port with that of the OPSAT's.

CONNECTING . . .
CAPTURE . . .
ENCODING . . .
DONE.

Fisher reached up, lightly placed one clamped end of the loop switch to the camera's feed cable, and the other a few inches away. Satisfied with the setup, Fisher tightened both clamps simultaneously. He then again aligned the loop switch's IR port with the OPSAT's and read the screen: LOOP ESTABLISHED. If there were eyes watching Stewart's camera, now all they would see was a replayed loop of him sleeping.

Fisher crept to the bed and knelt down beside it. He placed a hand on Stewart's shoulder and squeezed gently. "Calvin. Calvin, wake up."

Stewart groaned, and his eyelids fluttered open. It took a few seconds, but he focused on Fisher and then said, groggily, "Sam."

"How're you holding up?"

"Well, I've got a bed. That's an improvement."

"Still with the jewelry, I see."

Stewart glanced at his cuffed hand. "Day and night."

"Let me see your thumb." Stewart extended it, and Fisher examined the fake nail. All looked good. "We pinned down the identity of your minder. He's a North Korean agent."

"Any clue what they want with me?"

"We're working on it. Anything on your end?"

"Same questions, different angles. It almost feels like a job interview—like they're trying to decide if they've got the right guy."

"Encourage that."

"Why?"

"A couple reasons," Fisher replied. "One, the more useful you are to them, the more valuable you are. And two, if they're convinced you can do the job for them—whatever that is—they'll send you farther down the pipeline, and I can track you. Hopefully to the source of all this. Hopefully to the PuH-19."

"God, how long is this going to last?"

"I don't know, Calvin. Not much longer, I would bet. Hang in there. As soon as it's safe to pull you out, I'll do it."

"I guess I don't have much choice but to trust you, do I?"

"Well," Fisher said with a half grin, "it just so happens you're in luck: I'm a trustworthy guy. You're doing fine, Calvin. Get some sleep. I won't be far away."

FISHER returned to Pak's door, and in the flexicam's lens he could see the North Korean had turned out his light and now appeared to be asleep. Fisher watched for another five minutes; Pak didn't stir. Fisher lightly scratched at the door with his fingernail. Nothing. Another scratch, this time louder. Still, Pak remained motionless.

Fisher withdrew the flexicam, then picked the lock and slipped inside. On flat feet, he crept to the edge of the bed. Pak lay on his right side, facing away from Fisher. His chest was rising and falling rhythmically. To be on the safe side, Fisher drew his pistol, removed a Level 1 dart from the magazine, then moved to the end of the bed. Pak's bare left foot poked out from under the covers. Fisher knelt down below the footboard and scratched the sole of Pak's foot with the dart. Pak stirred slightly, then turned onto his left side and went back to sleep.

Fisher searched his room but found nothing of interest,

so he turned his attention to Pak's smart phone—a Palm Treo 700—on the nightstand. The keypad was password-locked. He called Grimsdottir. "I've got a Treo that needs a crack and dump," he said.

"Connect me."

Fisher did so. As if by magic, the Treo powered up and began a rapid-fire scroll through its programs and folders. After twenty seconds of this, the screen went dark again.

"Got it," said Grimsdottir. "I'll take a look at it and get back to you."

"Roger. I'm heading to the server room, then I'm out."

HE found it on the top floor of the southern tower—the one he'd seen Bakiyev emerge from earlier—slipped inside, and then tapped into each server in turn and waited for the OPSAT to download the data. He was about to leave when he heard the door to Bakiyev's room open, then slam shut.

"I know that, yes, I know," Bakiyev was saying into what Fisher guessed was a phone, "but it wasn't scheduled until morning. I understand . . . yes, I'll get it ready. How long? Okay, I'll have the pad lights on. Ten minutes."

Footsteps pounded down the spiral staircase. Another door slammed, then silence.

Someone was coming for Stewart, Fisher assumed. *Pad lights* . . . The roof.

Fisher climbed the spiral staircase all the way to the top, where it ended at a roof hatch. It was unlocked. He pushed through it and into the archer's gallery, a domed enclosure with a chest-high, square-serrated stone wall. He looked down. Forty feet below lay the roof of the fort, itself encircled by a crenellated wall. In the center of the roof was a white-painted circle overlaid with an X. Fisher zoomed in on it and could see lights embedded in the roof.

He scanned the north tower, looking for movement, but saw nothing. Instead, he spied a roof door set into the base of the tower.

Damn. Second floor. Go, go, go.

He climbed back through the hatch, picked his way down the spiral staircase to the second floor and, following his internal compass, located the right room. It, too, was unlocked. He slipped inside and looked around. On the far wall, hidden behind a floor-to-ceiling armoire, he found the door. He stepped inside the armoire, flipped the door's dead bolt, and opened it enough for the flexicam. Nothing was moving. He checked his watch: Five minutes to go.

The opposite tower door opened. Tolkun Bakiyev strode out, trotted to the center of the roof, and raised a pair of binoculars. He scanned the sky to the northwest for ten seconds, then started back to the door. Chin-Hwa Pak poked his head out. Bakiyev waved him back inside, then followed.

Four minutes later, Fisher heard the barely perceptible thumping of helicopter rotors. He switched to NV and zoomed in to the northwest just in time to see a pair of navigation strobes appear out of the darkness, followed seconds later by the white nose cone and Plexiglas windshield of a Sikorsky S-76. Fisher flipped up his goggles.

The landing pad lights glowed to life, outlining the circle and cross. Forty seconds later, the S-76 swept in over the roof, barely clearing the wall, and touched down.

Sticking to the shadows along the wall, Fisher ran,

crouched over, until the Sikorsky lay between him and the north tower door. He drew the SC-20 from its back holster and dropped to his belly. Beneath the S-76's cabin and through the landing skids Fisher saw two pair of legs emerge from the tower door and start jogging toward the helicopter. Through the cabin's tinted windows he saw the lights come on as the opposite door slid open to receive the passengers.

Fisher changed the SC-20's fire selector to Sticky Cam, then pulled one off his belt. The standard color for a Sticky Cam was black; Fisher pulled off the outer laminate to expose the white coating. Better match for the Sikorsky's paint scheme. He toggled the Sticky Cam's switch to GPS ENABLED, then loaded it. He tucked the rifle's stock to his cheek and peered through the scope, panning and zooming until he'd found his target.

Wait . . . The thump of the Sticky Cam would likely go unnoticed over the Sikorsky's engines, but Fisher didn't want to take a chance. Pak and Stewart reached the helicopter and took turns climbing in.

Wait . . .

Through the cabin window he saw an arm reach for the cabin's latch. The door started sliding shut. *Now.*

Fisher fired. The Sticky Cam flew true and popped onto the S-76's tail boom just as the cabin door thumped shut. He waited, breath held, half expecting one of the crew to climb out, but nothing happened. Ten seconds passed, then twenty. Thirty. Then the engines increased in pitch, and the S-76 lifted off the pad, rose up twenty feet, wheeled, and disappeared over the north tower. The landing pad lights went dark.

Fisher let out his breath and checked the OPSAT:

STICKY CAM > GPS ENABLED > ONLINE >TRACKING

Fisher smiled grimly to himself. *You can run, but you can't hide.*

23

LESS than a day after the first mortar round landed in Bishkek, the moderate government collapsed from within. With most of its armored vehicles destroyed along with what few strike aircraft it could field, the government forces had taken a crippling blow, and the battle for Bishkek quickly turned into a house-to-house fight as the insurgent army poured down from the mountains surrounding the capital and drove into the city proper under a steady stream of mortar fire that sometimes simply blanketed an area, wiping it clean of soldiers and vehicles alike, while other times taking out single targets, but always doing so with frightening speed and precision.

By the time the government forces recovered from the initial assault and managed to regroup, half the city was already lost, under insurgent control as thousands of Bishkek residents took to the streets and marched on government buildings and the presidential residence.

The Kyrgyz government's pleas for intervention from its neighbors fell on deaf ears, as did an official request to the U.S. State Department for immediate relief. What few forces the U.S. Army had on ready-alert were bogged down in Afghanistan's Hindu Kush mountain range, where the resurrected Taliban had begun to push south toward Kabul.

And so, twenty hours after it began, the Kyrgyz president appeared, pale and haggard, before the podium in his private office and announced his resignation.

The world's news networks had immediately picked up the BBC feed of the Battle for Bishkek and the president's surrender and began playing it on a near constant loop, along with commentary from an alphabet soup of experts, both military and civilian alike.

The monitors behind the situation room's conference table, set to mute, were tuned to CNN, MSNBC, and BBC World.

"Well, that was quick and tidy," Lambert said.

"Like they were being led by a resurrected God," Fisher murmured, taking a sip of coffee.

An hour after ex-filtrating Ingonish, he had met the Osprey at an airstrip in Grand River, and four hours after that he arrived back at Fort Meade, having caught a shower and an hour's nap.

His planting of the Sticky Cam on the Sikorsky was an insurance policy. The truth was, there was no guarantee Stewart, an untrained civilian, would hold up under even the lightest of interrogation. And if he broke, one of the first things he would do was give up the thumbnail beacon. Similarly, the beacon might not pass an electronic frisking. Their grasp on Stewart was tenuous at best. The Sikorsky was a poor substitute, but it was better than nothing.

"Any numbers on casualties?" Redding asked.

"None yet," Lambert replied. "The DIA is working on it."

"Well," Grimsdottir said from her workstation at the other end of the table, "if the satellite BDA is any indication, civilian casualties are likely to be low." As soon as the fighting had started, the entire U.S. intelligence community had turned its collective eyes and ears toward Kyrgyzstan. Overhead satellite battle damage assessments had begun pouring into the National Reconnaissance Office. "Take a look," Grimsdottir said.

She pointed the remote at one of the LCD screens and a black-and-white satellite image of what Fisher assumed was Bishkek appeared. Throughout the city hundreds of tiny craters had been highlighted in blue.

"Mortar strikes?" Lambert asked.

Grimsdottir nodded. "Current as of an hour ago. According to the Pentagon, about eighty percent of those craters were sites of ammunition and weapons depots, truck and APC parks, fuel dumps, and command-and-control centers. The rest were likely cover-for-fire barrages for when the insurgents moved in.

"The Brits have agreed to attach a plainclothes SAS team to a Red Cross mission that's on its way there. With luck, they'll be able to bring back shell fragments, unspent rounds, tubes—anything that might tell us where and who the mortars came from."

"If they get in," Fisher replied. "Those Kyrgyz insurgents

could give the Taliban a run for their money for Extremist
Group of the Year. First thing they'll do is close down every
border outpost."

"Agreed," Lambert said. "Grim, how about it? Anything?"

Eyes fixed on the computer monitor, she held a finger up
for quiet, then punched a few more keys and looked up.
"Maybe. Chin-Hwa Pak's Treo phone had a lot of goodies,
but one thing in particular interested me. In a couple of
phone calls we intercepted, both incoming and outgoing,
Pak mentions someplace called Site Seventeen. Sam, about
an hour before you heard Bakiyev get his call—which also
came from Pak—Pak himself got a call. I'm tracking down
the origin, but I can tell you it came from Asia. Listen to
this. I had to do a quick and dirty translation from Korean,
so it's a tad rough, and it hasn't been verified."

She tapped a key on her keyboard, and from the wall
speakers came a Stephen Hawking–esque voice of the computer's recitation software:

"Can he do it? Does he have the knowledge?"

"Yes. He has the knowledge, and he seems cooperative."

"We're sending for you . . ."

The speakers began hissing.

Grimsdottir said, "Here we got some interference for a
few seconds."

". . . which one?"

". . . teen. St. John's to to a pot then to the site."

Grimsdottir tapped another key. "That's pretty much it.
I'm guessing the 'teen' is Seventeen—as in Site Seventeen."

"'To a pot'," Fisher said. "What is that? A computer
glitch?"

"No, I double-checked it; it's a verbatim quote, which means it's a word the computer couldn't find in its linguistic database. Assuming Pak and the other man are talking about flying somewhere, and assuming the St. John's they're talking about is St. John's, Newfoundland—which is the only St. John's within range of the Sikorsky—that means they touched down there, either for refueling or for an aircraft change.

"I took the former first," Grimsdottir continued, "and did a search for any location within the Sikorsky's range that the computer might have mistaken for the words 'to a pot.' Came up with zilch. So that means they probably changed aircraft in St. John's for something with a longer range. Plus, Sam, your Sticky Cam beacon hasn't moved from St. John's since it arrived. So I expanded my search, spiraling outward from St. John's, until I found a village on very southern tip of Greenland called . . . drumroll, please . . . Tuapaat—*to a pot*."

She gave them a grin and spread her hands.

"Grim, you're a wonder," Fisher said. "Okay, so what's in Tuapaat?"

"Another aircraft change, I'm guessing, this time back to a helicopter. They'd need it for where they were going."

"Explain," Lambert said.

"For the last two hours I've been scouring every database I can beg, borrow, steal, or hack my way into. Five minutes ago I finally found mention of a Site Seventeen: a decommissioned Exxon deep-water oil exploration platform in the Labrador Sea, about a hundred eighty miles east of Tuapaat."

"Owned by?" Lambert asked.

"Working on that right now. The title on the deed belongs to an environmental group out of Australia, but I'm betting that's just a front."

Redding said, "Why in the world are they taking Stewart there?"

No one answered for a few seconds, then Fisher said, "Safety buffer."

"Huh?"

"Where better to handle and experiment with something like PuH-19." Fisher turned to Lambert. "Colonel?"

Lambert thought for a moment, thumbs tapping the rim of the coffee cup clasped in his hands. "Okay. Suit up. I'll get Bird and Sandy prepping."

He reached for the phone.

24

THE Osprey bucked to one side, rain slashing the fuselage. Fisher tightened his seat belt and gripped the armrests a little tighter. Into his headset microphone he said, "How're we looking, guys?"

"Not good," Sandy replied.

In the background, Fisher could hear Bird muttering to himself, which he did during only the most perilous of situations. "Come on, sweetie, don't be like that . . . Ah, now, that's not nice . . ."

Sandy said to Fisher, "You hear?"

"I hear."

Since leaving St. John's, Newfoundland, with every mile northward the weather had deteriorated, until finally eighty miles south of the Site 17 platform, the Osprey was being battered by sixty miles per hour gusts and horizontal rain. Ten thousand feet below them, the ocean was roiling with fifteen-foot waves.

"Can you get me there?" Fisher asked.

Bird answered: "Hell, yes, I can get you there. Getting there ain't the problem. The problem is, getting *Lulu* here to sit still in the crosswind long enough for you to fast-rope to the deck. Odds are, you'd get bashed to a pulp on the cranes and derricks as soon as you went out the darn door."

"In that case, how about we call that plan B," Fisher said.

"Suits me. We aborting?"

"Nope," Fisher said. "New plan A."

"Which is?"

"If we can't come in from the top, we'll come in from the bottom."

TWENTY-FIVE minutes later, Bird called, "About three miles out, Sam. Slowing to one fifty and descending through five thousand feet."

"Any radar?" Fisher asked. However unlikely it may be, Bird and Sandy had been watching their gauges for any EM transmissions coming from the platform.

"Not a peep."

Fisher reached above his head and hooked his safety tether to the overhead cable, then unclipped his seat belt and made his way to the rear of the cabin. In the middle of the ramp, secured to the deck by quick-release ratchet straps, was a Mark IX ISDS, or individual swimmer delivery sled. To Fisher, the sled looked like a miniature version of a Jet Ski whose tail end had been hacked off, leaving only the nose cone—containing a pair of horizontally mounted propellers driven by four marine batteries—a dash panel, a tapered fairing, and a throttle bar/rudder. Attached to the sled's underside was a pair of streamlined scuba tanks; attached to each side of the nose cone, a bow plane for depth control.

Fisher pressed the dash's power button, and the digital gauges lit up, amber on black. A thumb-size screen in the middle of the dash flashed the words SELF-DIAGNOSIS RUNNING. Sixty seconds later the screen flashed again: SELF-DIAGNOSIS COMPLETE. NO ERRORS FOUND.

"Sled checks out," Fisher told Sandy and Bird. "Prepping."

"Roger."

Fisher slipped a one-piece dry diving suit over his tac suit, made sure all the cuffs were sealed tight, then took off his headset, pulled on his hood and face mask, which he tightened for fit, then knelt beside the sled and hooked the loose end of his mask hose into the air-port. He pressed the dash button labeled AIRFLOW ON. Cool, metallic air gushed into his mask. He punched AIRFLOW OFF, then pushed the mask back onto his forehead and put the headset back on.

"Two miles," Bird called. "Three minutes."

"Sea state?"

"Running between five and six," Sandy replied. "Crests to sixteen feet."

"Give me half ramp," Fisher called.

"Half ramp."

"Switching to SVT." He took off his headset and hooked it on the bulkhead, then keyed the SVT. "Read me?"

"Loud and clear," replied Bird.

With a hum, the ramp's hydraulics engaged. The ramp

parted from the fuselage's curved upper rim, revealing a crescent of black sky. Sea spray burst through the opening and misted Fisher's face. The rain sounded like shrapnel striking the Osprey's aluminum skin.

"Hold ramp," Fisher ordered. The ramp stopped. "Lovely evening out there."

"I love your sunny disposition," Bird said.

"Everyone docs."

"One mile out. Coming to hover." The Osprey's engines changed pitch, and Fisher felt their forward momentum begin to slow, then stop altogether. "Hovering. Stand by . . . Couplers engaged."

Sandy said, "We're at thirty feet, Sam. Sorry. Any lower, and we might net some water."

"No problem."

Fisher knelt behind the sled. From the left calf pouch on his dry suit, he pulled a D-ring knotted to some blaze-orange 4mm parachute cord. In his pouch was another 100 feet of it. The sled was buoyant, and in these seas, Fisher wanted to be able to reel it to him—or vice versa—should they get separated during the drop.

"Ready," Fisher called. "On my mark."

"Roger," Bird replied. "We'll be nearby. Call when you're done playing."

"Will do. Give me full ramp."

The ramp groaned downward until it locked fully open with a dull clunk. Rain whipped through the opening. Fisher could see the sea below heaving and breaking, the wave crests serrated edges of white water.

He popped the sled's release toggle, watched it slide into the darkness, then counted five seconds and followed after it.

25

FISHER pushed the throttle bar downward. The bow planes responded, tilting forward and driving the sled deeper. The sled's twin headlights arced through the darkness, illuminating drifting plankton and the occasional curious fish.

When his depth gauge read thirty feet, he evened out, then checked his compass: on course. Above his head the surface of the ocean boiled, a ceiling of undulating white water, but here, a mere ten yards below the surface, the water was calm, with only a slight east-to-west current. Fisher could feel the press of the water against his dry suit, a bone-chilling cold that would have killed him long ago if not for the protective layers.

He saw something—a hazy vertical shape—appear in the

headlights, then fade away. Seconds later it reappeared and slowly took shape until Fisher could make it out: one of the platform's pilings.

Each of the platform's four main pilings, as big around as a tanker truck, were connected by a series of smaller, horizontal cross-pilings, and diagonal I-beam steel girders. Descending vertically between this maze of steel all the way to the ocean floor would be the platform's producing wells, which could number as many as twenty. This platform, long ago decommissioned, would have withdrawn its well pipes and drilling sleeves, leaving only the remnants dangling from the underside of the platform like a massive wind chime.

Fisher kept the sled steady until the rest of the support structure came into view. He curved around the piling, then turned parallel to the cross-piling until his headlights illuminated the next piling. This one, though identical to the first, was on the platform's west side, which put it in the lee of the current. He pushed the throttle bar up and ascended alongside the piling until the headlights illuminated a vertical steel ladder. This was the lower access ladder, used by divers to inspect the platform's submerged structures. He reached out and gave the lowermost rung a firm tug; it held.

He unhooked his face mask's hose from the sled's tanks and hooked into his chest rebreather, then lifted a thumb-size plastic cover on the dash and pressed a red button. On either side of the sled's nose cone, the buoyancy chambers opened. Seconds later the sled tipped over nose first and slid into the depths.

Fisher grabbed the ladder and started climbing.

The ladder rose thirty feet, the last ten out of the water, and ended at a square catwalk bordered by safety rails. Another ladder, this one enclosed by a cage, continued up the piling to another catwalk, encircling the piling. He paused here to strip off his dry suit and toss it over the side, then followed the catwalk to the back side of the piling where he found a set of grated steps that continued up the piling, switchbacking until it ended at a door-size horizontal hatch.

He climbed to the second to last step and tried the lever. It swiveled to the open position with a dull *thunk*. Fisher switched his goggles to NV, drew his pistol, put his back against the hatch, tightened his legs, then stood up a few inches. The hatch squeaked open. The room beyond was a changing area; tiled floors, shower cubicles, and lockers on one side, sinks and toilet stalls on the other. Fisher stood up, careful to keep his right arm on the hatch's edge so it didn't bang open. He climbed the last step into the room, then closed the hatch behind him.

At the far end of the room was a door with a porthole window set at chin height. To his left, a line of four porthole windows; he walked to one of them and looked out over the platform's open deck.

Like most exploration and drilling platforms, this one was built around the drilling and well head equipment, all of which descended through a square, hundred-foot-by-hundred-foot opening in the center of the platform. On either side of this opening were stacked three levels of work shacks joined together by enclosed walkways. Rising from each shack at opposite ends from one another were rotatable cranes. On the far north side of the platform was a raised helicopter pad encircled by a railing. Sitting on the pad was a helicopter. Fisher tried to make out the model, but the horizontal rain made it impossible.

Fisher called up his OPSAT blueprint of the platform and oriented himself on it. This changing room was on the lowermost level of the western-side shack. He checked for Stewart's beacon; it was still active, somewhere above him and to the east.

He walked to the door and peeked through the window. Beyond was a short, unlit hallway that ended at a stairwell. Out of habit, he scanned the hall in both IR and EM and saw nothing unusual. He opened the door and climbed the stairs to the next level. This floor was mostly open, with a solid wall to his left and a half wall to his right through which he could see hanging drilling pipes and cables. He walked to the wall and looked down. Eighty feet below, the sea churned around the pilings. He continued to the third and top level, which was similar to the one below, save one feature. At the far end he found an enclosed walkway to the eastern-side shacks.

He started across the walkway. As he neared the opposite end, he stopped, listened. Nothing. He was about to keep going, when the sound came again, more distinct this time. Voices. He crept to the end of the walkway, pressed himself flat against the wall, and peered around the corner.

The space he was seeing was only half as long—about thirty feet—and the layout was that of a makeshift laboratory, with a rectangular, laminate-topped worktable running down each wall and three tables spaced perpendicularly down the center. Fluorescent shop lights hung from the ceiling at ten-foot intervals, casting the space in cold gray light.

Beyond the tables Fisher could see what looked like a mobile hyperbaric chamber running lengthwise to the opposite wall; sitting before the chamber on a table was a device. It was approximately ten feet long and comprised of parallel conduits of various diameters, from a quarter inch to four inches, and intertwined electrical cables, all of which came together in a steel ring that seemed to have been welded into the chamber's door just below the porthole window through which Fisher could see dim light. He'd seen pictures of a similar device. It was a crude LINAC, a linear particle accelerator.

Three men were sitting in chairs before the LINAC having an animated discussion. A fourth man in a thigh-length black leather coat stood behind the group, arms folded across his chest. Fisher zoomed in. It was Chin-Hwa Pak.

Stewart was sitting in the middle chair, flanked on both sides by Koreans. The man to Stewart's left was holding a clipboard, which he was tapping with a pen and waving in front of Stewart, who pushed it away.

Behind him, Pak pulled out a pistol and put it to Stewart's head. He leaned over and whispered something in Stewart's ear.

Stewart reluctantly took the clipboard and started leafing through pages.

Fisher took pictures, getting all the men's faces, the LINAC, and the hyperbaric chamber. He scanned the room for a place to plant a Sticky Ear, but it was too confined. Pak would hear the placement.

Stewart had stopped leafing through the clipboard's pages and seemed to be studying something intently. He gestured to one of the men, who pulled a calculator from a briefcase on the floor and handed it over. Stewart started punching numbers, writing notations, and leafing back and forth through the pages.

He handed the clipboard back to the first man and tapped something on the page with his pen, then started gesturing to various parts of the LINAC. The men listened closely until Stewart finished, then began talking to one another across him.

A fourth Korean entered the room through the door beside the chamber. He whispered something to Pak, then handed him what looked like a thin remote control. Pak nodded and pocketed the device.

Suddenly, behind Fisher in the walkway, he heard a creaking. He spun around, gun coming up. A Korean was standing in the walkway. Obviously startled and uncertain, the man squinted, trying to make out the figure half hidden in the shadows. The man's hand shot into his coat and came out with a pistol. Fisher fired. The man stumbled backward, the hand holding the gun still coming up. The barrel flashed, and the shot boomed through the walkway.

Fisher spun again, bringing the pistol around. Pak and his partner were already moving—the latter drawing a pistol and taking aim on Fisher while Pak barked orders at the two other Koreans as he shoved them toward the door. Shots peppered the wall behind Fisher. He crab-walked left, squeezing off a trio of shots as he moved. Pak, having gotten the two other Koreans out the door, turned back to Stewart, who was trying to rise to his knees. Pak drew a pistol from his pocket and leveled it at Stewart's head. Stewart let out a scream that Fisher could only describe as half-angry, half-desperate, then launched himself at Pak. The other Korean, distracted by the scream, turned toward them. Fisher rose up, took aim, and drilled a shot into the side of the man's head.

Pak, startled by Stewart's move, backpedaled toward the door. His gun roared once, then again. Stewart stumbled, but kept coming. He wrapped Pak in a bear hug, and together they tumbled through the door.

Fisher holstered the pistol, drew the SC-20 from his back sling, and sprinted down the space, dodging and leaping tables until he reached the downed Korean. He checked the man; he was dead. On flat feet, Fisher slowly crept to the door and peeked his head around the corner. Pak was gone, but lying headfirst halfway down the steps was Stewart. Fisher rushed to him, knelt down.

He was still alive, but just barely. Fisher unzipped his jacket, ripped open his shirt. One bullet had entered just above his navel; the other in the center of the sternum, just below the breastbone.

"It's a LINAC," Stewart rasped, reaching for Fisher's hand and pulling him closer. "They're using it . . . using it . . ." Stewart coughed. He opened his mouth to speak again, but it was full of bubbling blood.

"I'm sorry, Calvin."

Stewart gave the barest shake of his head, then he went still.

From somewhere below, Fisher heard a muffled *crump*, then another, then a third. A vibrating rumble rose through the stairs and shook the walls, followed seconds later by the shriek of tortured steel.

The remote, Fisher thought. Getting rid of the evidence.

Fisher gave Stewart's hand a final squeeze, then laid it

across his chest and started down the stairs. He stopped. Turned back. One last thing . . .

He rushed back up the stairs into the laboratory. He took close-up pictures of the LINAC and the welded ring connector on the chamber's door, then pressed his face to the porthole window. The angle was tight and the single bulb inside the chamber dim, but he took three quick shots of the interior connectors, hoping to catch enough detail.

Below his feet the deck was canting to the left. Somewhere he could hear the rapid-fire *pop pop pop* of rivets giving way and the wrenching of steel on steel.

He was about to turn away from the chamber when something caught his eye. He pressed his face back to the porthole. It took him a full ten seconds to register what he was seeing. Up and down both of the chamber's walls were crisscrossing streaks of blood, and here and there, also stamped in blood, partial palm prints.

Fisher felt his stomach rise into his throat.

Peter's fingertips had been shredded nearly to the bone.

This is it. This is where it had happened. Where they killed him.

The deck was slanting badly now. Behind him, chairs and desks were skittering across the floor and crashing into the wall. Still staring into the chamber, Fisher grabbed the wheel to steady himself. Somewhere in the back of his head a faint voice prodded him: *Get out . . . get out!*

He tore his eyes from the porthole and headed for the door.

26

AFTER a night of observation and restless sleep in Bethesda, Fisher drove himself home, a 1940s farmhouse surrounded by two acres of red maple and pine about thirty minutes northwest of Washington. At Fisher Farms, as Grimsdottir called it, his closest neighbor wasn't within a stone's throw, and the road he lived on simply wound deeper into the Germantown countryside, so the only traffic he saw was that of neighbors or the occasional wanderer. There was no hum of car engines, no honking of horns—few noises, in fact, save those produced by nature: the chirping of chickadees, the croaking of frogs, the wind fluttering through the maples.

He'd bought the property on the cheap from the former owner, who had moved out of state years earlier and let it fall into disrepair. Fisher's home improvement list never seemed to shorten, but that didn't bother him. He found the "unextraordinariness" of retiling a bathroom or fixing a broken shutter therapeutic—the perfect antidote to a job that was anything but workaday.

Fisher climbed out of the car and mounted the front porch steps. Sitting at the foot of the front door was a round hatbox brimming with envelopes. On the way home he'd called Mrs. Stinson, the retired librarian who lived half a mile down the road. Taped to the side of the box was a note:

> *Welcome back. An apple pie on the back porch for you.*
>
> *Edna*

Fisher smiled. *No place like home.*

HE took a shower, made some coffee and a plate of ham and eggs, then stretched out on the couch under the bay window and read for a while—*The White Rhino Hotel* by Bartle Bull—then dozed fitfully for an hour, so he got up, changed clothes, and went outside to weed the garden. He gave up after ten minutes. He took off his gloves and walked to the middle of the lawn and sat down cross-legged in the sun.

His mind wouldn't turn off and kept returning to the platform, to Calvin Stewart, to the claw marks on the chamber wall, the bloody, shredded fingernails . . .

He should have never promised Stewart he would get him out. He knew better. There were few sure things, and even fewer in his line of work. What bothered him most is he couldn't decide whether he'd made the promise to secure Stewart's cooperation or because he'd truly meant it. To survive and thrive in special operations you had to have a mission mind-set: whatever it took to do the job. It wasn't a matter of setting aside your morals, per se, but a level of dedication, a silent oath to *get the job done*, regardless of hurdle or hardship.

Had he subconsciously been following this oath when he made the promise to Stewart? Before he'd dropped aboard the *Gosselin*, he'd known Stewart had a wife and a seven-year-old daughter. Now they didn't have him. Had Stewart died still believing Fisher was going to save him?

Peter. Fisher tried to imagine what it must have been like for his brother, trapped inside that chamber, that iron coffin, listening to the accelerator's motors spool up, and then . . . what? What had he felt? Had he—?

Stop, Sam. Just stop.

He squeezed his eyes shut, then opened them and stared at the sky, seeing but not seeing the clouds.

This was another hazard of the job. Some operators never let themselves think like this; they simply wiped their mental slate clean after a mission and moved on. Others, like Fisher, did just that but only after a mission. Shove your worries, fears, and emotional speed bumps into a mental vault, lock it shut, then reopen it later when you're safe at home. Opinions varied about which method was the healthiest, but for Fisher there'd never been any doubt. There's only so much stuff you can shove in the vault before it starts leaking. Better to keep it swept out.

No, he decided, he hadn't lied to Stewart. He'd meant

what he'd said, and he'd tried to get him out. He'd failed. Period. It was a promise he shouldn't have made, but he had, and it was done. His intentions had been good; his follow-through, not so much.

And as for Peter . . . Come what may, scores would be settled. Anyone and everyone who'd been a party to Peter's death would pay in full.

Fisher's cell phone vibrated in his pocket. He flipped it open. It was Grimsdottir: "So, what's your preference? Morton's or Outback?"

"You've lost me, Grim."

"For your steak. Never mind, just turn on your TV and call me back."

Fisher walked back inside and flipped on the kitchen set; it was already tuned to MSNBC.

". . . again, stunning news out of war-torn Kyrgyz-stan . . ." The inset image beside the anchorwoman changed to show a podium, the same one the Kyrgyz president had stood behind while resigning two days ago. Standing behind it now was Bolot Omurbai. "Let's listen," the anchor said.

". . . the grace of Allah and the will of the Kyrgyz people, I have returned to lead our country back to the ways of Islam—the ancient ways of Manas, before all was poisoned by the West, by technology, by modern soullessness." Omurbai's eyes seemed to glaze over as he spoke, his gaze fixed straight ahead as though he were in his own world. "Turn your eyes to Kyrgyzstan and behold our greatness. Watch the scourge of Manas return the lost Kyrgyz race back to greatness!"

Omurbai stopped suddenly. He blinked several times,

emerging from his trance, then continued. "I am told that most of the world believed me dead." Here Omurbai offered a disarming smile and a spread of his hands. "As they say, news of my demise was misreported.

"The outlaw government, backed by the evil forces of the United States, foisted a lie upon the world and the people of Kyrgyzstan—a lie meant to crush the spirit of my people . . ."

Fisher muted the television. *Good Christ.* Until now, his suspicion that Omurbai was still alive had been notional; now it was tangible.

Of course, Omurbai was lying. The man captured by the U.S. Army Rangers in that cave had been dressed in Omurbai's uniform, had answered to his name, and stood by it throughout his trial.

Had Omurbai already left the country by then? Fisher suspected so. He'd probably fled across the Kazak border even before the bombs started falling. Then, aided by loyalists in the stans, he'd made his way to Little Bishkek and disappeared into Tolkun Bakiyev's Ingonish. What remained to be answered was the nature of Omurbai's connection to the North Korean government. What was driving that partnership?

Fisher flipped open his cell phone to call Grimsdottir, then stopped, hesitated, and flipped it closed again. On the kitchen table was his hatbox full of mail. One of the envelopes jutting from the stack had caught Fisher's eye; he walked over and slid it out.

He felt his heart lurch. He knew the handwriting on the envelope.

Peter.

27

"**NO** doubts?" Lambert asked.

Fisher, his eyes fixed on the cellophane-sealed letter lying in the center of the conference table under a circle of light, seemed not to hear. Redding and Grimsdottir, also leaning over the letter, waited for Fisher to respond.

After a few moments, Fisher turned to Lambert. "I'm sorry?"

"The letter. No doubt it's Peter's handwriting?"

"No, it's his."

Quashing his urge to tear open the letter as soon as he'd seen it, Fisher had instead immediately called Lambert, who'd called the Department of Energy operations center, which in turn dispatched NEST (Nuclear Emergency Search Team) to Fisher's home. Though primarily tasked with the identification and handling of nuclear weapons, NESTs were also the best general-circumstances radioactive response teams in the country. However unlikely, if the letter contained even the barest trace of PuH-19, it needed to be handled appropriately.

With the letter on its way to Brookhaven National Laboratory in New York, Fisher himself was whisked to Georgetown University Hospital, where the doctors, already made aware of the nature of the possible contamination, gave him a full physical, from head to toe, inside and out. No trace of PuH-19 was found.

Four hours later the letter, too, was declared clean of any contamination, so it was transported to the FBI's Quantico labs, where it was pushed through Latent Prints and Trace Evidence units, then returned to Fort Meade. Peter's prints were found on the letter; no remarkable trace findings.

The letter had been postmarked in Nuuk, where Peter had been first taken after being picked up by the fishing boat, about four days before Peter had been transferred to Johns Hopkins. How the letter had gotten mailed Fisher could only guess, but the most likely answer was a kind-hearted nurse or orderly. What remained a true mystery was how Peter had escaped the chamber aboard the platform and made his way into a life raft.

"That's not his normal handwriting, I assume," Grimsdottir said.

Fisher shook his head. "He must have already been sick. Plus, he never wrote anything down. He had a snapshot memory."

The handwriting, while clearly belonging to Peter, was shaky, as though written by a palsied hand. Even the letter itself, which was headed by the words, *"Sam . . . important . . . piece together . . . answers here,"* wasn't so much a letter as it was a disjointed collection of doodles, some writing along the ruled lines, some in the margins, some upside down and trailing off the page into nowhere. It was as though Peter were trying to prize from his fevered and failing mind the most pertinent pieces of his investigation in hopes that Fisher could pick up the trail.

There were references to Site 17, the now-destroyed drilling platform; to Little Bishkek; to the missing Carmen Hayes—all of which Fisher understood. But then there were other notations, words and numbers that seemed unconnected to anything he'd encountered:

Sun
Star
Nile
Wonder ash
49- 2303253/1443622
Oziri
Red . . . tri . . . my . . . cota

"The problem is," Redding said, "we don't know how far the PuH-19 had spread through him when he wrote this. All this could be nonsense. It might have made sense to him at the time, but we have to at least consider it's meaningless." Redding caught Fisher's eye and grimaced. "Sorry, Sam, no offense."

"None taken. You're right; it's possible."

"Maybe," Grimsdottir said, tapping a pencil on the table, "but maybe not." She turned around, walked to a computer workstation, and started tapping keys. They watched her in silence for a couple minutes, and then Lambert said, "Grim . . ."

"Hang on . . . Okay, thought so." She curled an index finger at them, and they walked over and clustered around the monitor. On-screen was a Discovery Channel website article entitled "The Lost *Sunstar*."

> . . . *a mystery that has remained unsolved for almost sixty years. The* Sunstar, *a civilian version of the World War II Curtiss C-46 Commando transport plane owned by millionaire geologist-adventurer Niles Wondrash, took off from Mwanza, Tanzania, on the evening of November 17, 1949, with his manservant Oziri. The* Sunstar, *flown by Wondrash himself, never reached its destination, Addis Ababa, nine hundred miles to the north in Ethiopia. Extensive search and rescue efforts failed to find any trace of Wondrash and the* Sunstar. *They had simply vanished from existence . . .*

Lambert straightened up and whistled softly. "I'll be damned."

Grimsdottir said, "I knew those words sounded familiar."

"Those numbers," Fisher said. "The first two before the dash match the year Wondrash disappeared. The others— two sets of seven numbers divided by a slash—latitude and longitude?"

"Could be," Redding said. "What about the other words—'Red . . . tri . . . my . . . cota'?"

"No idea," Grimsdottir said. "I'll have to do some digging. But here's the real shocker, boys," she added, hands flying over the keyboard as she brought up Google, typed a word, and hit ENTER. She pointed triumphantly to the screen, which displayed a genealogy website's database. "Wondrash's manservant . . . Oziri? That's a traditional Kyrgyz name."

"**WHAT** we have to decide," Lambert said as they retook their seats around the conference table, "is whether any of this is worth pursuing. Grim, where do we stand on putting the puzzle together?"

Grimsdottir sighed and spread her hands. "Stewart's gone, sunk in six thousand feet of freezing water, along with any evidence we might have found on Site 17; right now, we have zero leads on Carmen Hayes; Chin-Hwa Pak and his cohorts have disappeared. I'm still working on both Legard's and Bakiyev's financials and data dumps Sam got, as well as the intercepts I got from Ingonish, but . . . In a word, we're dead in the water."

"On the other hand," Redding said, "we've got Peter's doodle letter, which turns out to be not as disjointed as we thought—"

Grimsdottir interrupted. "And those numbers could be lat and long coordinates. They do match up with real sites—one in Tanzania and one in Kenya—"

"And we've got Oziri, which *is* a connection to Kyrgyzstan, albeit a tenuous one. Or it could be a dumb coincidence and mean nothing."

There was a long ten seconds of silence around the table, and then Lambert turned to Fisher. "Sam?"

"It all comes down to what we know and what we're left

with. We know Bolot Omurbai and the North Koreans are working together. What that is, we don't know, but you can be sure it's not pretty, and it's not going to stop on its own. We also know every lead we've uncovered so far came from Peter's investigation. And what's in this letter"— Fisher nodded toward the cellophane sleeve in the center of the table—"was important enough that it was probably one of the last things Peter did before he died. With nothing else to go on, I say we see where it takes us."

Lambert considered this, then nodded. "I agree. How's your Swahili?"

"Niliumwa na papasi. Kichwa kinauma," Fisher replied.

"Wow, I'm impressed," Grimsdottir said. "What's it mean?"

"I have been bitten by a centipede. I need to see the doctor."

Lambert sighed heavily, trying to hide a smile, and shook his head. "Okay, let's find you a cover." He reached for the phone.

28

FISHER tapped the driver on the shoulder, who turned and looked back over the seat. Bob Marley's "Trenchtown Rock" blasted from the front seat's speakers, vibrating the taxi's doors. On the upside, the Pcugeot's air conditioner worked like an industrial freezer, chilling the interior to sixty-five degrees. Fisher, in a short-sleeve shirt and cargo shorts, had been wearing goose bumps on his forearms and thighs since leaving the airport.

"Pull over here."

"Eh?"

Fisher pointed toward the curb. "Here!"

"Yeah, yeah, okay."

The driver pulled over. Fisher counted out four hundred Kenyan shillings—about six dollars—and handed it to the driver, then grabbed his backpack and climbed out onto the sidewalk—what passed for a sidewalk here—a shelf of dirt about four inches higher than the dirt street. Fisher felt the heat enshroud him like a quilt straight from a dryer. With a wave of his arm, the driver pulled away in a geyser of oily blue smoke, Bob Marley shaking the windows.

Fisher looked around to get his bearings. If he was reading the map correctly—which was hand-drawn and blurred by a static-filled fax line—he was standing on Bukumbi Road. Despite a population of nearly two million and a cosmopolitan reputation, Nairobi off the main thoroughfares felt much smaller, with few buildings over five stories and little of the glitz and glitter that usually accompanies modern architecture. As Kenya's capital, Nairobi was the country's cultural, economic, and political hub.

A trio of giggling black children—two girls and a boy—ran down the sidewalk toward him, dodging and weaving as they tried to catch a chicken, then stopped suddenly. They stared up at him, wide-eyed, mouths agape.

Fisher smiled. *"Jambo,"* he said.

For a few seconds the children continued to ogle him, then one of the little girls offered a tentative smile; her teeth were perfect and white. *"Jambo.* Good day, sir."

"Your English is very good," Fisher said.

"Thank you, sir."

"I'm looking for someone. Can you help me?" The little girl nodded, and Fisher said, "Her name is Alysyn Wallace—"

"Miss Aly?"

Fisher nodded.

Behind him Fisher heard a woman say, "You've found me, I'd say."

Fisher turned around. The woman the kids had called Miss Aly wore khaki Capri pants and a blue T-shirt bearing the U.S. Air Force logo and the words, ALL AIR FORCE BIL- LIARDS CHAMPION. Her mouth seemed perpetually on the edge of a wry smile.

Fisher nodded. "Sam."

She extended her hand, and Fisher shook it. "Aly," she said. "Run along children, your chicken is getting away." With waves and giggles, the children scampered away.

"*Ahsante,*" Fisher called.

"You are welcome, sir," the little girl answered over her shoulder.

"Your Swahili's not bad," Aly said.

"Thanks. A few dozen phrases is all I know."

"Come on. I'm not far from here."

THEY walked to her home a few blocks away and sat on her back patio overlooking Lake Naivasha. The low stone wall was surrounded by sawback fronds that rattled in the breeze. Aly offered him a glass of iced tea, then leaned back in her wing-backed rattan chair.

"So tell me again," she said, "how do you know Butch?"

In truth, Fisher wouldn't know Butch if he passed him on the street. The man Aly had known as Butch Green, a Red Cross legal aid worker, was in fact Butch Mandt, a CIA case officer who had been assigned to Nairobi up until six months earlier.

Lambert's request to Langley for a local contact in Nairobi had led to Mandt, who in turn gave them Aly's name. Aly, herself a former relief worker with the Christian Children's Fund, had come to Kenya in 1982 and just never left.

"Now," she told him, "I teach English in St. Mary's School during the week, and on weekends it's billiards and paddleboat races on the Kisembe River."

According to Mandt, Aly knew Kenya better than most blacks who'd lived there all their lives. As far as she knew, Fisher was a real estate developer who'd retired early and now globe-hopped in search of adventure.

"Met him at a fund-raiser in Baltimore a couple years ago," Fisher replied. "I meant to ask you. What's with the paddleboat racing?"

"It's mostly for the kids. We get together, tool around the lake, have a picnic."

"Not a bad way to spend a Sunday."

"Join us."

Fisher shrugged, took a sip of tea. "I'll give it some thought."

"So, you're after the *Sunstar*, huh?"

"I am."

"A lot of people have already looked, Sam. Sixty years' worth of people."

Fisher smiled. "I love a challenge."

"You got a vehicle?"

Fisher dug into his shirt pocket and came up with a business card; he handed it over. "My travel agent set it up for me. A Range Rover."

Aly nodded and handed it back. "I know this man. He'll treat you right. You know where you're going?"

"More or less."

Less rather than more, Fisher thought. All he had were a pair of latitude and longitude coordinates, the first two hundred miles to the northwest, deep inside the Great Rift Valley in the Kenyan highlands; the second a hundred fifty miles to the east near Lake Victoria's Winam Gulf. What he would find, if anything, at these spots he didn't know, but he was trusting that Peter had known and that somehow, someway, these two spots were connected to Carmen Hayes's disappearance, North Korea, Bolot Omurbai, and the PuH-19.

Fisher was ready for some answers. He, Lambert, Grimsdottir, and Redding had been staring at this seemingly unsolvable puzzle for too long, and Fisher's instincts told him that whatever was happening, it wasn't far off.

"Gear, rations, et cetera?" asked Aly.

Fisher nodded to his Granite Gear Stratus lying beside his chair.

"Gun?" she said.

"They confiscated my bazooka at the airport."

She clucked her tongue. "We've got highway bandits in the backcountry. They'll steal your skin if they think they can sell it," she said solemnly, then gave him a wink. "No worries, I'll fix you up. You know how to handle a gun?"

"Just point the end with the hole in it at the bad guy and pull the trigger."

She narrowed her eyes at him, then decided he was kidding and laughed. "Right." She checked her watch. "Go catch a nap. When you wake up, I'll take you to supper. I know a place that serves a parrot fish that'll knock your socks off."

THE parrot fish had in fact been fantastic. They returned to her home just as the sun was setting. As promised, the rental agent had delivered his Range Rover to the house, complete with extra jerricans of water and fuel.

Fisher went to his bedroom, turned on the bedside lamp, and stretched out. His satellite phone chimed, and he checked the screen: Grimsdottir. "Morning, Grim."

"Evening, for you."

"Feels like morning to me. What's up?"

"I've got the colonel on the line, too."

"Lamb."

"When do you leave?" Lambert asked.

"Five in the morning."

"Omurbai's been on the air again doing his Hitler imitation. Remember he mentioned Manas? 'The scourge of Manas'?"

"Yes."

Grimsdottir said, "That's a reference to something called the *Epic of Manas*. It's a traditional Kyrgyz myth-slash-poem set in the ninth century. It's a cornerstone to Kyrgyz national identity. It runs almost half a million verses, twenty times longer than Homer's *Odyssey* and *Iliad* combined."

"Should I put it on my reading list," Fisher said, "or are there CliffsNotes?"

"Well, here's the condensed version: Manas and descendants go on a variety of adventures, waging war, looking for a homeland, and just generally being heroic. Harvard's got an electronic version, which I downloaded. I've scanned the thing from start to finish, and I can't find any mention of the phrase 'the scourge of Manas.'"

"So Omurbai's taken some creative license," Fisher replied.

Lambert said, "The shrinks at the CIA don't think so. Omurbai's used it seven more times in press conferences. They think it's more than just a catchphrase he's using to stir the masses. They think it has tangible meaning for him."

Fisher was silent for a few moments. "Scourge," he said. "Could have two meanings. Scourge, as in a tormentor, in which case he's probably talking about himself. Or, he's using it in the literal sense: scourge, as in a flail, or a whip."

"In other words," Lambert said, "a weapon."

"Not just a weapon," Fisher corrected him. "A weapon worthy of an epic, nation-saving hero."

—*29*——————————

KAPEDO, KENYA

FISHER pulled the Range Rover off the dirt track and beneath the canopy of trees hanging over the plank shack. The hand-painted red and white sign was so faded it was barely legible, but he could just make it out: JIMIYU'S. A scrawny, marginally feathered chicken jumped off the shack's tin roof and landed with a squawk on the Rover's hood.

"*Adede*, go, go!" a male voice called. A black man, standing at least six and a half feet tall, ducked out of the shack's doorway, waving his hands at the chicken. "Bad girl, bad!" His English had only a slight accent.

The chicken stalked across the hood and hopped down.

Fisher opened the Rover's door and climbed out. "Mr. Jimiyu?"

"Mr. Barnes?" the man replied, walking forward to shake

hands. Jimiyu was rail thin, the bones at his elbows and wrists knobby, and he had perfect, white teeth and lively eyes. "Welcome to Kapedo. How was your drive?"

Fisher had left Nairobi just before dawn. It had taken him nearly six hours to cover the one hundred seventy-five miles to Kapedo. Aly's warning about highway bandits had been prescient. Twice he'd had to use the vintage M-14 rifle she'd loaned him, once on the road between Nakuru and Nyahururu Falls when an ancient Subaru Brat full of panga-wielding teenagers had started tailgating him and gesturing for him to pull over; then again north of Nosoguru, where a trio of men had demanded a toll (they'd wanted the Range Rover itself) for crossing a bridge. In each case, Fisher's casual brandishing of the M-14 had resolved the debate.

"You had no trouble, yes?" Jimiyu said.

"No trouble."

"Good, good. And tell me: How is Irving?"

Surprisingly, Fisher's contact for this final leg of the journey to what he assumed/hoped was the *Sunstar*'s crash site had come not from the CIA but from Lambert himself, who'd simply given Fisher Jimiyu's name and a four-word guarantee: "You can trust him." No explanation offered. When Fisher had pressed him for an explanation, Lambert simply winked and said, "Another time."

"He sends his regards." Fisher walked to the rear of the Rover, lifted the hatch, and pulled out his backpack. "He had a message for you."

"Oh?"

"He said, 'Barasa is doing fine.'"

Jimiyu clapped his hands once and grinned broadly. "Excellent. Come, follow me. We'll have something to eat, then be on our way. With great luck, I will have you there before nightfall."

AN hour later, Jimiyu led Fisher down a jungle trail to a plank-and-tire dock at the river's edge. Bobbing gently on the river's muddy brown surface was a circa World War II eighteen-foot U.S. Navy motor whaleboat sporting a fresh coat of battleship gray paint and a pair of trolling motors sitting on a transom board in the stern.

"Nice," Fisher said. "Where'd you get it?"

"I found it," Jimiyu said proudly, his teeth flashing. Fisher cocked his head at the Kenyan. "Truly," Jimiyu added. "I was fishing near Tangulbe when it came floating down the river. It was empty and barely afloat. A ghost dhow. I swam out, towed it back to shore, then a friend with a truck helped me bring it here. I fixed it, and here it is," he finished, spreading his hands as though unveiling a magic trick.

"How fast?"

"Twenty-four kilometers per hour. With extra fuel cans, we can go nearly two hundred forty kilometers."

Fisher did the conversion in his head: about fourteen miles per hour for 150 miles. It would be just enough to reach the crash site and get back to Kapedo. From here all the way to Lake Turkana they would be crossing through the Eastern Rift Valley and Great Rift Valley, which as a whole ran over 3,500 miles, from Syria in the north to Mozambique in south. Formed by the sinking and tearing of the earth's crust along a tectonic plate that was fifty million years old, the Rift Valley was an ecosystem unto it- self, ranging in elevation from 6,000 feet above sea level here in Kenya to 1,400 feet below sea level at the shores of the Dead Sea, and ranging in width from less than a mile to more than one hundred miles.

On the flight to Nairobi, Fisher had studied satellite maps of the area. The seventy miles of river from Kapedo to Peter's mystery coordinates flowed ever downward through thick, triple-canopy jungle, boiling gorges, and past towering escarpments, until bottoming out at nearly six hundred feet below sea level in a valley that probably hadn't seen more than a hundred white footprints in its history. If that's where the *Sunstar* had gone down, it was no wonder it had remained lost for almost sixty years.

Jimiyu climbed into the stern, and Fisher handed him the extra fuel and water cans, four steel ammunition boxes full of rations and supplies, then cast off the lines and jumped in. Jimiyu braced his bony leg against the dock, pushed off, then pull-started the engines and opened the throttle.

For the next two hours they glided down the river, passing villages and other boats, most of them narrow-beamed fishing dhows. Jimiyu seemed to know everyone, waving and smiling and calling out in Swahili as they passed by, but for the most part the river was empty of traffic. Jimiyu whistled to himself, one hand on the throttle, the other resting on the stock of a vintage Mauser bolt-action rifle. Though his expression was one of contentment, Fisher could see his eyes constantly scanning, from the riverbanks and across the muddy brown water ahead and to the sides.

"Crocodiles?" Fisher asked at one point.

"Oh, yes, very big. And *koboku*," he said, and opened his mouth wide and chomped down. "Hippo, too. Watch for floating logs. They might not be logs, understand?"

"I understand," Fisher said and fingered his own rifle. Though opinions varied, it was widely accepted that hippos killed more people in Africa than all other animals combined. A bull hippo can weigh as much as six thousand pounds, has razor-sharp tusks, a nasty disposition, and can run, at a sprint, over thirty miles per hour.

Fisher couldn't help but smile. Throughout his career he'd been shot at, stabbed, clubbed, and everything in between. He'd jumped from airplanes at thirty-five thousand feet, piloted minisubmarines, and technically invaded dozens of countries. For some reason, the idea of being killed by a hippo while tooling down a jungle river in the Great Rift Valley while trying to solve one of the twentieth century's most enduring mysteries amused him. All things considered, there were worse ways to go.

Sam Fisher, koboku fodder.

"There!" Jimiyu called, pointing toward the bank. *"Koboku!"*

To the left in a shallow cove, were a dozen curved brown backs jutting from the water. As one, lined up as though waiting for a show to start, the hippos studied them, eyes barely visible above the surface of the water, ears twitching.

Jimiyu put the rudder over, steering right to give the pod a wide berth. He caught Fisher's astonished expression and grinned. "Impressive, are they not?"

Fisher could only nod, eyes still fixed on the gallery of hippos receding in their wake. Each one had been the size of a VW Beetle.

A few minutes later, Jimiyu said, "Irving tells me you are looking for a plane."

"That's true."

"The *Sunstar*."

"Yes."

"Old legend, that one."

"What's your opinion?" Fisher asked. "You know the area we're headed?"

Jimiyu thought for a moment, biting the inside of his lip. "Yes, very well. Many people have come looking for the *Sunstar*, but no one's looked in this place yet." He shrugged. "Who knows?"

Fisher didn't respond. From his expression, Jimiyu seemed to be still considering his answer. "I think it is either lost in the Rift or somewhere in Turkana. Lake Turkana, you know."

"I know."

"That lake—everyone thinks it is very shallow. Mostly it is, but there are parts that aren't so shallow." He grinned knowingly. "If we do not find it here, you and I, we will rent a submarine and look in Turkana, okay?"

Fisher smiled back. "Okay."

30

THEY'D arrived at their campsite—a flat section of beach in a gorge—in the late afternoon the day before, and though there was still four hours of daylight left, they both decided to get a fresh start the next morning. Peter's coordinates were four miles away, to the northwest. With luck, they could start at dawn, reach the site by midday, and be back to the campsite by nightfall.

They spent the remaining hours of daylight gathering firewood, and then, as Fisher got the fire started, Jimiyu disappeared into the jungle for an hour and returned carrying what looked like a large rat. It was, in fact, a rat, Fisher learned, but charred over the fire it tasted, predictably, like rubbery chicken. After supper, Jimiyu made coffee in a rust-spotted enamel pot, then tossed the remaining wood on the fire and slung a pair of netted sleeping hammocks from trees along the edge of the beach.

FISHER eased the strap off his shoulder, shifted the M-14 to his right, and then stopped on the trail and gave Jimiyu a soft *tsst*. On either side of Fisher the jungle was a thick wall of green. He sat down on his haunches. Jimiyu, walking ten feet ahead, stopped and looked over his shoulder. Fisher curled a finger at him, and he walked back.

"We're being followed," Fisher said.

"Yes, I assumed so," Jimiyu replied. "We're on the border between the Samburu and Turkana tribes. Do not worry; they are simply curious. We are not one or the other tribe, so our presence should not upset them." Jimiyu smiled and placed a hand on Fisher's shoulder.

"Is that a hard-and-fast rule?"

Jimiyu shrugged. "I see the jungle is not foreign to you."

More like an old friend, Fisher thought.

"Perhaps you are Samburu or Turkana," the Kenyan said. "How did you know?"

"Because there's a pair of eyes watching us. Ten feet to your left."

Very slowly, Jimiyu rotated his head to the left and scanned the foliage. As Fisher had said, a pair of white-rimmed brown eyes were peering at them from behind a palm trunk.

"Turkana," Jimiyu whispered. He raised a hand to chest level, palm out and said, *"Hujambo?"* Which means: How do you do?

The figure ducked out of sight and a few seconds later

soundlessly emerged from the jungle ten feet down the trail. The man was wearing denim shorts and a faded red T-shirt bearing the words THE CLASH ANARCHY TOUR 1976. A butcher knife with a rope-wrapped handle jutted from the front belt loop on his shorts.

"*Jambo,*" he said.

Jimiyu stood up and walked forward. The men shook hands and began speaking in rapid-fire Swahili. Most Kenyan tribes, Fisher had learned, speak at least two languages—Swahili and their own native dialect, of which there are more than thirty—and many speak a modicum of English. Jimiyu and the man spoke for another few minutes, then shook hands again, and the man stepped off the trail and disappeared.

"What's the verdict?" Fisher asked.

"He's Turkana; they and the Samburu have already talked about our presence. As long as we do not hunt here, we have safe passage."

"He didn't want to know why we're here?"

"I told him you were a . . ." Jimiyu paused and scratched his head. "The word does not translate so well. I told him you were a spoiled white adventurer."

Fisher laughed, and Jimiyu gave a pained shrug. "Apologies. It was a convenience on my part. Better that than try to explain. I also asked about the plane. Both tribes are aware of the legend, but neither have seen any sign of it."

THEY walked for another three hours, sometimes on well-worn paths, sometimes on narrow game trails, and other times through the thick of the jungle Fisher navigated via his GPS unit. The purist orienteer in him resented the gizmo, but the pragmatist in him knew it was a necessary evil. With limited time on his hands, a compass was a luxury he couldn't afford.

Jimiyu, armed with a long Ghurka knife, sliced his way through the foliage with practiced swings of his long arms, ducking and weaving like a boxer as he stepped over roots and ducked under branches and pointed out various plants and animals beside the trail along with a running, colorful commentary: *"Very rare . . . do not touch that . . . not poisonous . . . tasty, but hard to catch . . ."*

At noon they swung back to the northeast, and after another hour's walk Fisher heard the muffled roar of water through the trees. The landscape sloped downward until they were picking their way along switchbacked hillside. At last the slope evened out, the trees gave way to low scrub foliage, and they found themselves standing at the edge of a cliff.

Fifty feet below, the river surged down a narrow gorge. The water was a clear blue and in the still pools formed behind the boulders he could see the riverbed covered in smooth, round stones. A hundred yards to their right was a twenty-foot tall waterfall that split into three channels over a jagged rock face before splashing into a pool below.

Fisher studied the GPS unit. "This is the place." He lifted his binoculars to his eyes and scanned the length of the gorge, tracking along both tree lines as far as he could see in both directions. "I don't see anything," he said.

"You are not looking in the right place," Jimiyu murmured beside him.

"What?"

Jimiyu raised a bony hand and pointed straight ahead at a thick, vine-encrusted tree jutting from the edge of the cliff. Fisher stared at it, seeing nothing for a full thirty seconds, until finally his eyes detected a too-symmetrical shape hidden in the branches: a straight vertical line, another horizontal, a gentle curve . . .

Good God . . .

What he was seeing wasn't a tree. It was the inverted tail section of an airplane.

Fisher was dumbfounded. Of course, the brother in Fisher had prayed Peter's letter had been more than the ramblings of a sick and dying man, but with the thoughts so seemingly incoherent and far removed from the core of the Carmen Hayes/PuH-19 puzzle, he'd also had his doubts.

But here it was, exactly where the latitude and longitude indicated: a plane. Now seeing it for what it was, Fisher understood how even the Turkana and Samburu, so intimately familiar with the area, had missed it. While the jungle had long ago erased any sign of the impact itself, it was clear the *Sunstar* had crashed not far from here and ripped through the forest, slowing until the forward half of its fuselage had come to rest perched, hovering, at the edge of this cliff until finally, minutes or hours or days later, physics took over and it tipped over nose first and slid down the cliff face into the river below. Almost six decades of jungle foliage, mold, and lichens had enshrouded the aluminum fuselage, turning it into just another tree trunk.

Fisher dropped his pack and rifle, then pulled a sixty-foot coil of 10mm climbing rope from his pack. As Jimiyu secured the line to a nearby tree, Fisher looped together a makeshift rappelling rig. He stepped to the edge of the cliff and started down.

Pausing every few feet to poke through the vines and leaves with his knife, Fisher walked himself down the cliff until the jabbing of his knife returned not the hollow gong of aluminum, but the screeching of steel on glass. This version of Niles Wondrash's plane, a Curtiss C-46 Commando, had four fuselage windows, starting at the wing and moving forward to the cockpit windows. The cabin door was set behind these, just forward of the tail fin. Fisher saw no wings, and he assumed they'd been sheared off during the crash.

Now with a point of reference, he scaled upward, again tapping his knife. The windows were set roughly ten feet apart, so . . . He stopped climbing and studied the fuselage, trying to discern angles and shapes until finally he could make out an up-sloping curve he felt certain was the rear vertical fin. He spun his body and wedged his feet into the vines, then began cutting at the foliage with his knife until slowly, foot by foot, a patch of fuselage appeared, followed soon after by an inset hatch handle and a vertical seam. He wedged the point of his knife into the seam and began prying, moving inch by inch as though prying open a paint can. After five minutes of work, he heard a groaning screech of metal on metal. The hatch gave way and fell open. Fisher pushed off, avoiding the swinging metal, then swung back and kicked his legs through the opening and wriggled forward until his butt was resting on the hatch jamb.

"I'm in!" he called up to Jimiyu.

On hands and knees the Kenyan leaned over the cliff face

and offered him a smile and a thumbs-up. "Be very careful, Sam. Many creatures have probably made that their home, you know."

Great, Fisher thought. He hadn't considered that.

He pulled the LED headlamp from his belt, settled it on his head, and toggled the ON button. The beam illuminated the opposite cabin wall, its smooth aluminum surface mottled with mildew. He played the light down the vertical shaft of the cabin. The wall and floor were empty. No seats, no storage racks, no nothing. All of that, either knocked loose during the crash or simply loosened by time and gravity, had likely tumbled down the length of the cabin and into the cockpit below. Fisher did some mental measurements: The cliff was roughly fifty feet tall and about ten feet of the plane's tail had been jutting above the rim of the cliff. The C-46 Commando was seventy-five feet long, which meant the forward fifteen feet of the craft, including the cockpit, was submerged in the river.

The interior was surprisingly clear of jungle growth. Sealed as it was, with the only breaches probably being the shattered cockpit windows, nothing had had a chance to take root. The Commando was a virtual time capsule. He aimed the headlamp down the length of the cabin, but the walls, having lost their sheen, reflected nothing back. It was like staring down a mine shaft.

Fisher reeled in the rope below him, bunched it in one hand, then tossed it into the cabin. The loose end gave a hollow *ting* as it bounced off the aluminum, then there was silence.

He lowered himself through the darkness, scanning the light over the walls as he went, until finally his feet touched a horizontal surface—a section of the cockpit bulkhead. Stacked in a jumble around him were the Commando's seats. Through the tangle of braces and armrests and skeletal seat backs he could see the upper curve of the cockpit door opening; a few feet through that, his headlamp beam glinted off water. Just outside the plane's thin aluminum skin he could hear the gurgle of the river's current. The stench of mold was pervasive now, stinging his eyes and making it hard to breathe as though the air itself had grown thick.

It took fifteen minutes to shift and precariously restack the seats enough to allow him access to the cockpit. He lowered himself into a kneeling position, knees braced on either side of the door, rotated the rappelling rig around until it was facing backward, then he lowered himself again until he was lying splayed across the doorway.

Partially blinded by the glare of his flashlight on the water, which had filled the cockpit to a point just below the windshield, Fisher didn't immediately see the skulls.

There were two of them, one on either side of him in the pilot's and copilot's seats. Each was devoid of all traces of flesh, save a few desiccated chunks that hung like beef jerky from the facial bones. The torsos, which were submerged from the waist down, were clothed in tatters and in between the strips of fabric Fisher could see glimpses of white bone. Each skeleton hung suspended from its seat belt and harness, arms dangling and fingertips dipped in the water.

Fisher scanned the interior, looking for anything that might positively identify the craft or its occupants. Then he saw it, jutting from the pilot's inside jacket pocket, a brown rectangular package. Right arm braced for support on the cockpit bulkhead, Fisher leaned forward and gingerly removed the package.

It was oilskin. Fisher opened the folds. Inside was a well-preserved paperback-size leather journal. On the cover in faded, gold-embossed letters were the initials NW.

Niles Wondrash.

Fisher rewrapped the journal and slid it into the thigh pocket of his cargo pants. He was about to turn and leave, when he saw the glint of steel behind Wondrash's seat back. Fisher carefully tore away a section of the seat's moldering fabric until he could see the object.

It was a screw-top stainless steel canister, roughly the size of two soda cans stacked atop one another.

He grabbed it, then turned and started climbing.

31

"I assume you haven't opened it?" Lambert said.

Fisher switched the satellite phone to his left ear and moved out of the sun beneath the low-hanging branches of an olive tree. In the distance, over some scattered *kopjes*—low, rocky mounds—and forested savanna, he could see the surface of Lake Victoria shimmering blue in the heat. Fifty feet away Jimiyu sat in the Range Rover's driver's seat on the shoulder of the road.

"Which one?" Fisher asked. "The journal or the canister?"

"The canister."

Fisher smiled into the phone. "A mysterious sixty-year-old stainless steel canister I found inside a plane in the middle of the jungle. No, Lamb, I didn't open it."

"Didn't think so."

"As for the journal, the cover looks to be in good shape, but the edges of the pages feel spongy. I think it's best we wait for Quantico. If I open it, there's a good chance we'll lose whatever's in there."

"I agree."

"Anything more from Omurbai?" Fisher asked.

"More of the same, but his speeches are taking on a hysterical tone—the evils of the West, of 'infidel' cultures, of technology, and so on. As we'd guessed, he's sealed the border to all non-Muslims but has extended an invitation to all Muslims who want to, and I quote, 'partake in the jihad to end all jihads and to live in harmony in the true way of Islam,' unquote."

"Gracious of him." Fisher checked his watch. "Jimiyu and I just fueled up, and we're on our way to the second set of coordinates. I'll be in touch."

FROM Kusa they followed the C19, a heavily potholed road that meandered along the coastline southeast for a few miles before curving northwest into the Winam Gulf Peninsula, then on to Kendu Bay. On both shoulders, scrub grass, freshly green with spring, spread over rolling savanna. Here and there Fisher could see cones of earth rising from the landscape. Volcanic plugs, Jimiyu explained, exposed by erosion.

Four miles from the coordinates, Fisher's satellite phone chimed. He answered it and barely got one word out before Aly's panicked voice came over the line: "Sam, I'm sorry, I didn't want to tell them, but—"

"Aly, what—"

"They said they were going—"

"Aly, stop, slow down," Fisher commanded. "What's happened?"

There were a few seconds of silence. Fisher could hear her trying to catch her breath. "They came the night after you left. They broke into the house, tied me up, wanted to know where you'd gone. They had knives. They said they would—"

Fisher clutched the phone tighter. "Did they hurt you, are you hurt?"

"No, I'm fine, but I told them, Sam. I'm sorry, but—"

The driver's side window shattered. Jimiyu cried out and fell sideways into Fisher, who dropped the satellite phone; it clattered across the floorboards and disappeared. The Rover veered left, off the road, bumped up onto the shoulder, down into a depression, and began tipping onto its side. Fisher reached across Jimiyu's body, grabbed the wheel, straightened the Rover out, then groped with his foot until he felt the gas pedal and stomped on it. The engine roared. The Rover lurched up the hill.

"Jimiyu, can you hear me?" Fisher yelled. Using his free hand, he grabbed the Kenyan's shoulder and shook him. "Jimiyu!"

Jimiyu groaned.

A second bullet punched through the rear window and slammed into the dashboard. Fisher ducked down. Somewhere he could hear Aly's tinny voice calling, "Sam . . . Sam . . . are you there . . . ?" A third and fourth bullet tore through the back window, shattering it and spiderwebbing the windshield. Through the cracks he saw a kopje looming.

He jerked the wheel to the right, felt the left front tire bump over a rock, then they were tipping, the sky canting through the windshield.

FISHER forced open his eyes—one of his lids felt glued shut with what he assumed was blood—and looked around. The Rover had rolled once and come to rest on its roof, but the solid-cage construction had kept the interior intact, save his side window, which had shattered with the compression. Through the side window Fisher could see scrub grass. Jimiyu, whose seat belt had been demolished by the first bullet, lay in a heap, wedged between the dashboard and the windshield. Fisher realized the Rover's engine was still running. He vaguely thought, *Gas leak*, then *Fire*, then reached over and switched off the ignition. He undid his own seat belt, then rolled onto his side and reached toward Jimiyu. He found his hand and gave it a squeeze.

"Jimiyu," Fisher whispered. "Can you hear me?"

". . . es . . ."

"Stay still, don't move. Squeeze my hand if you understand."

Squeeze.

"Play dead. They'll be coming to finish us off."

Squeeze.

Fisher rolled over. He looked between the seats, searching for the M-14, and spotted the stock between the center console, which had detached itself during the rollover, and the roof. He grabbed the stock, gave it a tug. It didn't budge.

From outside came the roaring of an engine, then tires

skidding on dirt. Three car doors opened and slammed, and Fisher heard boots crunching on gravel.

He reached out, wrapped both hands around the stock, took in a deep breath, and heaved. The M-14 came loose, the butt smacking him in the lip. He tasted blood. Rifle held lengthwise down his body, he pushed off the dash with his legs, squirming until his torso was out the side window, then pushed again and drew his knees out.

On the other side of the Rover he heard a whispered voice say something, then once more. It took a moment for Fisher to realize it was Kyrgyz—something about going around.

Slowly, quietly, Fisher rose into a crouch. He flipped off the M-14's safety, took a few breaths to clear his head, then crab-walked to the rear of the Rover. Around the corner post he heard footsteps chafing the grass. He switched the M-14 to his left hand, drew the Applegate, flipped it open, and clenched it in his right hand, blade down and pointing back along his forearm. A thought popped into his head: *Crime scene*. He laid the M-14 in the grass.

The footsteps came closer. Fisher saw a man-shaped shadow fall across the grass. In one smooth motion, Fisher stepped around the Rover's corner post and rose up, grabbing and lifting the man's rifle stock while sweeping the Applegate up in a tight arc. He jammed it hilt-deep into the hollow spot behind the man's jaw and beneath his ear. The man never made a sound, dead before he hit the ground.

Fisher kept moving. He reversed the man's rifle—a FAMAS 5.56mm—shouldered it, took three quick steps out from behind the Rover, and saw a man turning toward him. He fired twice. Both rounds punched through the man's sternum. Even as he fell, Fisher was moving again, this time in the opposite direction, back across the rear of the Rover, where he dropped to one knee and leaned out, rifle at his shoulder. The last man was moving down the passenger side, his FAMAS coming up. Fisher fired. The bullet caught the man in the hip and spun him around. He screamed and toppled onto his side and kept rolling, trying to bring the FAMAS to bear. Fisher fired again. The bullet drilled a neat hole in the man's forehead. His head snapped back, and he went limp.

Moving on instinct, he checked each man to ensure he was dead and for any identifying papers (there were none), then crouched down and took ten seconds to catch his breath. He looked around. No cars on the road, none visible. He thought for a moment, running scenarios in his head, then made his decision. He dropped the FAMAS in the dirt, then hurried back to the driver's side window and dropped to his belly.

"Jimiyu, can you hear me?"

There were a few seconds of silence, the Kenyan cleared his throat and said softly, "I can hear you. Is it safe to no longer be dead?"

32

HE pulled Jimiyu from the Rover and checked him over. The bullet, moving slightly backward to forward, had carved a groove in the bony tip of his shoulder, then punched cleanly through the skin of his neck between a tendon and his jugular vein. There was a lot of blood but only superficial damage. A half inch to the right, and Jimiyu would be dead.

Fisher dug the first aid kit from the Rover's glove compartment, then dressed both his wounds and covered him with a blanket.

Next he picked up the M-14 and jogged the quarter mile to a rocky outcrop overlooking the lake. He hurled the rifle far into the water, then ran back to the Rover.

"Who were those men?" Jimiyu asked.

"The less you know, the better," Fisher said. "They were highway bandits. They ambushed us, and we never saw them coming. When you woke up, the Rover was lying on its side, and the men were already dead. You didn't see anything, didn't hear anything, and you don't remember anything after your window shattered. Got it?"

Jimiyu nodded. "I understand." Then, softly: "You killed them, Sam." There was no reproach in the Kenyan's voice, only astonishment.

"I'm sorry I got you into this."

"No apologies necessary, my new friend. What do we do now?"

The police were going to be involved; there was no way around it, which is why he'd chosen to not use the M-14 and to dispose of it. The better he could play the lucky victim, the easier things would go.

He hit speed dial on his satellite phone. When Grimsdottir answered, he said simply, "Napper, three, mess. Stand by." Then he hung up and dialed Aly. She picked up on the first ring.

"My God, what happened?" she asked. "I heard shots over the phone—"

"Have you called the police?"

"No, I wanted to hear from you."

"Good. How do you feel about not calling them?"

She hesitated. "Do you want me to not call them?"

"I'd be grateful."

"Okay."

Fisher thanked her, promised to be in touch, then disconnected. He cleared the phone's call memory.

East down the road he saw a car round the bend toward

them. He jogged to the shoulder and started waving his arms.

THE Western District Police and an ambulance from Kendu Adventist Hospital in Kendu Bay were there in twenty minutes. As Jimiyu was loaded into the ambulance, Fisher walked the one constable through the shooting and the accident while the other covered the bodies of the Kyrgyz in green plastic tarps and searched both vehicles and jotted notes.

Fisher stopped and restarted his story a half dozen times as though confused, asked for water, to sit down, then wondered aloud if he should go to the hospital. At last, after fifteen minutes, he got the whole story out

"And you say these men just began firing at you?" The constable spoke perfect English with the barest hint of a British accent.

Fisher said, "I didn't even realize it until the third or fourth—or was it the fifth?—shot. I don't know; it was a blur."

"And this," the constable said, waving his pencil at the three bodies. "You did this?"

"Yeah . . . uh, I guess. I was in the . . . in the army, the U.S. Army—the first Gulf War. Training, I guess. It just took over. I don't know, it happened so fast. I don't feel so good . . . Can I sit down?" The constable cupped Fisher's elbow and guided him to a rock.

They watched as the ambulance finished loading Jimiyu aboard, then pulled away.

"Is he going to be okay?" Fisher asked.

"It appears so. So tell me again how his happened. From start to finish, if you please."

Fisher did so, telling the same story, but not the exact same way.

"And this knife you used . . . it's the one in the dirt there?"

"Yeah, that's it. Am I in trouble? They didn't really give me a chance. When I crawled out of the car, they were pulling up. I stumbled around the Rover, and there he was, with the gun . . ."

"I will forward my report to my chief, of course, but providing we find nothing contradictory here, a written statement from you and your friend should suffice. You are staying here locally?"

Fisher nodded. "In Nairobi, at a friend's." Fisher gave him Aly's contact information.

"Do you wish to go to the hospital?" the constable asked.

"Uh . . . no, I don't think so."

"I will call your rental car agency and inform them of the incident. They'll arrange another vehicle for you, I'm sure."

"Thank you."

"How long will you be staying in Kenya?"

"Another day or two, I guess. I'll go to the hospital, I think, and see how Jimiyu's doing, then . . . I don't know."

But he did know. More than ever he wanted to find out what was so important about Niles Wondrash and the *Sunstar* that Bolot Omurbai would send three killers halfway across the globe to keep secret.

33

FISHER steered the Toyota Highlander off the road and coasted to a stop, his tires crunching on gravel. Through his windshield was a chest-high stockade fence bearing a sun-bleached, vine-entangled sign: RAKWARA WHCP (WATER HYACINTH CONTROL PROJECT) HEADQUARTERS. Through the trees he could see a ranch-style building. Faint strains of Carly Simon's "You're So Vain," mixed with the chirps and buzzes of the jungle, filtered through the trees.

He checked his GPS unit. This was, literally, the end of the road. From here, he walked. He climbed out, walked to the rear of the Highlander, and pulled out his Granite Gear pack, then started sorting through the gear he'd managed to salvage from the Range Rover.

The constables had waited with him for the arrival of the

tow truck from Kusa and a replacement car from the rental agency in Kisumu. Ostensibly making conversation, Fisher had asked the constables about the area—terrain, geology, history—and gotten in return much more than he'd bargained for. Both men had grown up along the shores of Lake Victoria and knew it intimately. In fact, one of them said as boys they used to search some of the shallower caves for pirate treasure.

"Caves?" Fisher asked.

"Yes," replied the constable. "Our word for them does not translate well." He thought for a moment, then held up an index finger. "In Mexico, I think, they have something similar—deep ponds—like shafts—with underwater caves."

"*Cenotes*," Fisher said.

"Yes, that's it. *Cenotes*."

A lightbulb came on in Fisher's head. The climbing gear in Wondrash's plane . . . He'd assumed it was climbing gear, but in what direction? Up or down? According to the legend, Wondrash and Oziri had flown straight into Kisumu then set off for Addis Ababa a few days later.

"No mountain climbing nearby?" Fisher asked.

"Mountain climbing? No, not near the lake. Mount Kenya, perhaps, but that's closer to Nairobi."

So, what, Fisher thought, *had Wondrash and Oziri been doing with climbing gear?*

ONCE satisfied with his pack's contents and weight distribution, Fisher set it aside and dialed Grimsdottir. Lambert was also on the line: "What's going on? What happened?"

Fisher explained, then said, "Jimiyu's going to be fine.

I called the hospital and talked to the doctor personally. As for the police, I'm pretty sure they bought it. I'm due in the Kisumu District headquarters day after tomorrow to write my statement."

"And you're sure they were Kyrgyz?"

"I'm sure."

"Then clearly we've touched a nerve. The very fact that he sent his own men rather than hiring locally says something. Grim, what can you give us on topography?"

"Not much, I'm afraid. If there are *cenote*-like caves in the area, they are not listed, and they don't show up on satellite. Sorry, Sam."

"If there's something there, I'll find it," Fisher said.

THE path led him away from the WHCP Headquarters building and deeper into the forest, winding northwest toward Lake Victoria. The terrain steadily lost elevation, and the forest slowly turned more junglelike. On either side of the trail, the ground appeared spongy, and soon Fisher heard the croaking of frogs.

After an hour's walk, he stopped and studied the GPS's screen. This was the area. He was a quarter mile from the lakeshore. He turned his body, checking each of the cardinal directions, until he was oriented, then pulled Jimiyu's machete from his belt, stepped off the trail, and started hacking.

Twenty minutes later, he emerged from the trees and found himself facing a craggy rock wall entwined with vines and dotted with pockets of bright red flowers. He craned his neck upward. The wall, only ten feet high, was topped by a berm of shrubs. He climbed to the top, then boosted himself over the lip, wriggled through the foliage, and found himself lying on a narrow stone shelf. Across from him, six feet away, was a matching shelf, and between the two, a ten-foot-wide crevice. Fisher peered over the edge. The crevice dropped away into darkness. He picked up a stone and dropped it in. A second later he heard a faint splash.

TEN minutes later, with a few essential items transferred from his Granite Gear to his waist pack, he secured the rope to a nearby tree, rigged his rappelling harness, and started down the crevice. After twenty feet the light dimmed enough that he flipped on his headlamp. The walls were comprised of jagged, volcanic rock mottled gray brown by lichen and molds. Above, the mouth of the crevice was a sun-filled slash through which Fisher could see overhanging branches. As his hand bumped over the thirty-foot knot in the rope, he stopped and sniffed the air. Water. Stagnant water. Somewhere below he heard dripping, echoing through a larger space. His heart rate increased. Then at fifty feet, with only ten feet of rope remaining, his groping foot plunged into water. Carefully, a few inches at a time, he lowered himself until his feet touched solid stone. The water, surprisingly cold, came up to his knees.

He unraveled the rope from the descender ring, then shined his headlamp left, down the length of the crevice, then right. He saw nothing but darkness. *Which way?* He thought.

He tossed a mental coin: heads for right; tails, left.
Right.

He set out.

AFTER fifty feet he bumped into a solid wall. The water
here was hip-deep. He felt a slight current swirling around
his thighs, so he scooted down until he was kneeling, then
probed the wall with his right hand. At the bottom of the
crevice where it met the wall, he found a jagged plate-size
hole through which cold water was gushing.

He reversed course. Ten feet past his dangling rope the
crevice walls began narrowing, and soon he was pressed flat
against the rock, his face turned to the side as he shuffled
along.

He stopped. Ahead, he could hear the distant splattering
of water on rock. He pressed on, stepping and sliding, stepping and sliding.

His left foot plunged into open space.

He jerked back and went still, his heart pounding.

He stepped left again, foot probing, until he found the
opening again. He probed with the toe of his boot until
he'd circumscribed the opening. It was a fissure, two feet
wide, beginning just below the surface of the water and
dropping vertically through the rock floor. He stepped left
until he was straddling the slash and pressed his back
against the wall. He had a decision to make. He had no idea
how far this main crevice extended or what might lie ahead.
He pulled the GPS unit off his belt and checked the screen:
According to the extrapolation buffer, he was precisely on
top of the coordinates, but with a margin of error of six to

eight feet horizontally and who knew how much vertically, this fissure could be what he was looking for, or it could be nothing at all.

Then he saw it. Jutting from a quarter-inch crack in the wall before his eyes was a rock screw—a rock screw identical to the ones he'd seen aboard the *Sunstar*.

HE pulled the twenty-foot coil of emergency 7mm climbing line from his waist pack, looped it through the rock screw's eyelet, tied it off with a modified clove hitch, then grabbed the rope with both hands and lifted his feet off the ground. The screw held.

Fisher didn't give himself time to think, didn't give himself time to fully acknowledge that tingle of fear in his belly, but rather stuck both feet through the fissure and began lowering himself. When the water reached his chin, he took a deep breath, ducked under the surface, and began forcing his way through the opening, wriggling his legs, then his torso, and finally his shoulders until at last he slid through and suddenly found himself hanging in the open air.

He looked up. From this angle the fissure was shaped like a jagged, narrow triangle and through the opening he could see diffused sunlight. Water poured through, crashing over his head and shoulders before plunging into the darkness and spattering against unseen rocks below.

Fisher extended his legs and felt his boots touch rock. He kicked off, swung out from under the waterfall, then glanced down. Ten feet down, his headlamp illuminated a flat shelf of rock off which the water was splashing. He lowered himself to it, then sidestepped left, out from under the waterfall, and looked around. Off the side of the shelf was a natural switchback stone staircase, worn smooth by millennia of water. At the bottom was a pool, roughly oval, and measuring twenty feet by twenty feet, and across from this a gravel beach that backed up to a sheer rock wall.

There was something different about the wall, Fisher realized. Unlike the rest of the cave and the crevice above, this wall was not mottled with brownish gray lichen but covered from top to bottom in a scabrous red growth.

Fisher felt the skin on his arms and on the back of his neck tingle with goose bumps. And then, for reasons he'd never quite be able to explain, four words from Peter's mystery note popped into his head: *"Red . . . tri . . . my . . . cota."*

34

FISHER sat sipping coffee in one of the leather club chairs beneath the windows and watched as the attendees, looking frustrated and haggard, wandered back into the room one by one and retook their seats at the conference table. The first hour of the meeting had been little more than a circuitous debate, going nowhere and revealing nothing, so the DCI (Director, Central Intelligence) had called for a break.

The others present were Lambert, three biologists from the CMLS (Chemicals, Materials, and Life Sciences) Directorate of Lawrence Livermore National Laboratory, and the Department of Energy's undersecretary for science and two of her deputies, one from the office of Biological and Environmental Research, the other from High Energy Physics.

"Okay, let's get back to it," the DCI called, and everyone took their seats.

Round two, Fisher thought, his mind drifting back to that cold, dark cave . . .

AGAINST his every instinct, after staring at the red growth for five solid minutes, he'd waded across the pool, which he found was only knee-deep, and walked up the beach to the wall. He wasn't sure what he expected to happen, but of course the growth hadn't leapt off the wall at him, nor did it explode into a lethal powder when he'd taken the tip of his Applegate and gently pried loose a quarter-size chunk of it from the wall and deposited it in an empty trail mix Baggie he'd found in the bottom of his waist pack.

He'd then reversed his course, climbing back through the fissure and then up the crevice and hiked back to the Highlander, where he'd called Grimsdottir and had her conference in Lambert.

"Remember Peter's words, 'Red . . . tri . . . my . . . cota'?" Fisher asked.

"I remember," Lambert said.

"It's just a gut feeling on my part, but I think it's a biological reference. A fungus of some kind, I'm guessing." He explained what he'd found in the cave. "And I'm willing to bet this stuff—whatever it is—is what's inside the canister I found aboard Wondrash's plane."

"Curiouser and curiouser," Grimsdottir said. Fisher could hear her tapping her keyboard. "We've got a compiled biological database here somewhere . . ." she muttered. "Yeah, here it is . . . Okay, I'm doing a fuzzy search using those key words. Hang on . . ." Thirty seconds later she was back. "Whoa, give that man a gold star."

"What?" Lambert asked.

"It's called Chytridiomycota—*tri . . . my . . . cota*. Peter was close; he had most of it, right down to the color, with just a few letters transposed. Chytridiomycota is a kind of fungus. Comes from the Greek *chytridion*, which means 'little pot'—or a structure that contains dormant spores. Approximately a thousand species in a hundred twenty or so genera, distributed among—"

"Bottom line it, Grim," Lambert said. "What is it?"

"A fungus. A motile, spore-producing fungus."

"And it does what?"

"Specifically? I don't know. That's over my head," Grimsdottir replied. "According to what's in front of me, there are about seventy thousand known species of fungi in the world, but that's estimated to be only about five percent of what's likely out there. So, we're talking about maybe two million species of fungi—most of which we haven't even found."

"Give me a comparison," Fisher said.

"Birds: five thousand species in the world. Insects: There are about nine hundred thousand different types. Compared to those, they know nothing—absolutely *nothing*—about fungi or what they can do. In fact, I just read a CDC report last month: Fungal-based diseases are on the rise, and a lot of the medical community think it's the next big, bad epidemiological nightmare."

"Christ," said Lambert.

The scourge of Manas, Fisher thought.

THE second half of the meeting picked up where it had left off: an argument between the biologists over what exactly Chytridiomycota was, its classification, its cellular makeup, and so on. Fisher noticed one of the biologists, a woman named Shirley Russo from the CMLS, wasn't partaking in the debate but rather jotting notes, grimacing, and shaking her head.

As had most of Washington's elite, Fisher had heard of Russo. The sole heiress to an old-money Connecticut family fortune, Russo had broken the mold and instead of letting herself ease into the role of überrich benefactor-socialite, had at the age of fifty gotten her Ph.D. in biology. Rumor had it she donated every penny of her salary to the International Dragon Boat League, which sponsored fund-raising dragon boat races for breast cancer survivors. Looking at her slim frame, Fisher guessed Russo had spent a fair amount of time at the oars herself.

He caught Lambert's gaze and gestured with his eyes toward Russo.

Lambert broke in. "Dr. Russo, you look like you have something to say."

Russo looked up from her pad and cleared her throat. "I have a theory," she said.

"A fringe theory," one of her fellow biologists said.

The DCI gave him a hard stare. "Why don't you let us worry about that. Dr. Russo."

She hesitated, then said, "One of the areas I study is called petro-parasitology. I think this fungus you—or whoever—found is a petro-parasitic organism. I agree with the others: I think it belongs to Chytridiomycota, but that's like saying birds and bees are alike because they both have wings."

"Petro-parasitic," Lambert said. "I assume that means what I think it means?"

Russo nodded. "That it eats petroleum-based substances? Yes, that's exactly what it does."

Fisher and Lambert exchanged worried looks.

The other biologists began talking, arguing back and forth across the table. Russo simply folded her hands on her legal pad and waited. The DCI brought the meeting back under control and then said to Russo, "Go on, Doctor."

"The problem is," she said, "that we've never seen a fungi that does this. Technically, there's no reason why it couldn't exist. There are enzymes we use to clean up oil spills all the time. They feed on the oil, neutralize it, then die and degrade and become part of the food chain."

"But you're not talking about that, are you?" said Lambert.

"No. I'm talking about a self-sustaining organism that feeds on petroleum-based substances—from crude oil, to kerosene, to the gas we put in our cars—then replicates and spreads, just like a fungal colony would. See, the thing about fungus is that it's hearty, tenacious stuff. It's hard to kill and harder still to make sure you've killed it all. It can lie dormant for years—for *millennia*—then just flip itself back on and pick up where it left off."

"Okay," the DCI said, "clearly the rest of you have

concerns about Dr. Russo's theory. Am I correct?" There were emphatic nods around the table. "But let me ask you this—and I want to hear it straight—is her theory plausible? Could there be something to it?"

No one responded.

"Goddamn it," the DCI barked. "I don't care about your egos, or your funding woes, or whether a theory is mainstream or fringe. If anyone at this table either doesn't believe Dr. Russo's theory is plausible or has a better theory, speak up right now, or I'll make sure you spend the rest of your careers counting fly turds."

Again, none of the scientists responded. Some looked at their hands; others shifted nervously in their seats. The DCI looked at each one in turn. "No? No one?" He turned to Russo again. "Doctor, I assume you have some ideas how we can confirm or refute whether this stuff is . . . What did you call it?"

"Petro-parasitic."

"Right."

Russo thought for a moment, then nodded. "I'll have an answer for you in the morning."

THE DCI thanked and excused the group, save Fisher, Lambert, the DOE undersecretary, and the scientist from the High Energy Physics division, a tall, balding man with thick, wiry eyebrows named Weldon Shoals.

"There's another component to this issue we need to discuss," the DCI said. "I know everyone here has top secret and above clearance, but I'll remind you that whatever we discuss stays here."

The undersecretary and Shoals nodded.

The DCI turned to Lambert. "Irv, if you would."

Lambert spent the next ten minutes outlining what they knew and what they suspected about PuH-19. He left out any mention of Peter, Calvin Stewart, Bolot Omurbai, or the North Koreans. Top secret clearances or not, these men didn't have the need to know.

"The question we have," the DCI said, "is what could someone with technical know-how do with this fungus, some PuH-19, and a linear particle accelerator?"

"You mean, could they create a giant fungus monster, or some kind of cancer supercure?" Shoals said, straight-faced.

Fisher chuckled. The DCI, hiding his own smile, replied, "No, what I'm asking is could the fungus's characteristics be enhanced—altered."

"In other words, mutated?" Shoals asked.

"Yes."

"Absolutely. Mutation has gotten a bad rap. Hollywood horror directors have made it a boogie word, but mutation is just another way of saying 'change.'

"But if I understand you correctly, what you want to know is, could someone, using PuH-19, a linear accelerator, and some high-energy physics principles, turn Dr. Russo's strain of Chytridiomycota—a theory I believe has real credibility, by the way—into something worse than it might otherwise be? Something that not only eats oil but uses it for fuel, then replicates and spreads like a plague?"

The DCI nodded.

"The answer is yes. Without a doubt. See, the trick is, you don't shoot radioactive junk at something and it suddenly mutates into whatever you want it to be. It's not alchemy. It would take years of trial and error to find the right balance—the right recipe that gives you what you want.

"Most man-made mutations—both bad and good—are discovered by accident. So, back to the essence of your question: Could these notional someones you're talking about have come up with the right combination of ingredients to create a weaponized, petro-parasitic fungus? Again, I'm sorry to say, the answer is yes."

"I was afraid you were going to say that," Lambert said.

"And it gets worse," Shoals said. "If in fact something like this überfungus existed, the only sure way to kill it or stop it would be to have access to the process that created it. Without that, you're just stumbling around in the dark, hoping you find the right recipe to shut the thing off. And, if by some miracle, you found it, would it be too late?"

35

"**AND** *I tell you, as surely as Allah's will binds us all, the modern world and the disease of technology cleaves us from all that is holy. It is a pervasive evil, one that infects every person and every culture it touches. Above all others, this is the greatest danger to Islam—*"

Fisher pressed the remote's REWIND button and watched Bolot Omurbai's latest speech for the third time. He paused it, Omurbai's face filling the screen.

"That's what you've got in mind, isn't it?" Fisher murmured.

Unable to sleep, he'd driven to Fort Meade at three a.m., signed in with the duty officer, and then went to the situation room and made coffee. Two hours and four cups later, he'd reviewed all the speeches Omurbai had given since beginning his second reign as Kyrgyzstan's president.

"*Technology cleaves us from all that is holy . . .*"

"*A pervasive evil . . .*"

"*Infects every person and every culture . . .*"

Omurbai was insane, that much seemed clear, but however irrational his thoughts, his reasoning was well-ordered: The modern world is evil; technology is an infectious agent—it is the greatest enemy of Islam.

And what, Fisher thought, is the essence of the modern world? Of technology? What is the engine behind it all? Answer: oil, and everything that flows from it. A plus B equals C. Oil is the enemy of Islam; oil itself must be destroyed.

The scourge of Munas.

And where better to launch the opening salvo in his war but beneath his own country, which shares one of the world's greatest untapped reservoirs of oil? Conservatively, the fields beneath Central Asia were estimated to contain three hundred billion barrels—a third of a trillion—of recoverable oil.

It was a mind-boggling number, Fisher admitted, and without the Chytridiomycota (or, as Fisher and Lambert had started calling it, *Manas*), Omurbai would have as much luck destroying the fields as he would trying to knock the air from the sky. But now . . .

He laid the remote aside, sat back, and rubbed his temples. How had all this started? With one man, his brother, dead. It seemed surreal, the twisting course he'd followed to this point, and somewhere along the way Peter's death had been pushed into the background. Despite what his instincts had told him, Fisher had hoped, in some small part of his mind, that Peter's death would turn out to be a simple—if that word could be used—murder. Faced with that, Fisher would have simply tracked down those responsible and seen them either dead or locked up. Done. But it had turned out to be anything but a simple, thoughtless murder, hadn't it?

Instead, here he was, sitting alone in the dark and staring at the face of a madman who planned to let loose a plague that could in one fell swoop turn the planet back to the Stone Age.

FISHER awoke to a hand shaking his shoulder. He opened his eyes and saw Lambert standing beside his chair. "Morning," Lambert said. "How long have you been here?"

"What time is it?"

"Six."

"A few hours. Couldn't sleep."

"Join the club." Lambert nodded at Omurbai's frozen face on the screen. "Not a good image to have in your head when trying to nod off."

Fisher took a sip from his coffee cup; it was cold. "You know what he's got planned, don't you, Lamb?"

Lambert nodded and sat down in the next chair. "There are still a lot of ifs. We don't even know if that stuff is what we think it is. Or if they've managed to enhance it. That's what they needed Stewart for. Something wasn't working, something they couldn't get right. The question is, did they fix it?"

"Good question. I've also been thinking about Carmen Hayes," Fisher said. "She's gotten lost in all this."

"And Peter."

"Him, too. But at least now we know why they grabbed her in the first place."

The biggest hurdle Omurbai and the North Koreans would have with Manas was deployment: how to introduce it where it would have the biggest impact and spread the quickest. Fisher assumed they'd long ago broken Carmen down and that she'd been cooperating. She'd been gone four months—plenty of time to study the subterranean rivers and streams beneath Kyrgyzstan and its neighboring countries, then map the points where they intersected the oil fields and tell Omurbai exactly where to drop Manas.

Like a virus in the bloodstream, Fisher thought.

"You have any thoughts on the North Koreans?" he asked Lambert.

"I do. There are three reasons for them getting involved, I think: one, a sword to hang over our heads; two, a preemptive move for an invasion of South Korea."

"And the third?"

"Kim Jong-il is nuts, and he just feels like wreaking havoc."

"I've got a fourth scenario," Fisher said. "It's a little bit out there, but it may fit."

"Tell me."

"North Korea's found its own oil reserves, but as long as they're a pariah, they've got no chance to exploit them. Then along comes Omurbai. Somehow, somewhere, he's gotten ahold of this very interesting fungus that does a very interesting thing: It eats oil, which just happens to be the devil's own invention. He wants to use the fungus, but as long as he's an outcast from his homeland, he can't.

"So the North Koreans help him retake Kyrgyzstan, which happens to sit smack-dab on top of one of the world's greatest deposits, then sit back and watch as Omurbai releases Manas and destroys three hundred billion barrels of untapped oil. The world panics. North Korea announces it just happens to have found its own reserves."

Lambert considered this for a few moments, then said with a grim smile, "Any other country or leader, and I'd say that's an exceedingly implausible scenario. Well, since we're playing doom-and-gloom, try this: North Korea watches Omurbai release Manas in Central Asia, then they secretly do the same elsewhere—in the Middle East, in Africa, in Russia—but North Korea's fields remain untouched. Omurbai gets the blame, and suddenly they've got the only surviving oil source on the planet."

Fisher caught on, finishing the scenario. "Because, while they were working on Manas, they also found a neutralizing agent for it."

"You got it."

Fisher squeezed the bridge of his nose between his index finger and his thumb. "And right now, we've got nothing. No leads, no clues, no idea where Manas is—nothing."

Lambert gave him a weary smile, then stood up and placed a hand on his shoulder. "Sam, we've had less than that before and still come through the other side."

REDDING arrived twenty minutes later, poured himself a cup of coffee, and joined them at the table. "Who wants to know how Omurbai probably found out about Chytridiomycota?"

Fisher raised a weary finger.

"Remember Oziri, Wondrash's man Friday?"

Fisher and Lambert nodded.

"Well, Grim asked me to do a little genealogy detective work. Here's the short version: Oziri was the grandfather of Samet, Omurbai's right-hand man and second-in-command of the KRLA. My guess, Oziri knew what Wondrash was looking for and had bragged or blabbed to a family member before they headed to Africa."

"Which means Wondrash had had some inkling of what Chytridiomycota was capable of even before he found the source," Fisher said.

Redding nodded. "That's part two. Quantico was able to restore most of Wondrash's journal you found aboard the *Sunstar*. He doesn't describe how they found the cave in the first place, or how he got onto the trail of the fungus in the first place, but he talks about the night they spent inside there. Evidently, some of the stuff must have rubbed off on their gear. The next morning they woke up, and everything made of rubber or plastic had dissolved."

A few minutes later, Lambert's cell phone trilled. He picked it up, listened for a moment, said thanks, and disconnected. He walked to the nearest computer workstation, tapped a few keys, and one of the monitors glowed to life. The DCI's face filled the screen.

"Morning," he said. "I've got Dr. Russo's report in front of me. She's confident that Chytridiomycota is a type of petro-parasite."

Lambert told the DCI about Wondrash's journal and Omurbai's link to Oziri.

"Then I'd say that's proof enough," the DCI replied. "Russo also sent along a computer simulation. Worst-case scenario. I asked her to make some assumptions—namely that Manas has been enhanced for longevity and reproduction. Take a look."

The DCI's face disappeared and was replaced with a computer-generated Mercator projection of Earth. The camera zoomed in until it was focused on Central Asia, then paused. A clock graphic in the right-hand corner appeared and, beside it, the notation, DAY 1. A red dot appeared in the center of Kyrgyzstan, then expanded, doubling in size. The clock changed to DAY 5. The red dot expanded again, doubling again, and then again, and again, until the whole of Kyrgyzstan was covered, and the clock read DAY 11.

Fisher and the others continued to watch as Manas spread beyond the borders of Kyrgyzstan, north into Kazakhstan, east into China, south into Tajikistan, then India . . .

Thirty seconds later, half the globe had turned red, and the area was still increasing in size.

The clock read DAY 26.

Grimsdottir pushed through the door ten minutes later and stopped short as she saw the three of them sitting around the table. "Did I miss a memo?" she asked.

Lambert shook his head. "The Insomniacs' Club."

"Sign me up," she said, then poured her own cup of coffee, sat down, and powered up her laptop. Lambert briefed her on their discussion so far. She paused a few moments to take it all in, then said to Fisher, "Sam, you're sure that Stewart died at Site Seventeen?"

Fisher nodded. "Either there or in the water a few minutes later."

"Then we've got a mystery on our hands. I just heard from the comm center. Stewart's beacon is still active, and it's transmitting from Pyongyang, North Korea."

36

FISHER had gotten up at dawn and taken the Metro train to the Rungnado station, where he got off, stopped at a street kiosk to buy some green tea, then walked to a park and found a bench overlooking the Taedong River, which ran through the center of the North Korean capital. Beyond the river's opposite bank, Pyongyang's skyscrapers and gray cinder-block Soviet-style buildings spread across the horizon.

The sun was bright, glistening off the dew-covered grass. A hundred yards away, a group of thirty or so teenage boys and girls were practicing hapkido under the watchful eyes of North Korean People's Army officers. They barked orders, and the students answered *"Ye!"* Whether the teenagers were bothered by the rigorous early morning training,

Fisher couldn't tell. Each teenager wore the same expression: thin-set mouths and narrowed eyes. Their collective breathing, which itself seemed to have a disciplined rhythm to it, steamed in the chilled, early morning air.

One of the officers barked another order, and the group bent at the waist, en masse, and picked up their rifles, old World War II–era Soviet Mosin-Nagant carbines, and began a drill routine.

The future of North Korea, Fisher thought. And, if Omurbai's Manas plan succeeded, perhaps the future of the world. Since Lambert had suggested the scenario, Fisher had been trying to wrap his head around the idea of North Korea as the world's only oil superpower. It was a frightening thought.

From the corner of his eye Fisher saw his escorts, a pair of plainclothes State Security Department officers, which he'd dubbed Flim and Flam, enter the park's west entrance and take up station at the railing along the river's edge.

Good morning, boys, Fisher thought. *Like clockwork.*

Since his arrival two days earlier, the SSD had thoroughly, if not imaginatively, watched his every movement. The pair that had just walked into the park was the day shift; the night shift came on at six p.m.

So far, every prediction he'd received about North Korean's security agencies had been proved true.

FIVE days earlier and just two hours after Grimsdottir's revelation about Stewart's still-active beacon (which, Fisher suspected, Stewart had planted on Chin-Hwa Pak during the chaos aboard the Site 17 platform), he, Lambert, and

Grimsdottir had been ordered to report to Camp Perry, the CIA's legendary training facility outside Williamsburg, Virginia. Waiting for them in the main conference room was Langley's DDO, or deputy directorate of operations, Tom Richards. Fisher knew Richards from the Iranian crisis the year before.

"I'll get to the point," Richards said. "We don't have any field people in North Korea, which puts us in a pickle."

The pickle to which Richards was referring was Fisher himself. Lambert had already pitched Third Echelon's plan directly to the president, who had approved it and ordered the CIA to act in a support role.

Accomplished as he was at covert operations, Fisher's expertise was of a more military nature, and despite his recent graduation from CROSSCUT, his bona fides as a field intelligence operative were nonexistent. For Fisher's part, his head was already in North Korea. A covert operation was a covert operation; the nuts and bolts of how Third Echelon and the CIA's DO did their jobs might be different, but the mind-set was the same: Get in, do the job, and get out, leaving as few footprints as possible.

"Sam, you'll be completely on your own."

Fisher nodded. "I know."

"You get caught there, you're done. You'll either end up with a bullet in your head or living out the rest of your life in a windowless underground cell. The North Koreans don't do prisoner exchanges, and they don't PNG people," Richards said, referring to persona non grata, the official process of expelling suspected spies from First World countries. "North Korea is true Indian country. In a lot of ways they're worse than the Soviets ever were."

Fisher smiled at Richards; there was no warmth in it. "Gosh golly, Tom, are you trying to scare me?"

"Yeah, I am."

"Consider your job done."

"Just want to make sure you've got your head right for this."

"I do."

"Okay." Richards shrugged and said, "I'm going to turn you over to a familiar face. You've got just two days to prep; they'll get you as ready as they can." Richards turned to Lambert. "Irv, if you and Ms. Grimsdottir will follow me, I'll show you what we've got for you."

Thirty seconds after they filed out, a door on the opposite side of the conference room opened, and a man walked in. Fisher did in fact recognize the face: Frederick, one of the watchers who'd dogged him during his final CROSS-CUT field exam.

"Hi, Sam. Heard they were tossing you to the sharks already."

"So it seems."

"Well, let's see what we can do about bite-proofing you."

AND, despite the narrow time line he'd had to work with, Frederick did just that, spending eighteen hours a day taking him through his paces, from the details of his cover, to communication protocols, to what he could expect from the myriad North Korean counterintelligence agencies.

Though predictably Frederick admitted nothing, it was immediately clear to Fisher that the man had had a lot of time in Pyongyang, and as the U.S. had no official diplomatic presence there, it meant he'd survived "naked"—without cover or backup—and come home to tell about it.

On the final day, just hours before Fisher was to enter the pipeline, Frederick proclaimed him as ready as he would ever be and sealed it with a handshake. "If you remember only one thing," Frederick said, "it's this: Always assume. Assume you're being watched; assume they know exactly who and what you are; assume they're going to pluck you off the street any second."

Fisher smiled. "Fred, if this is your version of a pep talk, it needs a little work."

"It's my keep-you-alive talk. I tell you to assume these things for two reasons: one, because it'll all be true; and two, they're going to be assuming the same thing about you: that you need to be watched; that you're an enemy agent; that you're probably doing something that deserves arrest."

"And if they do?" Fisher asked.

"Arrest you?"

Fisher nodded.

"Then God help you. My advice . . ." Frederick paused. "If it were me going back there . . . I'd go to ground before I let them get their hands on me. If you know they're coming for you, run."

NOW, sitting on the bench, watching the two SSD officers watching him, Fisher realized he agreed with Fred's advice. However steep the odds against success, he'd go to ground the second they made a move for him.

After ten more minutes of watching the soldier-students, Fisher stood up, tossed his cup in a nearby trash barrel, and set off down the sidewalk. He didn't look back, and he didn't need to. Before he got a hundred yards, either Flim or Flam would be digging his cup out of the garbage for later examination.

FISHER'S cover was that of a photographer from the German newspaper *Stern*, a choice that was based partially on Fisher's fluency in German but also because of *Stern*'s often anti-American slant and for decrying what it called the United States's "Bully Administration." Moreover, *Stern* had for the last few years been courting the youth of North Korea, who were starving for a connection with their European counterparts. North Korea's leaders had decided *Stern* might be a safe way to satisfy that craving and perhaps make political inroads with European countries that oftentimes adopted a contrarian outlook to cultural affairs: If America thinks you're bad, maybe you're worth a second look to us.

And so Fisher, speaking nearly flawless German and hailing from a country that had little love for the current American administration, received only a cursory questioning upon his arrival at Pyongyang's airport. Even so, his passport had been collected at the hotel, and he'd been assigned an SSD shadow detail. How long it would last, he didn't know, but Frederick had felt confident the two-day rule would likely be in effect: If after two days the SSD decided you weren't there to topple the government or foment antisocial behavior, they would scale back the surveillance—or at least the overt surveillance.

FISHER spent the rest of the morning touring the city's landmarks: the Arch of Triumph, a grander replica of Paris's Arc de Triomphe; Mangyongdae Hill, Kim Il-sung's birthplace; Juche Tower; the Korean Workers' Party Monument; and Namsan Hill, also known as the Grand People's Study House. These would be expected stops of any tourist and certainly the kinds of photo opportunities a *Stern* photographer wouldn't forgo, Frederick had told him.

By late afternoon Fisher was back at his hotel—the Yanggakdo—having an early supper. Ten minutes before Flim and Flam were to be relieved by the night shift team, Flip and Flop, Fisher had retired to the hotel's bar overlooking the Taedong to enjoy a cup of coffee, as he had each night since arriving.

Right on time, at six o'clock, Flim and Flam, who were seated inside near a window, stood up and disappeared. Fisher watched and waited. Five minutes passed, then ten, then fifteen. Usually by now either Flip or Flop would have made an appearance, either walking to the railing and watching the river for a few minutes or actually taking a table and enjoying a meal while Fisher finished his coffee.

After thirty minutes, Fisher realized no one was coming. He called for the waitress, signed his tab, then went through the lobby and out onto the sidewalk, where he turned left and started walking. He strolled along the shop fronts for the next hour, stopping occasionally to price gifts, ducking into and out of doorways, hailing taxis, then riding only a block before getting out. Satisfied that Frederick's prediction about the two-day rule had been accurate and that he was no longer under close surveillance, he walked back to the hotel and took the elevator to his room.

Inside, he picked up the phone and asked for an outside line. The number he dialed, though prefaced by Germany's country code, 49, and Berlin's city code, 30, in fact took him to an NSA monitoring and intercept station in Misawa, Japan.

Grimsdottir answered in German on the third ring: "*Stern*, how can I help you?"

"Extension forty-two nineteen," Fisher replied in German.

"Wait, please." Ten seconds later, Lambert, who'd undergone his own crash course in German, picked up the line. "Kaufmann! How is Pyongyang?"

"Fine. The weather is what you'd expect," Fisher replied. "Did some tourist sites today; tomorrow I hope to get some street interviews."

"Outstanding! Keep us posted."

Fisher hung up.

The conversation was scripted, and it told Lambert three things: one, Fisher had encountered no complications; two, the SSD was behaving as expected and surveillance had been scaled back; and three, tomorrow he was going after the RDEI agent, Chin-Hwa Pak.

37

FISHER stepped backward into the alley, ducked behind a garbage can, and watched, breath held, as the jeep rolled past him at a walking pace. Sitting in the back of the open vehicle were three soldiers, one on either side shining flashlights along the sidewalks and a third standing behind a mounted .50-caliber machine gun. They passed Fisher's alley, then rolled to a stop at the next intersection, brakes squealing softly in the darkness. In the distance, toward Kyonghung Street, he could hear disco music.

After a few seconds the jeep rolled forward and turned left out of sight. Fisher let out his breath. He ran both hands through his sweat-dampened hair, then checked his watch: two a.m. He'd been moving for two hours. He was within a quarter mile of his destination.

He'd left his room just before midnight and taken the elevator to the parking garage, where'd he'd tucked himself in the shadows behind a concrete pillar and waited for the garage attendant shift change. When the replacement showed up, both men stepped into the adjoining security room, leaving the barrier arm unguarded. He'd watched this changeover process six times since he'd arrived at the hotel and never more than thirty seconds passed before the two attendants emerged from the security room.

When he'd heard the door click shut, he stepped out from behind the pillar and walked, shoeless, up the ramp, then ducked down and crab-walked below the security room's single window, then around the barrier's post. He stood up, glanced left then right and, seeing nothing, walked straight across the street and around the corner.

Pyongyang's nightlife was scarce and confined to only a few pockets of bars and dance clubs around the city, so most of Fisher's journey was done on vacant streets and empty sidewalks, which had turned out to be both a blessing and a curse: the former because he felt more in his natural element; the latter because he would quickly draw attention if spotted. A Caucasian, walking alone on the streets at two in the morning . . . The police would snatch him up without so much as a question and deposit him at the nearest SSD office for questioning. Of course, the same curse that applied to him would apply to any watchers on his tail. Unless they were very, very good, they would be easy to spot. The playing field was even. Or at least he hoped so.

*   *   *

TWENTY minutes later he was lying in the undergrowth bordering the governor's residence, studying the street through a pair of miniature binoculars. As bad luck would have it, Pak's four-story apartment building, which sat on the opposite side of the street and fifty yards to Fisher's right, was located in a Pyongyang neighborhood reserved for established North Korean politicians, military officers, and civil servants. Fisher was now in one of the most protected single square miles of the capital. From where he lay he could see the mayor's residence, three semiprivate banks reserved for party luminaries, an antiaircraft battery, an ammunition depot, and the barracks for the seventy-seventh Infantry Regiment, all illuminated by floodlights and guarded by somber, rifle-toting soldiers, both roving and stationary.

There was an upside, however. As well-guarded as the area was, most of the protection was focused on private residences. Pak's building, two blocks from the barracks, sat on a relatively dark and quiet street surrounded by dogwood trees and lilac hedges. Whether Pak was at home Fisher didn't know; all he knew was Stewart's beacon was there, probably still attached to the clothing Pak was wearing aboard the platform.

Fisher checked his watch again.

Patience, Sam.

HE forced himself to lie still for another hour, watching the comings and goings of the guards, looking for that one defect, that one gap in coverage he could exploit. And, as he'd expected, when he finally spotted his opening, it came not from flawed logistics or training but from individual idio-syncrasy. One soldier, a boy in his late teens, was a chain-smoker, and he clearly lacked the self-discipline to wait for scheduled breaks.

On every third patrol around the block that encompassed the governor's and mayor's residences, as well as Pak's apart-ment, the boy would stop, duck behind a tree, and greedily smoke a cigarette before completing his round. It gave Fisher an extra two minutes to do what he needed to do.

Fisher watched the soldier stroll past his hiding spot, then turn the corner and start back toward the mayor's resi-dence. Then, like clockwork, he stopped, furtively glanced around, then stepped behind a tree and lit up.

Fisher rose to his knees and padded, hunched over, across the street, moving diagonally away from the smok-ing soldier until he was behind the screen of lilac hedges that bracketed the covered walkway that led to the door to Pak's building. Fisher slipped along the wall to where the walkway and front wall met, then turned around and pressed his back into the corner. Now he would see if his daily exercise routine, which included seven hundred single-leg squats for just such occasions as this one, would pay off.

He took a deep breath, planted the rubber sole of his left shoe against the wall, and pushed hard. He leaned to the left, shifting his weight, and pressed his shoulder into the wall. Next he braced his right foot against the ad-joining wall, coiled his leg, and pushed again, lifting him-self off the ground. He was now in what's called the chimneying position. Used by mountaineers and rock climbers to navigate right-angle outcroppings and vertical rock chutes, chimneying took patience, stamina, and brute strength, but it came as close to defying gravity as one could without the aid of pitons and carabiners.

Luckily for Fisher, he had to cover only twelve vertical feet, which he did in forty seconds, pulling himself level with the walkway's roof. He reached out with his left hand, hooked his fingertips in the eaves trough, then froze.

Beyond the hedge he could hear footsteps echoing on the sidewalk and coming this way. Over the top of the hedge he saw the peaked cap of his smoking soldier glide past the apartment's walkway gate, then continue down the sidewalk, where he eventually disappeared into the darkness.

Fisher shifted some weight to his left, testing the eaves trough. It groaned softly, sagged slightly, but held. He pushed off with his right foot, swung it upward, hooked his heel on the trough, then boosted his body onto the roof. He spread himself flat and went still and stayed that way for a few minutes until certain he'd attracted no attention.

He was now within arm's reach of the building's first-floor hallway, which in a curious break with the communist gray architecture that seemed to dominate most of Pyongyang's older neighborhoods, circumnavigated the building. Bordered on the exterior side by a waist-high railing and arched openings, and on the interior side by apartment doors, the style was more Mediterranean than Soviet-industrial. Beside each apartment door was a wall sconce, a lengthwise-cut cylinder of brushed stainless steel that cast light on the ceiling. Whatever else Pak had done for the RDEI, he must have succeeded; in North Korea, apartments of this quality were reserved for political stars. This was luxury, North Korean style.

Fisher was about to reach for the railing when he stopped. *Cameras*. He pulled back and spread himself flat again. *Almost slipped up, Sam*. In his earlier surveillance of Pak's building, he'd seen a doorman sitting behind a desk in the lobby. Judging from the flickering glow Fisher had seen reflected in the doorman's glasses, he'd been watching a small, unseen television. But what kind? Regular, close-circuit security, or both?

He pulled his DARPA-enhanced iPhone from his pocket and scrolled through to his Images folder, typed in the password, and called up the blueprint of Pak's building. It was incomplete and partially speculative, cobbled together by Grimsdottir using a collage of sources: satellite imagery, tourist photos, electrical grid maps, similar buildings in other parts of the country . . . She'd used it all to give Fisher at least a sketch of what he'd be facing.

Looking at it now, his best guess put the elevator directly behind the wall at his back. He looked up. The wall, ten feet wide—typical of an elevator shaft—extended all the way to the roof. If there were cameras in the building, the first place he would likely find them would be on each floor, facing the elevators.

After waiting for his smoking soldier to pass by once again, Fisher rose into a crouch, then reached up, grabbed the railing, chinned himself up, scanned the hall for cameras and, seeing none, rolled over onto the floor, where he pressed himself flat against the elevator shaft's wall and sidestepped up to the corner.

He heard the whirring of the camera before he saw the camera itself. He stopped short, went still.

Long before his days with Third Echelon, Fisher had

dealt with more than his fair share of surveillance cameras using only his ears and his good timing. Faint though they were, camera motors had a distinct aural signature, especially at their range stops, the point at which a rotating camera reaches its panning limit to the left or right. It is at this point, as the motor pauses then reverses the camera's direction, that a well-tuned ear can detect the barely perceptible strain on the motor. And it was this sound Fisher was listening for as he stood motionless, back pressed against the wall, eyes closed . . .

There . . . there . . . there . . . there. Twelve seconds from range stop to range stop. Which stop was which—facing left or facing right—didn't matter. With no other cameras in the hall, this one would be calibrated to full rotation so it could see down the length of each hall. It was at this point when the camera's blind spot was most accessible. Stand directly beneath the camera's mount, and you're as good as invisible.

Fisher waited, listening and counting, then stepped out from the wall and centered himself under the mount. Above him, the camera, which had been panning right, reversed course and started coming around. Fisher looked left and counted doors. Pak's apartment number was 9, the third door down. The trick would be reaching that door and getting inside in the time it took the camera to complete a full pan.

Suddenly, Fisher's decision was made for him.

Pak's door opened, and Pak himself stepped out.

38

PAK, juggling a bag of garbage in each hand, leaned back into his apartment, trying to get the door closed.

Fisher glanced up. The camera was pointed directly at Pak. It paused, then started panning in the other direction. Fisher counted *One one thousand, two one thousand,* then pushed off the wall and sprinted, hunched over, straight at Pak. He covered the distance in less than three seconds, but at the last moment, either sensing Fisher's presence or hearing his approach, Pak spun to face him.

Fisher's earlier hunch about the man's physical condition and training was dead-on. In the blink of an eye, Pak, still holding the garbage bags, lashed out with a front heel kick. It was perfectly aimed and delivered, a strike that could easily snap a neck or crush a skull. But Fisher, having registered

Pak's slight shifting of weight to his back leg, was ready for the kick. Still moving at a sprint, he dropped his shoulder, somersaulted beneath the leg, caught the raised heel with his right hand, then rose up and caught Pak squarely in the chin with a short jab. Pak stumbled backward into the apartment, stunned. Fisher didn't give him a chance to react but kept driving forward, raising Pak's leg until he toppled over sideways, sliding back-first down the wall and landing with an *"Umph"* on the floor. Fisher twisted Pak's foot, flipping him onto his stomach, then dropped to one knee, grabbed a handful of his hair, and slammed his head against the floor once, twice, three times. Pak went limp.

Fisher grabbed him by the foot again and spun his limp body around and dragged him farther into the apartment, then shut the door. He pulled a pair of plastic flexicuffs from their hiding place in his jacket's lining and bound Pak's wrists and ankles, dragged him into the living room, laid him faceup on the floor, then picked up a nearby coffee table and placed it over his body. He found a narrow-based vase and placed it on top of the table. The rudimentary early warning system would give Fisher a few seconds' notice should Pak regain consciousness and get frisky. Knowing now how dangerous the North Korean was, Fisher wasn't going to give him even the slightest advantage.

He did a quick search of Pak's studio apartment and found no one else home. In the bedroom, however, he did find a portrait of Pak sitting with a woman and two young girls. Many North Korean political up-and-comers were given two residences: a working apartment in Pyongyang for use during the week and a private rural home for weekends. This, Fisher suspected, was where Pak's family was. Also in the bedroom he found a wireless-capable laptop and, in Pak's nightstand, a Type 69 7.62mm pistol in a leather holster along with two fully loaded magazines. He pocketed the pistol and the magazines and turned his attention to Pak's closet. He found what he was looking for almost immediately: the thigh-length black leather coat Pak had been wearing at the Site 17 platform. In the coat's left pocket he found Stewart's thumbnail beacon. He stared at it a moment. *Thanks, Calvin.* He stuck it in his pocket, grabbed the laptop, and returned to the living room.

He pulled the iPhone from his pocket, called up the iPod feature, scrolled to the Eagles' "Hotel California," and punched a code into the keypad. The screen changed to an amber-on-black compasslike display with the words ENGAGED > SEEKING SIGNAL flashing near the bottom edge of the screen. Fisher spent the next ten minutes sweeping the apartment for audio and video devices. He found none, so he went into the kitchen, found an English-version of Diet Coke, then returned to the living room and sat down in a wing-back club chair a few feet from Pak's head. He stuck a magazine into the pistol, chambered a round, and waited.

FISHER was almost finished with his Diet Coke when Pak began stirring. He groaned, and his eyelids blinked open, then closed again as he tried to focus. He tried to raise his hands to his face; his knuckles rapped the underside of the coffee table with a dull *thud*, and the vase teetered, then went still.

"Just lie still," Fisher said. "It'll be easier for both of us."

Pak went still. He rotated his eyes and craned his neck until he could see Fisher. Instead of the typical "Who are you" and "What do you want," Pak said simply, "You're an American." His English was only slightly accented; Fisher noted his use of the contraction. Pak had had extensive language training, which was to be expected from an RDEI agent.

"I am," Fisher said.

"Don't you know where you are? You'll never get out of the city alive. You probably won't get off this block alive."

"We," Fisher replied.

"What?"

"*We'll* never get out of the city alive." He held up Pak's pistol. "I guarantee you, if that time comes, you'll go before me."

"How'd you find me?"

"Western imperialist technology at its best."

"Why have you come here?"

"Complicated question." *Too complicated*, Fisher thought. If not for Omurbai and Manas, Pak would have gotten a bullet a long time ago. But that wasn't the situation, was it? He needed Pak alive. "I want you to tell me where Carmen Hayes is, and I want you to tell me everything you know about Manas: Where it is, where Omurbai plans to use it, and how to neutralize it."

Pak offered him a condescending grin. "I'm not going to help you."

"I thought you'd say that," Fisher said. "And I'm sure I'd have a hard time changing your mind. Am I right?"

Pak nodded.

Fisher gestured to Pak's laptop, which sat, powered up, on a side table. An SD/USB card reader jutted from one of the laptop's side ports. "You've got some pretty good encryption on there. Unfortunately, it's not good enough. Right now, I'm loading a virus onto your hard drive. I won't pretend to know how it does what it does, but here's what I do know: Two hours from now, and every two hours after that, if a specially coded e-mail doesn't land in your in-box, the virus goes active."

"That's your plan?" Pak said, smiling smugly. "You're going to ruin my laptop?"

"No, I'm going to ruin your life. You see, you trusted your encryption a little too much—put too much dicey information on your hard drive. What that virus will do is plant digital tracks in every corner of your life—your e-mail accounts, your finances, your travel logs—and the story it will tell is that of a traitor, a trusted RDEI agent who volunteered to spy for the United States and has been feeding the CIA information for the past three years. You might not be afraid of what I can do to you, but I know you're afraid of what your bosses at the SSD do with traitors. I've seen video of their interrogation methods. It's not pretty. But, of course I'm sure you know that."

"I don't believe you," Pak said. "*They* won't believe it."

"Bad gamble," said Fisher.

And it was. This was no bluff. The CIA's biggest contribution to Fisher's mission was one of its most prized agents, an executive secretary in the comptroller's office at the State Security Department. While none of the information she'd passed to Langley had been of strategic value, it had given the CIA's Intelligence Directorate an invaluable glimpse into the administrative side of North Korea's security services, allowing it to build from the inside out profiles of more than a dozen RDEI agents: where they went, how they traveled, and through which banks and front companies money was moved. It had been a jigsaw puzzle of daunting complexity, but it had paid off. Fisher's threat to Pak was a case in point.

What Fisher did not tell Pak was that while he was unconscious another program on another SD card had plucked from the laptop's hard drive every piece of data within a certain range of file extensions, the passwords and log-ins to a half dozen SSD intranet portals, including Pak's office e-mail account. Once the program had completed its search, Fisher had loaded the contents onto his iPhone for encrypted burst transmission back to Third Echelon, where Grimsdottir and Redding, working at tandem workstations, were sorting through the data.

"That's not possible," Pak said. "You'll miss something."

Fisher smiled. "I doubt it. I happen to work with a woman who's frighteningly good at what she does, and right now you're her only project. Did I mention she was kind enough to open a private account at *Syndikus Treuhandanstalt* bank in Liechtenstein? You've got a small fortune in there. You'll never see it, of course, but your bosses will."

Pak's eyes shifted, and Fisher saw for the first time a hint of fear.

"Make no mistake," Fisher continued, "when we're done with you, you'll be the greatest traitor your country has ever seen. Or, option two: You agree to help us." Fisher spread his hands and gave Pak a friendly grin. "It's your call."

"How do I know I can trust—"

"You don't. There're only two things you can count on right now: one, that we can and will burn you; and two, whatever else happens, the first hint I get that you're double-dealing us, I'll put a bullet in your head. That's the deal. Take it or leave it."

Pak closed his eyes, took a deep breath, let it out. "I'll take it."

39

"**SLOW** down," Fisher ordered Pak. "You don't want to get a speeding ticket."

Pak eased up on the gas pedal, and the car—a 1990 Mercedes 300 Diesel that Fisher assumed was another RDEI perk—slowed to below 50 kph. The tires beat out a steady rhythm on the highway's expansion joints, lulling Fisher toward drowsiness. He shook it off and focused.

Knowing he was losing ground to exhaustion, Fisher had taken out some insurance against the inevitability of Pak trying to make a move: Tightened around the base of each of Pak's ring fingers was a wire-thin flexicuff. The other ends were secured around the steering wheel's lower half. He had enough length to operate the Mercedes but nothing else.

They'd been traveling for forty minutes. In the side mirror Fisher could see the lights of Pyongyang in the distance, but out here, just six miles outside the city, it was pitch-dark, save what little moonlight filtered through the low cloud cover. It was as though they'd passed through a curtain on the capital's eastern outskirts, from lighted skyscrapers and streetlamps to blackness.

With one eye trained on the iPhone's screen, which currently displayed a hybrid satellite/road map of North Korea, and one eye tuned toward Pak, Fisher ordered him to turn left off the two-lane highway onto a narrow gravel road that took them into a stretch of rolling hills covered by evergreen trees. Fisher watched the latitude and longitude coordinates at the edge of the iPhone's screen scroll until finally they stopped and started flashing.

"Stop here," Fisher ordered.

Pak pulled to the side of the road and shut off the engine. Fisher took the car keys.

"I'm taking a little walk," he told Pak. "If you can manage to gnaw your fingers off before I get back, you're free to go."

"You're a funny man," Pak grumbled.

"So I've been told."

Fisher climbed out, clicked on his penlight, then started up the hillside until he reached the tree line, where he stopped and reoriented himself to the iPhone's screen, and kept going, following a game trail higher into the trees. After sixty seconds he stopped, checked his position, then turned left, took four paces, and knelt down. He broomed the pine needles away with his hands. Lying there half buried in the dirt was a wood handled gardener's trowel.

Fisher started digging. It took only a minute to unearth a black Gore-Tex rucksack. He smiled to himself. *Hello, old friends*.

Fisher hadn't asked, and Lambert hadn't offered an explanation, but just before leaving Washington he'd given Fisher a set of latitude and longitude coordinates. "If you have to go to ground."

He didn't have to look inside the bag to know it contained his full mission equipment loadout: tac suit, goggles, SC-20 rifle and pistol, OPSAT, his Fairbairn-Sykes dagger—all of it would be there.

Fisher didn't need an explanation of how the bag found its way here; he had a solid hunch: Against every operational tradecraft rule in the book, Tom Richards had instructed their spy in the SSD's comptroller's office to take a drive in the country.

Thanks, whoever you are, Fisher thought.

He picked up the bag and started back down the path.

TWENTY minutes later, back on the main highway, Fisher's Bluetooth headset vibrated; he tapped the connect button.

"Sam, it's Grim. Will and I are almost done sorting through the dump from Pak's laptop. About two months before Carmen Hayes went missing, Pak was assigned a new password and log-in to an SSD intranet portal. The portal address has changed, but the e-mail account associated with it hasn't. There's a backlog of e-mail that shows spikes at times that correspond with some interesting events—namely the mortar bombardment in Bishkek, the

Kyrgyz president's resignation, Omurbai's reappearance, Calvin Stewart's transfer to the Site 17 platform . . . that sort of stuff. All related to Manas."

"Anything worthwhile?"

"The e-mails are encoded—some kind of digital one-time pad setup, which means only Pak and whoever he was exchanging e-mails with had the decryption algorithm, and it probably changed frequently. I've got enough messages with enough repeated phrases and references to start piecing it together from the back end, but it's going to take time.

"But here's what you need to know. First of all: Is Pak within earshot?"

"Yes."

"Then just listen; don't let on. All of the e-mails Pak sent through this portal go to a single routing station about ten miles east of Pyongyang. I've been tracking you, and I think he's taking you on a wild-goose hunt. You're about five miles southeast of the routing station and heading away from it."

"I see."

"And he's taking you straight into a military restriction zone."

"Huh."

"I'm looking at the sat pics right now. If you keep going down the road you're on, you'll run smack into a checkpoint, and within a half mile of you there's a dozen anti-aircraft sites, bunkers, infantry barracks, and radar sites. According to Langley, that whole area is a retreat for North Korean Workers' Party bigwigs. It's one of the most heavily guarded sites in the whole country."

"Good to know."

"What're you going to do?"

"I'll get back to you." Fisher disconnected. He turned in his seat and leveled the pistol with Pak's chest. "Stop the car."

"What?"

"You heard me. Stop the car."

In the corner of his eye, through the windshield, Fisher saw a glimmer of light. He turned. A quarter mile down the road a pair of floodlights came to life atop a guard shack that straddled the road. The lights pierced the windshield. Fisher squinted.

Pak slammed the gas pedal to the floor. The Mercedes's powerful engine roared, and the car lurched forward. A half second later, Pak spun the wheel hard left, and the car skidded, sliding sideways down the road, and then suddenly they were airborne. Fisher went weightless for a moment before he was slammed forward again. His forehead cracked against the dashboard, and everything dimmed.

Fisher was vaguely aware that the car had come to a stop. He opened his eyes and looked around. The Mercedes was sitting right side up, angled downward in a drainage ditch. Fisher touched his forehead and his hand came back red. Beside him, Pak was unconscious, sitting upright in his seat, his head leaning against the side window, both hands still tethered to the wheel. Down the road he heard voices calling in Korean, then an engine accelerating toward him.

Move, Sam, don't think. Move!

Fisher cast his eyes around the car for the pistol and spotted it lying on Pak's floorboard. He retrieved it. Using both hands he smeared blood from his forehead down over his face and neck. He opened the car door, rolled out onto his knees, and tried to stand, but fell. He took three quick breaths to clear his head, then tried again and forced himself upright. He looked left. Down the road, not more than a hundred yards away, a vehicle was speeding toward him. He tucked the pistol into his front waistband, then climbed up the embankment and ran around to Pak's side. He paused to wave his hands at the approaching vehicle in what he hoped was the universal *Help me* gesture, then stumbled to Pak's door and began fumbling for the handle.

The vehicle—a jeep with three soldiers, Fisher now saw—skidded to a stop. The headlights pinned Fisher. The soldiers climbed out, rifles in hand, and encircled him.

"Pak!" Fisher cried, mush-mouthing his marginal Korean. *"Jom do-wa-ju-se-yo!"* Help me! Fisher turned his face in quarter profile toward the soldiers. Fisher was hoping the sight of blood, combined with his obvious panic, would have the desired effect. *"Jom do-wa-ju-se-yo!"* he cried again, batting at the car's door handle and waving an arm toward the soldiers.

One of them, evidently the senior of the trio, barked an order. Fisher caught a snippet: ". . . go help . . . !"

It was exactly what Fisher had been waiting for. He drew the pistol from his waistband and spun. He ignored the two soldiers closest to him, who had lowered their rifles and were stepping forward to help, and focused instead on the third, who was holding his rifle at ready low. Fisher fired two shots, striking the man's center of mass, then sidestepped left, adjusted his aim, fired twice more, then again, dropping the two other soldiers in midstep. He hurried forward, kicking rifles away as he went, and checked for pulses. All three were dead.

Behind him, Fisher heard a groan, then Pak's voice: "You still won't get there."

Fisher turned around and walked back to the car.

Pak said, "In twenty minutes there will be a hundred soldiers looking for you. You won't make it." He coughed, then hawked up some mucus and spat it on the ground.

"Maybe," Fisher replied, "but I'm not inclined to take your word for it. One question before I go: There was a man who was looking for Carmen Hayes. You know who I'm talking about?"

Pak furrowed his brows, then nodded. "A private detective. So?"

"Were you the one who put him in that chamber at Site Seventeen?"

"Yes."

"Why?"

"Couldn't leave him alive."

"But why that way?" Fisher asked. He wasn't sure why any of this was important to him, but for some reason he couldn't pin down, he needed to hear the words. "Why kill him like that?"

Pak shrugged. "Why not? I was curious." Then Pak's face changed. His eyes focused on Fisher's, and he smiled smugly. "You knew him, didn't you?"

"I knew him. His name was Peter. He was my brother."

Pak laughed, a mocking snort. "Peter. Yes, I put him in there. Locked the door myself."

"Did you let him out?"

Pak frowned. "Let him out?" He laughed. "Why would I let him out?"

Peter must have somehow broken out after Pak and his

people had left, found a life raft, and set off, hoping against hope he'd be spotted. He probably had an idea he was already dying.

"So you just left him there to die," Fisher said.

"He deserved no better," Pak replied. "He wasn't a man. He cried. He begged and screamed like a—"

Fisher raised his pistol and shot Pak in the forehead.

Pak's head snapped back, his eyes bulging, mouth frozen open in midsentence.

40

FISHER slowed his pace, trotted down an embankment, and dropped belly first into the foot-wide stream there. Ten seconds later a convoy of two jeeps and four trucks roared by on the road and disappeared around a bend.

Fisher keyed his SVT. "Status," he said.

"I've got a real-time satellite feed," Grimsdottir said. "An NK expert from the DIA named Ben is sitting next to me."

"Morning, Ben," Fisher said pleasantly.

"Uh . . . morning, sir."

"He'll tell us what we're looking at," Grimsdottir said. "Lambert and Redding are here, too."

Lambert said, "Sam, it looks like Pak's prediction was dead-on. They're mobilizing everything in the area. Right now it's about a company's worth—maybe a hundred fifty men. On the plus side, they're not organized. I think your ruse at the checkpoint might buy you more time than we'd thought. We're seeing a good-size cluster of vehicles around the crash."

After dispatching Pak, Fisher had done a series of things in short order: picked up the shell casings he'd expended, stripped Pak's car of its license plate and any documentation inside, cut Pak's hands free of the wheel and pocketed the flexicuffs, maneuvered the dead soldiers, including their rifles, back to the jeep and arranged them as they'd arrived, then plucked a pair of grenades off one of their belts and pushed the jeep forward until it rolled down the embankment and bumped into Pak's door.

He'd then stepped back to check his handiwork. Satisfied, he'd shouldered his rucksack, then pulled and popped the grenades and dropped one each into the jeep's and Mercedes's gas tanks.

He was fifty yards away, crouched in the undergrowth, when the explosion turned the sky orange.

"Long shot as it is," Fisher said now, "with luck it'll take them a while to figure out it was more than an accident. With even more luck, they won't figure it out, but I'm not counting on that."

"Probably wise," Lambert said. "You've made good time. Three miles in twenty-two minutes."

Fisher had taken a previous five-minute break to strip out of his civilian clothes, bury them, and slip into his tac suit and gear. Tactically, the change had of course made sense, but on an intangible but no less important level, it had also helped him switch mental gears. He was on the run, deep inside Indian country. This was his element.

"Getting old," Fisher said. "Used to be a little faster."

Fisher checked his watch, then looked eastward. The horizon was fringed with orange light, but directly above him the sky was swollen with rain clouds. Daylight was fifty minutes away. He needed to find a bolt-hole.

"Any ideas?" Fisher asked. "I need to disappear in the next thirty minutes."

"We're looking," Grimsdottir said.

Ben's voice came on the line. "Sir, within a quarter mile of you—to the east and west—are two SAM sites," he said, referring to surface-to-air missiles. "The normal complement for these are twelve men apiece. They're not hardened soldiers, but I'd still give them a wide berth. To the south, where you just came from, is that NKWP retreat and checkpoint, another SAM site, a radar station, and a supply depot. To the north, where Miss Grimsdottir tells me you're headed, are some empty artillery positions—basically crescent-shaped sandbag revetments; a barracks, which we believe is only partially manned; and an abandoned sewage disposal plant."

"How far?" Fisher asked.

"Half a mile."

"Will is downloading a higher-resolution annotated map to your OPSAT right now," Lambert said.

Twenty seconds later it was on Fisher's screen. He studied it. Three hundred yards to the west of his position, at the end of the drainage ditch in which he lay, was a grove of trees running from north to south.

"What is that?" he asked.

"Pecan orchard," replied Ben. "It runs north for about a mile, right past the sewage plant."

"My kind of place," Fisher said. "I'm moving."

TWENTY minutes later, having picked his way from tree to tree through the pecan grove, Fisher dropped to his belly in the tall grass that bordered the sewage plant's fence. He switched his goggles first to NV, then infrared, scanning the plant's outbuildings and roads for activity. The plant, which roughly covered a square mile, was laid out in an L-shape, with a pair of rectangular Quonset hut–style buildings aligned on each arm of the L and a filtration pond situated between them. Running into the pond on a raised, cross-girdered platform was a six-foot-diameter sewage pipe.

He saw neither movement nor signs of habitation on the grounds. No lights, no cars. He zoomed in on one of the buildings. The windows were covered in an even layer of dust and grime. He studied the dirt parking lot and was about to zoom back out when something caught his eye: a pattern in the parking lot's dirt.

"Grim, do we have any data on the weather around here? Specifically, wind patterns."

"Hold on," Grimsdottir said. She came back thirty seconds later. "This time of year, steady winds; northerly; average speed, about twenty miles an hour."

"Bingo," Fisher muttered.

"What's that?"

"Tell you later." Fisher flipped a switch on his goggles,

linking them to his OPSAT. "Are you seeing this?" he asked.

"We see it," Lambert replied. "Bad feeling about those buildings, Sam."

"I agree. They'll eventually get to them. Grim, how long has this plant been abandoned?"

"Checking . . . Best guess, about two years. Why?"

"The sewage pipe running into the filtration pool . . . Just wondering how dry it's going to be."

There was a long pause, then Grimsdottir said, "Oh, boy. Better you than me."

"Lamb?"

"I agree. It's your best bet, Sam."

"Okay, I'm moving again."

RACING the coming dawn, Fisher scaled the fence and sprinted, hunched over, across the open ground to the edge of the parking lot, where he crouched down. He could now see the windblown streaks in the dirt lot. But in lee of the buildings, along their southern walls, the dirt showed no streaks. The plan Fisher had been contemplating solidified in his mind.

He sprinted across the lot to the nearest building's long wall and knelt at a mullioned window. He looked over his shoulder. Perfect. Where he'd passed over ground not shielded by the buildings, his footprints were clearly outlined in the dirt. Before long, with the coming of daylight, the wind would come up and hopefully wipe them clean.

Fisher drew the Sykes from its sheath and smacked the handle against the glass. The mullioned square shattered.

Fisher reached through the opening, unlatched the window, and slid it up. He crawled through, closed the window behind him, and looked around. The building's interior was dominated by three open, steel-sided storage pools topped by a catwalk.

He found what he needed almost immediately. Fisher ran forward, ducked between two of the pools, then to the opposite wall, where he crouched before a window. He unlatched the window, slid it up a half inch, then backstepped to the ladder, carefully stepping in his own footprints.

Fisher climbed the ladder to the catwalk and sprinted down its length to the far wall and the opposite ladder. Where the catwalk met the wall, there was a waist-high railing; above this, a louvered vent leading to the outside.

Fisher climbed the railing and balanced himself on the top rung as he wrestled the vent free from the wall. He placed the vent beside him on the railing so it was balanced against the wall, then pulled a six-foot length of parachute cord from one of his waist pouches. He secured one end to one of the vent's louvers, the other to his ankle.

Next he boosted himself in the opening, rolled onto his back, and wriggled through until he was suspended, his torso outside, his legs inside. A few feet above his head was the roof's peak. He grabbed the edge with both hands, then gradually drew his legs through the vent and slowly let them drop until the vent cover, still attached to his ankle, popped back into the opening. He gave the cord a firm tug to ensure the vent was locked into place, then released his right hand from the roof and undid the knot.

He placed his right hand to the roof, took a deep breath,

and chinned himself up to the roofline. He hooked a heel on the edge and rolled himself over.

Almost there, Sam.

He backed up twenty paces, then sprinted forward and leapt over the gap to the next building and kept running along the peak, his boots pounding on the tin roof until he reached the opposite edge, where he stopped.

He smiled. Love it when a plan comes together.

Ten feet below him was the raised sewage pipe; to his right, thirty feet away, it ended at the filtration pool. Fisher jumped down and headed for the opening.

— 41 —

FISHER'S eyes snapped open. *Trucks,* he thought. Took them long enough.

After sliding into the pipe, he'd crawled for a hundred feet until the opening was but a distant circle of gray light, then chose a patch of the pipe's corrugated bottom that looked slightly less sewage-encrusted than the rest, and settled in. He took off his rucksack, propped his head against it, and folded his hands across his chest. It took forty minutes for the adrenaline buzz in his limbs to wear off and for his mind to stop spinning. He drifted off to sleep.

He rolled onto his belly and looked down the length of the pipe to the opening. A gust of wind whipped around the opening, peppering the sides with grit. He caught the ozone scent of rain. He checked his watch: seven thirty.

From outside came the roar of engines—three, he estimated—followed by tires skidding in the dirt and barked orders in Korean.

He'd chosen the sewage plant as his bolt-hole not only for its proximity but because he was certain the North Koreans would consider it a worthy site to search. A critical part of E&E (escape and evasion), was to sometimes give your pursuers exactly what they expected.

Two minutes passed. An alarmed voiced shouted, followed by more barked orders. Fisher caught only one word: *window*. In his mind's eye, he saw the soldiers breaking down the building's door . . . men racing down the catwalk to search the storage pools, another one finding the open window on the opposite side of the room . . .

Their quarry had been here not long ago but had since moved on.

Fisher froze.

On the other side of the pipe's wall he heard scrabbling sounds: hands slapping on girders, followed by grunts of effort, then boots walking on the roof over his head and moving toward the opening. A pair of male voices muttered back and forth. Fisher waited until the footsteps were farther down the pipe, then shifted the rucksack so it sat in front of his face. He peered through the straps.

Moments later a pair of faces appeared, upside down, in the pipe's opening. Voices echoed down the pipe.

". . . anything?"

"No . . . light . . ."

A flashlight clicked on and played over the inside of the pipe for ten seconds, then clicked off.

From outside, nearer to ground level, a commanding

voice barked a question, and one of the men answered: "No, nothing."

The heads pulled out of sight.

THE search lasted another twenty minutes. Five minutes after the engines had faded into the distance, Fisher keyed his SVT. He brought Lambert and the others up to speed, then asked, "Any luck nailing down what the hell I'm looking for and where I can find it?"

"We think so," Grimsdottir replied. "We mapped the area using Pak's e-mail cluster and the routing station they went to, but that still leaves us a lot of ground to cover. We're studying the overheads right now. Be back to you as soon as possible."

Lambert came back on the line: "How're you holding up?"

"Good. Got a whole day's nap ahead of me. What more could a man want?"

"A whole day's nap in your own bed at home instead of a sewer pipe in the middle of North Korea?" Lambert offered.

"Killjoy. How's our friend, Omurbai? Still talking?"

"Almost constantly. He's running on all channels, all day, either live or repeats."

"Anything new?"

"More of the same. His Manas rhetoric is ramping up, though. That's got folks around here worried."

In this case, "folks" meant the CIA, the president, and the national security council.

"I can only imagine," Fisher replied. "How's our door replacement coming?"

Fisher was referring to DOORSTOP, the operational code name for a plan to deal with Omurbai and Manas should Fisher fail on his mission. While Fisher had been in the air on his way to Pyongyang, the Joint Chiefs had begun pre-positioning U.S. military assets to deal with Kyrgyzstan. AH-64 Apaches, AH-1 Cobras, and UH-60 Black Hawks had been put on ready alert at Bagram Air Base in Afghanistan, as had elements from the Seventy-fifth Ranger Regiment and Eighty-second Airborne Division, while in the Arabian Sea the aircraft carrier *Reagan* had taken up station off the Pakistani coast.

If Fisher managed to uncover the locations in which Omurbai planned to introduce Manas, DOORSTOP's forces would move in to secure the sites. If, however, Fisher failed, DOORSTOP's mission would be to attack Omurbai's forces in and around Bishkek in hopes of shutting Manas off at the tap. Of course, this plan made a dangerous but unavoidable assumption—that Omurbai would be keeping Manas in the capital and that he hadn't already dispatched it to pre-positioned teams throughout the country. If this was the case, the United States had little hope of stopping Manas.

"Almost have the hinges on," Lambert replied. "Hopefully, everything will fit."

Translation: Hopefully, DOORSTOP won't be necessary.

"A little bit of oil," Fisher said, "and everything will fit."

Translation: We find a neutralizing agent for Manas, and none of it will be necessary.

HE slept surprisingly well for a solid three hours and awoke to Grimsdottir's voice in his ear. "Sam, you there?"

"Yep. Dreaming of rats crawling on my face."

"Maybe it wasn't a dream."

"Don't ruin it for me, Grim. What've you got?"

"First thing: I've been monitoring Pyongyang's emergency frequencies. While this isn't proof positive, so far we've seen no activity at Pak's apartment. The remains of the jeep and Pak's Mercedes were towed to a civilian lot in Namsan-dong. Patrols are still pretty heavy in the area, but the radio chatter is dying down."

"Good news."

"Next, we spotted something that might be worth a look. I'll let Ben explain."

"Sir, we think we've found an anomaly in the terrain about a mile to your northwest. For a long time we've had the area under surveillance. We were pretty sure something's there, we just couldn't figure out what. We don't think it's military related, but beyond that, we've got no clue."

"Describe the anomaly."

"A two-lane paved highway that goes through a tunnel built into a hillside. But here's the thing: the last three hours I've been watching the real-time satellite feed. Forty-two vehicles have entered, but only thirty-eight have come out the other side."

"You're sure? No miscount?"

"No, sir."

"What types of vehicles?"

"Flatbed semitrailers. Actually, I misspoke: One of them did come back out, but it was two hours later, and it was carrying something."

"What?"

"It was under a tarp, but we got a glimpse. It would just be speculation—"

"Speculate away," Fisher said.

Ben cleared his throat. "The closest thing that I've seen that matches the dimensions and configuration is a LINAC or a cyclotron—those are kinds of particle accelerators—"

"I know what they are, Ben. So, we've got high-energy physics equipment coming out of this tunnel to nowhere. Okay, what else?"

"About a thousand feet north of the highway and the tunnel is what looks like a roofed dairy farm. Goat's milk and yogurt, we believe. Problem with that story is, we've never been able to detect any methane emissions and never seen any disposal trucks coming or going. Plenty of tanker trucks, but no dump trucks."

"No goat crap," Fisher said.

"No goat crap," Ben repeated.

"Anything else?"

"Saved the best for last. All throughout the area—around the highway tunnel and scattered around the goat farm are bushes, sitting all by their lonesome. They're natural to the area, but a little off color. Of course, the CIA has done soil and irrigation studies on the whole country, so we've got a good idea of what should grow where and how well. These bushes are a little too healthy. Somehow they're getting a little extra moisture."

Fisher thought for a moment, then said, "Air. Camouflaged air shafts. The air condenses and warms as it comes up from underground."

"That was my guess," Ben said.

"How many?"

Grimsdottir said, "Fourteen that we can see. I'm uploading them to your OPSAT now."

Fisher waited for the images, then looked them over, and said, "Patrols?"

"None visible," Grimsdottir said, "but nightfall could be a different story."

"Safe bet. Lamb, how're we doing on my ex-fil?"

With no idea where in North Korea Fisher's mission might take him, they'd left his ex-filtration uncomfortably open-ended. No operative liked going into Indian countr without a clear plan to get himself back out again. In this case, however, there'd been no choice.

"Assuming this goat farm is what we're looking for, think Delta is our best bet." They'd tagged possible ex-filtration scenarios alphabetically. Delta was dicey, Fisher knew, but Lambert was right: It offered his best hope of not only getting out, but getting out quickly.

"Delta it is. By the way, what's my ROE?"

"Weapons free," Lambert replied. "Gloves off. If you have to rack up a body count to get into that facility, so be it."

"About time. I'm signing off. I'm going to enjoy my accommodations, then come nightfall, we're going to see if we can solve the great goat farm mystery."

42

FISHER left his hiding place at the sewage plant at nine thirty, a full hour after dusk, and then made his way north and west toward the highway bridge. The rain that had seemed imminent during the day had never materialized, and now the sky was clear, save a high, crescent moon.

The maze of tree-lined dirt roads that wound through the area was heavily patrolled, but only by jeep and truck; no foot patrols. Three times Fisher had to stop, take cover, and watch as a slowly moving jeep or truck would roll by, flashlights in unseen hands playing over the edge of the road and through the trees. Sometimes in the distance he could hear soldiers calling to one another.

He'd begun to realize being trapped here, in such a heavily guarded zone, had a hidden benefit. Aside from the main highway, there was very little nonmilitary traffic. He'd seen no farmers nor laborers nor sightseers, so the likelihood of him running into a civilian, who would in turn alert the authorities, was slim. Civilians were like Yorkshire terriers guarding a backyard: mostly harmless, but quick to sound the alarm at the slightest provocation.

A quarter mile from the tunnel he reached a scrub-covered hillock. He dropped to his belly, crawled to the crest, and did an NV/IR scan of the terrain ahead. Across from his hillock, perhaps a hundred yards away, over a patch of dead ground, was a sloping dirt berm that ran perpendicularly, east to west, for about a quarter mile. Emerging from either end of it was the two-lane highway Ben and Grimsdottir had mentioned. It was well lit by rural North Korean standards, with sodium-vapor light poles placed every couple hundred yards, alternating from one side of the road to the other. He rechecked his OPSAT to be certain. This was the place. Though it was below his line of sight right now, beyond the berm was the dairy goat farm.

The berm itself, which he had to cross to reach the farm, was roughly twelve feet tall, rimmed with juniper bushes at the bottom, and topped by a dirt path. At each end, the path seemed to curve northward down the opposite slope.

Five minutes after he'd started watching, a soldier appeared atop the berm's far eastern edge and started down the path. Seconds later, another soldier, this one from the west side, appeared and also started down the path. The two men met in the middle, stopped to chat for half a minute, then continued past one another. Fisher kept watching, timing the patrols for the next hour, and got only frustration for his effort. Aside from two soldiers, one coming from each direction and passing in the middle, the timing was never the same. Twice he'd watched the soldiers disappear down the opposite slope only to see them return thirty seconds later for another stroll along the berm. Of course, the purpose of the random timing was to do exactly what it was doing to Fisher: frustrate him, or any other potential intruder.

He briefly considered picking his way north or south, parallel to the highway, but dismissed the idea. North would only take him closer to the NKWP retreat, which would be even more heavily guarded. To the south lay more SAM sites and radar installations, which meant more traffic. No, this was his best chance.

First, though, he needed to know what lay between the berm and the goat farm. He pulled out the SC-20 and flipped the selector to ASE, or All-Seeing Eye. Of all the tools at his disposal, this was one of Fisher's favorites. The ASE was a microcamera embedded in a tiny parachute made from a substance called aerogel.

Consisting of 90 percent air, aerogel could hold four thousand times its own weight and had a mind-bending amount of surface area: Spread flat, each cubic inch of aerogel—roughly the size of four nickels stacked atop one another—would cover a football field from end zone to end zone. The ASE's palm-size, self-deploying aerogel chute could, depending on weather conditions, keep it aloft for as long as ninety seconds, giving Fisher a high-resolution bird's-eye view of nearly a square mile.

This newest generation of ASE had been fitted with a self-destruct mechanism, à la *Mission Impossible*. The camera's interior, coated with a magnesium-lithium mixture, would ignite at a touch of a button on Fisher's OPSAT screen, turning the camera and its aerogel chute into a charred, unrecognizable lump of plastic.

He took a moment to gauge the wind, then raised the SC-20 and pulled the trigger. With a soft *thwump*, the ASE arched into the sky over the berm. Fisher tapped the OP-SAT, bringing up the ASE's screen. The view he had was a quarter mile above the berm, looking straight down. The wind was negligible, drifting southeast to northwest at a slow walking pace.

The ground on the north side of the berm was also mostly featureless, with scattered trees and scrub brush and the empty artillery revetments set in a semicircle, each one a crescent of stacked sandbags. Fifty yards to the east of these, a curving S-shaped road ran northward to the goat farm, where it turned sharply right and ended in what looked like a gravel parking lot.

Fisher switched to night vision. In the washed-out gray green he could immediately pick out his two berm guards, both of whom were walking along the base of the berm toward each other. North of them, a hundred feet away, two more soldiers sat smoking atop the revetment's sand-bags. He saw no one else. On the OPSAT screen he scrolled through the options until he came to SEQUENTIAL STILLS > ONE SECOND INTERVAL > OVERLAY TO MAP. He hit EXECUTE. High above him the ASE would be taking a sequence of ten photos, which it would transmit to the OP-SAT, which in turn would match the ASE's landmarks with its own map of the area, producing a layered NV/standard satellite image.

He switched to infrared and repeated the same process,

but as he was about to self-destruct the ASE, a gust of wind caught it. In the few seconds it took the camera's internal gyroscopes to steady the image, Fisher caught a glimpse of color. He panned the ASE around until he spotted it again.

Hello, friend . . .

A man-shaped figure outlined in the reds, blues, and greens of the IR lay prone in the scrub brush north of the artillery positions and beside the S-shaped road. This would be an observation post, he knew, probably a sniper equipped with a night-vision scope and a radio link to a command station somewhere. Anything that came up that road or over the berm would immediately fall into his crosshairs.

Damn. This complicated things. Then he thought about it. *Maybe not.*

He tapped the ASE's self-destruct button.

Having already picked his spot, he waited for each of the guards to disappear down his respective north slope, then got up and sprinted across the dead ground to the edge of the berm, where he dropped flat behind the juniper bushes. He parted the branches, wriggled through, and crawled up the slope until his head was three feet below the top. He waited. Two minutes passed. Four. At the five-minute mark, the guards reappeared on the path. From his vantage point, Fisher could see only their heads as they passed by one another, exchanged a few words, and kept going.

He waited for them to get fifty yards away, then checked his OPSAT one last time. Using his stylus and the IR overlay the ASE had taken for him, Fisher tapped his position on the map, then the sniper's. An annotated yellow diagonal line connected the two spots:

DISTANCE TO TARGET: 180 METERS
RISE/DROP: –9 METERS

Fisher gauged the wind. Two knots, moving diagonally left to right. He adjusted the SC-20's scope, crawled up the slope until he was even with the top, then scooted forward an inch at a time, stopping every few feet and focusing the scope on the sniper's position. He was halfway across the berm when the sniper appeared in the scope's NV. He was lying on his belly in the undergrowth, perpendicular to Fisher, his cheek resting on the rifle's butt. His attention seemed focused on the S-road.

Fisher zoomed in until only the man' head, shoulders, and upper torso filled the scope. He laid the crosshairs on a spot just behind the man's armpit—a heart shot—then took a breath, paused, let it out. He squeezed the trigger. The SC-20 gave a muted cough. Two hundred yards away, the sniper lay still, his head slumped forward on his rifle.

Fisher wriggled back across the path and down the slope and waited another seven minutes for the berm guards to pass by. He crawled back onto the path, again moving inches at a time, until through his scope he had a clear view of the two soldiers sitting atop the sandbag revetments. He checked the wind again, found it unchanged, so he zoomed in on the pair. They were sitting side by side, within two feet of one another. The sandbags, stacked to chest height, left their legs dangling in midair. Fisher saw one of them laugh, his head tilted back, teeth flashing white in the night-vision.

Sorry about this, boys.

Fisher laid the crosshairs on the center of the laughing

man's chest and squeezed the trigger. Even as he was falling backward into the revetment and his friend, wearing a surprised expression, was extending a hand toward him, Fisher fired again. The second man toppled behind the sandbags.

Fisher began scooting backward.

43

FISHER lay on his belly, perfectly still, his eyes fixed on the boot twelve inches before his face. Of all the places the soldier could have chosen for a bathroom break, the man chose this spot. Fisher closed his eyes for a moment, centering himself. Slowly, his heart rate returned to normal. The soldier unzipped his pants. Fisher heard liquid pattering the leaves beside his leg. After an agonizingly long thirty seconds, the guard rezipped, picked up his rifle from where it was leaning against the tree, turned around, and walked away.

After finishing off the two soldiers atop the revetment, it had been relatively simple to slip between the berm guard, crawl down the opposite embankment, then sprint to the revetment. From there he'd picked his way through the trees lining the S-road to the edge of the goat farm's gravel parking lot, where he settled in to wait and watch.

His two options to gain entrance into whatever kind of facility lay beneath the farm both had their pros and cons. The bush-camouflaged air vents, numerous and easier to reach, appealed to Fisher, but there was no telling where a vent would drop him, so he'd chosen the farm itself. If the farm was what they thought it was, there had to be access for staff. Clearly, there was an entrance somewhere in the highway tunnel, but Fisher knew he'd never make it past the checkpoints. That left the farm. Somewhere amid the collection of covered pens and miscellaneous rooms he would find what he was looking for.

The guard who had just nearly urinated on him had emerged from one of the farm's outbuildings, which was more of a raised construction trailer than a building. To the right of the trailer was a covered goat pen enclosed by a split-rail fence.

The guard climbed the wooden steps to the trailer and went inside. Through the window Fisher could see light and could make out voices speaking in Korean. Two, maybe three men, he estimated.

A quick check with the flexicam at the trailer's window revealed two men, both sitting at a folding table playing cards. Each one wore a sidearm, and leaning against the wall beside them were a pair of rifles. Sitting on the floor in the corner was a bronze tabletop reading lamp. Against the near wall, just below the window, was a countertop and sink.

Fisher drew the SC-20 from its holster and thumbed the selector to COTTONBALL.

Another favorite of his, the SC-20's Cottonball feature was made up of two parts: a slotted plastic cylinder—the sabot—which measured about two inches long and half an inch in diameter, and a spiked soft rubber ball roughly the size of a marble. Once fired, the sabot breaks away, leaving only the Cottonball, which, upon striking a hard object, shatters an inner pod of aerosol tranquilizer. Cottonball's effective radius was three feet; any living thing inside the cloud lost consciousness within four seconds and stayed that way for twenty to thirty minutes.

Fisher crept up the steps, turned the knob with his left hand, and stepped through the door, the SC-20 already to his shoulder. He swung the door shut with his boot. In unison, both men spun in their chairs. The one farthest from Fisher started to rise.

"Sit," Fisher barked in Korean.

The man hesitated.

Fisher shook his head and gestured with the SC-20.

The man sat down.

"Raise your hand if you speak English," Fisher asked in English.

Each men raised a hand. One man—a senior sergeant, judging by the patch on his sleeve—was in his forties; the other man was no older than twenty. Fisher studied them for a few moments and decided he didn't like the glint of anger in the younger one's eyes.

He fired a Cottonball in his chest. There was a *pfft* sound. The man staggered, then his eyes rolled back into his head, and he collapsed.

Fisher pointed the SC-20 at the sergeant, who already had his hands raised. "Please . . . no shoot," he said in stilted English.

"You've got a family, don't you?" Fisher asked.

"Yes. A family."

"And you're close to retirement."

"Yes. Uh . . . six . . . uh . . ."

"Months."

"Yes."

"You cooperate, and you'll live to see your family and your retirement. You don't cooperate, you're going to die in this trailer. Do you understand?"

The sergeant's bulging eyes told Fisher he understood perfectly.

"Yes, yes, please . . ."

Fisher stalked forward and knelt down before the sink. He opened the cabinet door, looked inside, then stood up and tossed the sergeant a pair of flexicuffs. "See that pipe bracket in there?"

The sergeant bent over and looked. "Yes."

"Tie him to that. Not the pipe, the bracket."

As the sergeant dragged his partner to the sink, Fisher walked to the floor lamp and unplugged it. He clicked on the SC-20's barrel light, then checked the sergeant's work and found it satisfactory.

"Empty your pockets on the table."

The sergeant did so. Fisher sorted through the contents. He found no keys, but on the back of the man's ID card he spotted a magnetic dot about half the diameter of a penny. Fisher pocketed the card. He gestured for the sergeant to sit down.

"What's your name?"

"Kim. I am Kim."

"Kim, there's a facility beneath this goat farm. How do I get into it?"

Kim hesitated. His eyes darted left, then right.

Fisher thumbed the SC-20's selector to SINGLE and fired a bullet into the wall beside his head. Kim started, nearly toppling sideways out of his chair.

"Next bullet goes between your eyes," Fisher said, tapping his index finger on his own forehead, then pointing at Kim's. "Understand?"

"Yes."

"Where's the entrance?"

Kim pointed vaguely. "There."

"Take me."

ONCE outside the trailer, Kim didn't turn right toward the outbuildings but walked straight into the goat pen, turned left, and stopped before a storage closet built into the wall. The doors were covered in peeling white paint, one latch hanging precariously by a rusted screw.

At Fisher's prompting, Kim opened the cabinet doors. He reached down and brushed away some hay from the floor, revealing a hinged O-ring. He pulled on it. The closet's entire floor lifted up on hinges and locked into the open position. A set of wood stairs dropped away into darkness.

Kim nodded and pointed. "There. Yes?"

Fisher nodded, then gestured with the SC-20. "Back to the trailer. It's nap time."

* * *

AFTER giving Kim a dose of Cottonball and securing him next to his partner, he locked the trailer door from the inside and returned to the hidden stairway.

At the bottom he found a long, dark corridor with white linoleum floor tiles and white cinder-block walls. With the SC-20 held at ready low he started down the corridor. He passed eight rooms, five to one side, three to the other. All were empty and dark. Not a piece of furniture, not a scrap of paper, not even the barest trace of dust on the floor.

He came to a T-intersection. To the left and right, more white walls, more white doors, more empty rooms. At the end of the right-hand corridor he found a freight elevator, gate wide open. To his right, the last door stood open. Inside, Fisher found an industrial-sized paper shredder plugged into the wall outlet and, lying on the floor beside it, an empty trash bag. He returned to the corridor. The door on the opposite side bore a white placard with Korean *Hangul* characters in red. Fisher opened the door. On the other side was a stairwell. He followed it down two flights to a landing and another door. Through it was a short corridor ending at yet another door. While this one was unlocked like all the rest, it had been secured by a hasp and a padlock, both of which hung open.

He opened the door.

The room was eight feet by eight feet and contained a narrow trundle bed with an inch-thick mattress, a tattered green wool blanket, a sink and a toilet, both bolted to the wall, and a hard-backed steel chair sitting in the corner.

A prison cell, Fisher thought.

With nothing else to search, Fisher used his Sykes to split the mattress and dump the foam batting onto the floor. Amid the fluff he found a thin rubber shoe insert. On its back, pressed into the foam with what Fisher guessed was a fingernail, was a block letter message:

IF YOU FIND THIS AND CARE MY NAME IS CARMEN HAYES

AMERICAN

MY PARENTS PRICE AND LORETTA

HOUSTON TEXAS

TELL THEM I LOVE THEM

TELL THEM WHAT HAPPENED TO ME

—CH

44

ON the screen, Lambert sat alone at the conference room table. Grimsdottir and Redding sat behind him at the periphery of the room, partially in the shadows. Fisher's own screen, a nineteen-inch computer monitor, sat on the desk before him. The room he'd been given was one of the base's tanks, an isolated, soundproof space in the commander's anteroom. Tanks were constantly monitored and scrubbed for listening devices.

Lambert took a moment to digest the brief Fisher had just given him, then nodded. "That poor girl," he said. "So there was nothing? Cleaned out completely?"

"A few trash bags," Fisher said. "And her message. Nothing more."

How long ago had that been? Fisher thought. It felt much longer than it was.

Four hours after clearing North Korean airspace, Fisher had landed in an NSA-owned Gulfstream jet at Misawa.

After searching the remainder of the facility beneath the goat farm and finding it also empty, Fisher had backed out the same way he'd come, paused briefly to update Lambert, then headed north, deeper into the countryside and away from the main roads until just before dawn when he found another bolt-hole—this time an overhang of rock choked with scrub brush—and waited out the day. At dusk he started moving again, following his OPSAT map until he came across a set of north-south railroad tracks. Two hours after he settled in at the edge of the track embankment, the coal train Grimsdottir had told him to expect chugged around the bend and passed by him. He hopped aboard, burrowed himself a dugout in one of the coal cars, and covered himself.

The train wound its way north and west through the countryside until, twelve miles later and two miles outside Pyongsong, Fisher hopped off and headed northwest, across the evergreen-covered slopes to the south of the city until he reached a dirt road, which he followed south until he reached a T-turn. He checked his coordinates to make sure he was on target, then hunkered down to wait.

An hour later, at three a.m., a lone car chugged its way up the road and stopped at the T-turn. The car was an older Renault. Fisher zoomed in on the license plate; the number matched. The driver, a woman with bright blond hair got out, walked to the front of the car, and popped the hood. Fisher stood up and walked to the side of the road.

The woman simply stared at him for a moment, then offered him a curt nod. She closed the hood, then walked around to the trunk, where Fisher joined her. In the trunk was a black duffel bag. Inside Fisher found worn black loafers, wrinkled brown corduroy pants, a white T-shirt, and a blue polyester suit coat. The bottom of the duffel bag was lined with dumbbell weights.

While the woman watched the road, Fisher stripped down to his underwear and socks, put his tac suit and all of his gear into the duffel, then donned the other outfit. The woman looked him over, nodded again, and gestured for him to get in the car.

She climbed into the driver's seat and turned on the ignition.

"Rules," she said.

"Okay."

"If I tell you to get out of the car, you are to get out immediately and without question. Do you understand?"

"Yes."

"I'll come back to this spot at the same time tomorrow night."

Fisher nodded.

She nodded back. "Good."

THEY drove in silence for fifteen minutes until they reached a single-lane bridge that crossed over a lake. She pulled onto the shoulder. "Here."

"How deep?" Fisher asked.

"Fifty, sixty meters. Mud bottom."

Fisher climbed out, opened the trunk, carried the duffel to the railing, and heaved it over the side.

TWO hours later, back in Pyongyang, the woman pulled over to the curb. "Two blocks to the east there is a park. Sit on the bench directly in front of the fountain. Someone will come for you in twenty-five minutes. His name is Alexandru."

"Thanks," Fisher said and got out.

The woman pulled away. The Renault disappeared around the corner.

EXACTLY twenty-five minutes later, a figure walked through the park's wrought-iron gate, circled the fountain once, then walked up to Fisher. "I'm Alexandru."

"And I'm glad to see you."

Alexandru was over sixty, five foot five, and bald save a fringe of gray hair over each ear and on his forehead. He smiled. "Would you like to go home now?"

THE entire affair had had a surreal quality to it, and Fisher, so accustomed to sneaking his way into and out of denied areas, was amazed at how simple it had been. For reasons he would probably never know, the Romanian *Serviciul de Informaţii Externe*, or Foreign Intelligence Service, which, as one of the United States's allies in Iraq, was in the rare position of still having not only an embassy in North Korea but an active intelligence apparatus. Plan Delta had involved nothing more than asking an ally for a no-questions-asked favor.

Four hours after Alexandru had escorted him through the Romanian embassy's service entrance, Fisher, armed with a Romanian diplomatic passport and escorted by the SIE's deputy chief of station, boarded a government chartered TAROM jet and lifted off.

A light beside Lambert's elbow started flashing yellow. "Time," he said.

Fisher's screen dissolved, then reappeared, this time looking down the length of the White House situation room's conference table, with the president at the far end beneath an American flag. On his left and right were the chairman of the Joint Chiefs from the Pentagon, and the DCI from CIA headquarters in Langley. There were no greetings exchanged, no smiles or small talk offered. Fisher knew the principals could see only Lambert.

"Colonel, I understand we struck out in North Korea," the president said.

"I'm afraid so, Mr. President. Our man found the facility, but it had been recently evacuated—along with Ms. Hayes, we believe."

"That leaves us one option, Mr. President," said the DCI on the screen. "We have no idea where this Hayes woman went or where Manas is, and according to the DIA and the U.S. Geological Survey, it'll take weeks—maybe months— to map out the underground hydrological strata in Kyrgyzstan."

"What about a neutralizing agent?"

"Dr. Russo from the CMLS at Lawrence Livermore is working on it, but the permutations she and her team have to run through just to nail down this fungus's cellular makeup and then reverse-engineer a neutralizer . . . Suffice it to say we shouldn't expect a save there."

"So," the president said to the chairman of the Joint Chiefs, "that takes us back to you, Admiral."

"DOORSTOP is ready to roll, Mr. President. Six hours after you give the word, our forces will cross the Kyrgyz border. Two hours after that, we'll have Rangers and Eighty-second Airborne on the ground in Bishkek. I can't talk to anything that gets out of the capital before we land, but once we're there, nothing will move without us seeing it."

The president sighed, stared at his clasped hands for ten seconds, then looked up. "Go ahead, Admiral. Activate DOORSTOP."

AFTER the meeting ended, Fisher stayed on the line for a postmortem with Lambert, Grimsdottir, and Redding. After a few minutes, Grimsdottir's cell phone trilled. She answered, listened for ten seconds, then said, "How long ago . . . no doubts? Okay . . . okay. Thanks, Ben, I owe you." She disconnected.

"Your DIA guy?" Lambert asked.

She nodded. "I was playing a long shot. It just paid off. Sam, after you found the goat farm abandoned, I figured they'd moved Carmen out at the same time those semi-trucks appeared. They probably emptied out the whole place in one fell swoop."

"I agree," Fisher said.

"So, assuming Carmen wasn't already in Kyrgyzstan, I figured she was on her way there, so I started running scenarios. Omurbai isn't a city person. He's lived and fought from the countryside all his life, so somehow it just didn't make sense to me that he'd stash her in Bishkek. So the question was, where?

"Back when he first took over the country, he opened a prison in the Tian Shan Mountains about two hundred miles east of Bishkek, then started dumping all his detractors into it. After he was ousted, the prison was shut down."

Redding said, "But now that he's back in power . . ."

"Exactly. The NRO's got four satellites tasked to Kyrgyzstan, so I've been having Ben monitor the prison site. Six hours ago, a platoon of troops arrived there. It looks like they're setting up shop again."

"Getting ready for a very important prisoner?" Fisher asked.

Grimsdottir smiled and shrugged.

Fisher said to Lambert, "Colonel . . ."

"Long shot," Lambert said.

"Better than nothing," Fisher replied. "Better than sitting on our hands."

"True. Okay, sit tight. Give us twenty minutes to get some assets moving, and we'll get back to you."

45

AGAIN Fisher felt the engines hiccup, fade, then roar to life again. Flying at 23,700 feet, the aircraft was approaching its maximum ceiling, and the sixty-year-old engines, though well-maintained, were starving for oxygen. The interior of the plane was like a museum, with canvas seats, many of them gone to dry rot, and an exposed aluminum deck that was missing a good quarter of its rivets, replaced by layers of dog-eared and edge-worn duct tape.

Fisher glanced out the porthole window but could see nothing through the frosted glass. He checked his OPSAT; on the screen was a map of northeastern Kyrgyzstan, most of which was dominated by the Tian Shan Mountain Range.

The Tian Shan, which was part of the same Himalayan orogenic belt that included Everest and K2, encompassed an enormous swath of the earth, from the Takla Makan desert in the border region of Kazakhstan, Kyrgyzstan, and the Xinjiang Uyghur region of western China, all the way south to the Pamir Mountains, and into Xinjiang, northern Pakistan, and Afghanistan's Hindu Kush.

True to her word, twenty minutes later Grimsdottir called back with his marching orders. Fisher had gathered his gear, caught a ride from the base commander's driver, who drove him to the tarmac.

Misawa was the home of the Thirty-fifth Fighter Wing, which flew two squadrons of the Block 50 model F-16CJ and F-16DJ Fighting Falcons, which is what sat fully prepped and waiting when Fisher stepped out of the car. Two minutes later he was suited up and bundled into the Falcon's rear seat.

The distance from Misawa to Peshawar, Pakistan— skirting China—was just shy of 5,800 miles, but with the Falcon's conformal fuel tanks and running at twice its normal cruising speed, it took only one midair refueling from a KC-135 Stratotanker over the Pacific Ocean. Six hours after he took off, Fisher touched down at Peshawar air base, where he was met by the base commander's chief of staff, a major, who took him to a hangar. Inside was a Douglas DC-3 Dakota transport plane. Decommissioned from the U.S. Air Force in the fifties, the first Dakotas came off the line in 1935. From what vintage this one hailed, Fisher had no idea, but best case, he was looking at a sixty-year-old aircraft. It looked well maintained, but he was reluctant to get any closer lest he notice something untoward.

"This is it, huh?" Fisher asked.

"Yes, sir, I'm sorry, but our forces are . . . otherwise engaged."

Fisher understood. The Taliban, hiding and fighting in Afghanistan's rugged mountain country, was using the turmoil in Kyrgyzstan to mount fresh offensives against Kabul, as well as cross-border raids into Pakistan's northwest frontier. Like the U.S. military, Pakistan had little to spare for the effort in Kyrgyzstan.

"It will get you to your drop zone," the major said with a smile. "Our special forces troops often use it on training missions. She's well equipped, despite her appearance. And I can assure you the door is perfectly good for jumping out of."

Though slow and lumbering, the Dakota had faithfully flown him north out of Pakistani airspace, over Tajikistan, then here, the southern fringe of the Tian Shan Mountain Range.

A voice came through Fisher's headset: "Sir, we are approaching the area."

"On my way."

Fisher unbuckled himself and walked hunched over to the cockpit opening, where he knelt down between the pilot's and copilot's seats. Both men were Pakistan Air Force reserve officers, called to duty especially for this mission.

The copilot jerked his thumb out the side window, which had been scraped free of frost. "There," he called over the engine noise.

Fisher stood up and leaned forward over the man's shoulder. Twenty thousand feet below and to the left he could see the dark blue, rounded rectangular shape of Issyk

Kul, a lake that ran through the Tian Shan roughly north-east to southwest for nearly 120 miles. Sitting at an altitude of 5,200 feet, Issyk Kul was one of the world's deepest mountain lakes at nearly 2,300 feet—nearly half a mile.

His destination, Omurbai's secret mountain prison, was located a mile from the lake's northeastern shore.

"Can you give me a flyover?" Fisher asked.

"No problem."

SEVEN minutes later, the Dakota had dropped to eight thousand feet in a wide spiral that aligned the nose with the lake's northern shoreline, which was covered in alpine meadow grasses and interspersed with rock outcroppings and stands of evergreen trees. Inland, ranging from a half mile to a mile from the shore, was a ten-mile-long granite escarpment that marked the start of Tian Shan's northern elevations. It was late afternoon, and the sun was already dropping behind some of the higher peaks, leaving the valleys and shoreline cloaked in fog.

"One mile," the pilot called.

Fisher raised his binoculars.

Where are you . . . ?

Suddenly they swept over a tree-lined ridge, and below Fisher caught a glimpse of a man-made structure in a clearing: dark rock, square shapes.

On the plane's console a red light started flashing, accompanied by a *beep beep beep*. The light was labeled EM WARNING. Fisher thought, *Fire control*.

"What, what—" the pilot called, head swiveling as he leaned toward the side window, looking.

The beeping turned to a steady whine.

"Lock!" the copilot called. "Fire control radar!"

"There," Fisher called, pointing out the right-side window.

Far below, from somewhere in the stand of trees there was a mushroom of light, followed by a streaming contrail that rose from the ground like a smoking finger, curving toward them. In the setting sun Fisher saw a glint of light on steel. *Missile nose cone*, he thought, followed by, *Too late*.

"Hang on!" the pilot called, and turned the wheel hard right. Fisher dropped to his knees and grabbed the copilot's seat bracket with both hands as the Dakota heeled onto its side and nosed over toward the ground.

It was a bold move on the pilot's part, and his only chance, but Fisher knew, as did the pilot, that it wasn't going to be enough. Recognizing that the Dakota had no chance of outrunning the missile, the pilot had chosen to turn into it in hopes of getting inside the missile's turning radius. If they had less altitude to work with, it may have worked, but the missile, having already locked onto the Dakota—either by solid radar contact or by heat signature—had plenty of sky in which to maneuver. If it didn't catch its quarry on the first pass, it would on the second.

Fisher's mind clicked over. If they went down on the shore, whoever had fired on them would be on them quickly. If they managed to crash-land or get out higher in the mountains . . .

"Can you reach the escarpment?" Fisher called.

"What? Why—"

"They'll be coming for us."

The pilot, face pinched with the strain, neck tendons standing out, nodded. "I see. I'll try!"

The missile flashed across the windscreen like a comet, and the pilot turned the wheel again, this time to the left as he and the copilot pulled back, trying to gain some altitude. Through the glass Fisher could see the escarpment's granite wall looming before them, a half mile away. To the right was a narrow valley bracketed by snowcapped peaks.

"I see it!" the pilot called and steered for the opening.

In his mind, Fisher was picturing the missile, its computer-chip brain having already registered the miss, making the turn, coming back around, and aligning on the Dakota's tail. *Ten seconds,* he thought. *No more.*

Eight . . . seven . . . six . . . five . . .

Unconsciously, he glanced over his shoulder.

The tail of the Dakota disintegrated in a flash of light.

46

FISHER stopped jogging, then stepped off the trail and dropped into a crouch behind a boulder. He'd been on the move without pause for forty minutes but had so far covered only a mile. He was still high up on the mountainside, well above the tree line, and still two thousand vertical feet above his destination. He checked his watch: just after one a.m. He glanced up and felt a moment of vertigo. The sky was clear, and at this altitude the number of visible stars was stunning, as though a giant cosmic hand had scattered diamond flakes across the black of space.

At lower elevations, the Tian Shan Mountains were alpine-esque with gently rolling hills and valleys covered in a lush blanket of green interspersed with wildflowers, but up here, amid the jagged granite peaks, towering spires, and plunging cliffs, the Tian Shan's terrain was as brutal as any Fisher had encountered. Then again, he thought, simply getting here had proved a tall—and costly—order all by itself.

THE missile had struck the Dakota's fuselage just below and behind the port engine, shearing off the wing and most of the tail capsule. The plane had immediately tipped over as the pilot and copilot had tried to regain level, but it was a lost cause. As the Dakota, smoking and shuddering, crossed over the escarpment and into the valley beyond, the pilot ordered Fisher and the copilot out, then followed them moments later as the Dakota nosed over and spiraled into a granite ice-veined spire jutting from one of the peaks.

Fisher's chute, a ram-air parafoil, had opened seconds after he leapt from the plane, but the pilot and copilot, equipped with old American MC1-1C series round parachutes, dropped like stones and weren't able to deploy in time. Gliding above them, Fisher watched in horror as they spiraled and tumbled, their chutes only partially inflated, into the spire a few hundred feet below the Dakota's impact point.

Once on the ground, Fisher briefly considered searching for them but reluctantly dismissed the idea; neither man would have survived the impact, let alone the fall down the mountainside. He'd gathered his parafoil, buried it, gave a silent thanks to the two pilots, and set off, heading east at as much of a sprint as the terrain would allow, hoping to put as much distance as he could between himself and the plane. However unlikely it was that whoever had shot down the Dakota would send searchers, Fisher didn't want to take the chance.

After two hours, having gained a couple thousand feet from the crash site, he'd stopped and studied the valley below. He took his time, looking for the slightest sign that he'd been followed. He saw none, so he set off again, this time on a curving course that took him south and west, back toward Omurbai's prison.

NOW, four hours from the crash site, he pulled out his binoculars and scanned the trail ahead, which wound its way down the boulder-littered mountainside to a shallow draw that ran east for two miles and terminated at a two-hundred-foot vertical escarpment overlooking Omurbai's mountain prison, which had no name as far as Grimsdottir could tell, and which sat at the foot of the escarpment a quarter mile from the lake.

In his ear came Grimsdottir's voice. "Sam, you there?"

"I'm here."

"You sound close."

"I'm about a mile and a half above sea level. That's got to help."

"I have some more info for you. Omurbai's prison has a long history. It's actually a fortified outpost that he revamped. In 1876, when the Russians invaded Kyrgyzstan and took it from the Quqon Khanate, they knew they were going to have a hard time with a multitude of tribes and warlords, so they built these outposts all over the country and garrisoned troops there to put down rebellions and general mischief."

Fisher could see it. From the satellite photos, the compound looked more like a Wild West cavalry fort than a prison, with high stone walls and rough mud-and-grass brick buildings. Most of the roofs appeared new, however, and were made from slate. Short wooden bridges connected each building's roof to the fighting catwalk that lined the interior side of the fort's stone walls. Fisher assumed that during battle the Russian soldiers would have climbed through some unseen trap in each building's roof, then crossed the bridge to take up defensive positions along the wall.

"Don't suppose you happened upon some Imperial Russian blueprints of the place, did you?" Fisher asked.

"After a fashion, I did," Grimsdottir replied. "Found a professor in Prague who wrote a book on Russia's time in Kyrgyzstan. He says most of the forts were constructed on three levels: the ground level, with bunkerlike buildings inside the walls, and two subterranean levels, the second for living spaces and stores, the lowermost for stables. In his book, he talked about—"

"You read it?" Fisher asked, amazed.

"Searched it. It's in e-book format on the university's website. He said the Russians were fond of a tactical trick they used on the natives laying siege to the fort: a flanking cavalry attack launched from a secret passage—"

"*Secret passage,*" Fisher said. "One of my favorite phrases."

"How well I know. Anyway, if this fort is anything like the others the Russians built there, the tunnel would lead away from the underground stables and come up about a hundred feet away—probably tucked into a stand of trees nearby. The passage wouldn't be very big. Just tall and wide enough to accommodate a horse and rider on foot."

"I'll look around. After a hundred and thirty years, I'm not counting on it, though."

"Worth a look. Okay, here's the colonel."

Lambert came on the line. "Sam, DOORSTOP is under way. The lead Apaches should be hitting Bishkek right now."

"Any luck prying anyone loose to send my way?"

"Sorry, no. We're spread paper thin as it is. The Joint Chiefs are confident we can take Bishkek, but holding it for any length of time is another thing."

"Understood," said Fisher. "I'm about two hours out. I'll call when—if—we find our girl."

"Luck," Lambert said.

NINETY minutes later, Fisher jogged over a rise, then trotted to a stop, his boots crunching and sliding on the scree. A few hundred yards ahead lay the edge of the cliff. He took his time now, moving on flat feet from boulder to boulder until he was within fifty yards of the edge. He crouched down and did an NV/IR scan. There was nothing moving, nothing visible, just the cool blue background of the rocks interspersed with the pale yellows of the still-warm foliage. He walked up a few feet from the edge, then dropped flat and crawled forward.

Two hundred feet below him, sitting a mere thirty feet from the face of the escarpment, was Omurbai's prison. It sat in a shallow draw above the lake, bracketed on the east and west by pine forests. As it appeared on the satellite photo, the compound was laid out as a square, with the brick buildings lining the perimeter of the wall and a single fifty-foot guard tower rising from the center. Two olive drab trucks were parked in the compound, one beside the guard tower, the other backed up to one of the buildings. A third vehicle, this tracked like a tank and parked alongside the first truck, answered a question Fisher had been pondering: What had taken the shot at the Dakota?

It was an SA 13 Gopher mobile SAM system. It carried Strela-10 missiles with infrared guidance systems and a ten-kilometer range. The Dakota had never had a chance.

Beyond the compound, a mile to the south, he could see the shore of Issyk Kul, its surface glass-flat and black, a perfect mirror for the star-sprinkled sky above. A narrow dirt road paralleled the shore, disappearing to the east and west. Fisher tracked it until he saw what he wanted: a fork in the road that wound up the hillside and ended at the fort's front gate.

Fisher switched his goggles to IR, scanned the grounds, then zoomed in on the guard tower until it filled his vision.

There you are . . .

The watchtower was a square perch surrounded by a waist-high wooden railing and topped by a sloped room. Fisher could just make out a pencil-thin line of red and green resting on the railing. A human index finger. A few seconds later, the finger moved, pulling back out of sight.

He checked the rest of the compound. Each building's roof had a chimney, but only two—a side-by-side pair closest to the escarpment—showed heat signatures. No fires burning in the other buildings. What did that mean, if anything? It was a toss-up. The temperature hovered in the mid-thirties. Did the guards care if their prisoner—if in fact there was a prisoner here—was cold and miserable? All questions he couldn't answer until he got down there.

He scooted back from the edge, stood up, and started jogging.

LACKING both the time and the equipment to tackle the escarpment, Fisher had picked out an alternative route on the OPSAT's satellite map: a narrow, hairpin trail that zigzagged its way down the eastern ridge of the escarpment. He started down it, moving with exaggerated slowness; a misplaced foot could not only mean a lethal fall but falling rocks. Moreover, the moon was at his back, so he had to be careful not to expose himself much beyond the edge of rock, lest an alert guard spot him.

Two-thirds the way down the trail, he stopped and crouched down, wedging himself in a saddle between two rocks. He was almost even with the watchtower, some two hundred meters away. He slid the SC-20 from its back holster, switched to NV, and zoomed in on the tower.

There were two guards, one standing at the east railing, facing away, and one at the west railing, facing Fisher. Both were standing stock-still, save the occasional shifting of weight from foot to foot and the rubbing of cold hands.

Fisher took a pinch of rock dust from a crevice and tossed it into the air, gauging the wind. Almost dead calm. He zoomed out, then in again, testing aiming points and practicing shifts until he was comfortable with the motions. The risk here was not only missing a shot and letting one of the guards sound the alarm, but perched as he was in open space with his attention focused on hitting the targets, he could easily shift his weight an inch or two in the wrong direction, lose his balance, and tumble down the ridge.

That, Lambert was fond of saying, was the kind of bump you don't recover from.

In itself, taking out these two guards was risky, but Fisher had decided his rationale was solid. If in his rescue of Carmen Hayes he raised any alarm or she was found missing quicker than he'd anticipated, the last thing he needed was a pair of sharpshooters in the tower guarding their escape route. With these two men gone, he and Carmen would have a better chance of reaching the nearby forest.

He zoomed in on the first guard, the one facing him, until the man's head filled the scope, then zoomed out until he could see, at the far left edge of the scope, the other man's blurred form.

He placed the crosshairs on the bridge of the man's nose, squeezed the trigger, then shifted left and down and squeezed the trigger again. The first man was already down, having fallen below the railing. The second man had also crumpled, but only to his knees. Concerned that a head or upper torso shot would send the man over the railing, Fisher had placed his first bullet in the man's lower back, severing the spinal column.

Fisher adjusted his aim, laid the crosshairs on the nape of the man's neck, and squeezed the trigger. The man's head snapped forward, bouncing off the railing, then he toppled sideways out of sight.

Two down.

He sat still, tracking the SC-20 back and forth across the compound, watching for signs that his shots had attracted attention. Two minutes passed. All remained quiet.

He reholstered the SC-20 and kept going.

47

FISHER knelt on the carpet of pine needles and used his hands to brush clear a patch of ground until he reached dirt. He took out his Sykes and gently probed the earth. Nothing. He moved over six inches and probed again. Nothing. The third time was the charm. A foot to the left of his original spot, the knife's tip scraped on wood.

I'll be damned, he thought.

As intriguing as he'd found Grimsdottir's cavalry secret tunnel, Fisher hadn't put much stock in it but, having learned to never discount anything Grim said, he'd set aside twenty minutes to search for it.

After a mental coin toss he'd picked his way down the rest of the ridgeline, then headed east into the pine forest, where he started picking his way through the trees, alternately scanning the ground with the goggle's IR setting. He was playing a hunch, and it had panned out. Fifteen minutes after he'd started out, he rounded a tree and found himself standing at the edge of a faint blue line in the pine needles. As he'd suspected, if the trapdoor existed, its entrance would show up on IR as the cooler air of the tunnel beneath seeped through the opening.

He carefully cleared the pine needles from the edges of the hatch, which measured four feet wide and six feet tall—just barely enough room for a dismounted rider and a horse walking head-down. The tunnel's engineers had set the hatch into the downslope of a small rise in the earth because, Fisher assumed, the angle had made it easier to fashion the earthen ramp necessary to accommodate the horses.

He switched his goggles to EM and scanned the edges of the hatch for any electrical emissions. Finding none, he went to work with the Sykes, clearing the cracks of dirt. Once done, he probed with his fingers until he found what he was looking for. On the high side of the hatch, he found a rusted metal D-ring set into the wood. Fisher stood up, bent at the knees, grabbed the ring with both hands, and gave it a test pull. To his astonishment, it took almost no effort; the hatch cracked open an inch with only the sound of shifting dirt. Fisher felt a stream of cool air gush from the crack and wash over his face.

He pulled the hatch open a few more inches. As he did so, the lower edge of it seemed to swivel into the hillside. And then he realized what the Russian engineers had done. The hatch, which he now saw was made up of cross-braced ten-inch-thick wood, was mounted on counterbalanced pivot hinges. Lift the upper edge, and the lower edge swivels down, coming to rest on the earth, like the ramp of a marine landing craft.

Ingenious, he thought.

He checked his watch. The DOORSTOP forces would be fully engaged by now. Assuming Omurbai hadn't already done so, the attack would likely spur him to release Manas. Fisher prayed Carmen Hayes was as integral to Omurbai's plan as they'd all assumed. Otherwise, he was on a disastrous wild-goose chase.

He pulled the hatch open another two feet, then crept down the hillside, switched his goggles to NV, then dropped to his belly and crawled beneath the lower edge. Five feet ahead lay a jumbled mass of wooden stanchions and joists. The tunnel had collapsed. But how badly? He held up his hand and could feel cool air rushing from the tunnel. The tunnel was completely blocked, but whether he could pick his way through this maze, he didn't know. He thought it over and decided to try. He'd come this far, and if his gamble paid off, he'd find himself inside the fort, right beneath the bad guys' feet.

He crawled inside.

BY smell and by feel, Fisher picked his way through the labyrinth, stepping over, ducking under, and crawling through the maze of fallen beams. Giant cobwebs crisscrossed the tunnel like threadbare gauze sheets, sometimes so thick he'd had to hack his way through with his knife. Somewhere in the darkness he could hear water dripping, and twice he thought he heard muffled, distant voices.

After an hour, his OPSAT told him he'd covered nearly

eighty feet, which meant he was nearing or already under the fort's outer wall. He wriggled belly first through a gap between a cracked beam and the earthen wall and suddenly found himself crawling over solid stone. He looked around. Here the tunnel was wider and taller, roughly twelve feet by eight feet. Down the length of the tunnel, which ran fifty feet and ended at an upsloping ramp, were what Fisher could only describe as horse stalls dug into the earth and shored up by stone. He caught a whiff of something sour in the air, and it took him a moment to place it: manure, rotting hay. Though the leavings of the Russian cavalry horses had long ago merged with the earth, their scent remained, if only faintly.

He rose into a crouch and scanned the tunnel ahead. Nothing. If Grimsdottir's Prague professor was correct, there was another subterranean level above him: living quarters and storage.

He headed for the ramp. At its foot he dropped flat and crawled upward until his eyes were level with the dirt floor above. This level was much wider than the stable floors below, nearly forty feet from wall to wall and a hundred long, Fisher judged. Jutting from each dirt wall was what Fisher could only describe as a row of wooden shacks, each about ten feet wide, eight tall, and sharing a wall with its neighbor. Aligned down the center of the space were a dozen or more telephone booth–size structures, each raised off the ground a few feet by stilts and fronted by wooden steps. Latrines, Fisher guessed.

He counted twelve doors to each row of shacks. Grimsdottir had said the fort's complement was 160, so figuring eight men to a shack, that left at most six shacks for food and ammunition stores.

He'd seen pictures of similar living arrangements in books about World War I, where soldiers had lived for months on end like moles in trench cave systems. The phrase, *sardines in a can,* didn't do this place justice, Fisher thought.

Tarnished oil lamps, their glass flutes black with soot, hung at six-foot intervals from chains in the ceiling. One of the lamps was lit.

At the far end of the level, near the far ramp, he could see a lone figure standing beneath the dim glow of the lamp. Fisher switched to NV. Standing in the shadows across from the man, leaning against the door of the last shack, were two more soldiers. All three were talking and smoking, and all three were armed with AK-47s.

On a break, or guarding something? Fisher wondered. *Or someone?*

Fisher crept down the center of the space, using the latrines as cover, until he reached the last one, some twenty feet short of where the soldiers stood. He crept around the back side of the latrine; here the glow of the oil lamp faintly illuminated the wooden wall. Fisher got down on his belly and peeked around the corner. The guards hadn't moved. He backed up, crept around the other side until he could see the stone ramp, which he now saw was two-tiered, jogging to the left and to what he assumed was the ground level. He could see light filtering down from above and could hear voices muttering in Kyrgyz. Fisher closed his eyes, concentrating, and listened. Four to five men, he judged.

Suddenly there came the squelch of radio static. Then a commanding voice shushing the other voices, followed by a tinny voice over the radio. Fisher strained to hear, but was unable to catch any of the transmission. Whatever it was, it provoked an immediate response. A soldier came trotting down the ramp, barked an order at the three chatting guards, then ran back up. Fisher caught a bit of it: ". . . ready . . . bring her . . ."

One of the guards standing against the door turned, lifted the latch, leaned inside, and said something. A moment later a diminutive figure shuffled out and into the lamp's light. *Carmen.* The hair was shorter—they had shaved her head at some point, Fisher guessed—and the face more gaunt, but it was her. Fisher was momentarily taken aback—not so much by her appearance but by simply having found her. From the start Carmen Hayes's disappearance had been the cornerstone to not only Peter's journey but his own. Fisher felt as though he'd been chasing a ghost all this time, and now here it—she—was, in the flesh.

And then Carmen did something that stunned Fisher. She looked up at the soldier who had released her and said something in Kyrgyz. Though he didn't catch what she said, there was no mistaking the authoritative tone of her voice. Similarly, her gaze wasn't that of a broken prisoner but that of a superior. Or was it simply defiance?

The soldier nodded to her and replied in Kyrgyz, "Yes."

What is going on? Fisher wondered. But he already knew the most likely answer.

They'd broken her. They'd broken her and turned her mind.

The North Koreans and/or Omurbai and his people had had Carmen Hayes for at least four months. Four months was plenty of time to break anyone, to turn their mind to a cause not their own. Whether by torture or conditioning or drug therapy or a combination of all three, they'd not only secured Carmen's help but her allegiance as well.

There was part of Fisher's mind that didn't want to believe it, but he had little choice. There was too much at stake to risk it.

In his mind, he shifted Carmen from one column to another: *friend* to *foe*.

48

FISHER waited until Carmen and the three soldiers walked up the ramp, turned the corner, and disappeared from view, then darted around the latrine, paused at the hanging lamp to turn down the wick to its lowest setting, then trotted in a half crouch to the foot of the ramp and crab-walked up to where it jogged left. He peeked around the corner.

And froze.

Six feet away, standing at the top of the ramp under a stone arch was a pair of guards, their AK-47s held at ready low.

With exaggerated slowness, Fisher pulled his head back around the corner. He pulled out the flexicam and snaked it around the corner. Past the two soldiers Fisher could see an open room with a stone floor and a vaulted, crossbeam ceiling. A pair of fluorescent shop lights hung from the center beam, casting the room in cold, milky light.

One of the walls was open, a pair of barnlike doors, and backed into the opening was the rear third of a truck. Fisher zoomed in on it. It was a Ural-4320, an old Soviet army utility truck: heavy-duty, made for mountainous terrain, with six wheels, two in the front and four in the rear on a double axle. Affixed to the rear step bumper was a winch drum wrapped in a hooked steel cable.

The Ural's tailgate was down and the canvas flaps thrown back. Dangling over the tailgate from a wheeled hoist was a white plastic fertilizer tank, elliptical in shape and measuring roughly four feet wide and five feet long, with a pair of toboggan-like runners affixed to the bottom. Three hundred gallon capacity, Fisher estimated.

He counted nine soldiers, all armed, and Carmen, who stood off to the left, watching.

As he watched, two of the soldiers began maneuvering the hoist forward, guiding the tank deeper into the truck's bed. Inside the tank Fisher could see a brownish red fluid, thick like molasses, sloshing against the interior walls.

Manas. The Chytridiomycota fungus.

He pulled back.

Think, Sam, . . . think . . .

Nine soldiers, all armed. However slim the danger, he was reluctant to risk penetrating the tank. They knew so little about Chytridiomycota—how long it lived, its potency. Better to secure the tank intact. That left him few options. No grenades, no stray bullets. And even if he managed to take out all of these men without dying in the process, or penetrating the tank, or letting anyone get off a warning shout or shot, there were at least two dozen more of Omurbai's troops in the compound outside that would be on him within seconds.

Even the odds. Wait for a better chance.

From around the corner came a *thud*, the creaking of heavy truck springs.

Fisher checked the flexicam. The tank was fully inside the truck now, the tailgate up. The hoist was pushed off to the side and one of the soldiers—a major, Fisher guessed—barked an order. The soldiers began climbing into the truck until all eight were inside, four to each bench seat alongside the tank. The officer closed the tailgate and the canvas flaps, then he and Carmen walked through the barn doors.

The truck's engine started, and a plume of blue gray exhaust burst from the muffler pipe.

Fisher sprinted forward, ducked down, wriggled beneath the truck's bumper, looked around. He wrapped his left arm over the bed's crossbeam support, his right over the winch drum's vertical post, then pulled himself off the ground and wedged his feet against the interior wheel fender.

With a growl, the engine revved, and the truck started moving.

After a brief stop at the gate, the truck turned left down the dirt road and descended toward the lakeshore, where it turned right, or west. Through the truck's step bumper Fisher watched the fort fade into the darkness.

THEY drove for fifteen minutes on the relatively flat shore road, then suddenly the truck ground to a stop, the brakes squealing softly. Under the wheel well fender, Fisher could just make out the gray granite wall of the escarpment, two hundred yards away.

Faintly, over the rumble of the engine, Fisher heard Carmen's higher-pitched voice, followed by that of what Fisher assumed was the major's. An argument. The exchange lasted thirty seconds or so, then the gears engaged, and the truck started moving again.

The truck rolled forward about a hundred yards, then turned right toward the escarpment. Beneath him, Fisher watched the dirt road turn into rutted parallel tracks in the meadow grass. After another hundred feet, he heard the gears change and the engine drop in pitch as the truck started up an incline. A few moments later, Fisher saw the granite wall roll past the side of the truck. Entering a canyon.

For the next twenty minutes the truck continued winding higher and deeper into the mountains, bumping and tipping over an increasingly undulating and rocky road. Finally they slowed and then ground to a stop, then started backing down an incline. Everything went dark, and Fisher caught a whiff of dank water, mold, wet soil.

A cave.

The truck rolled for what Fisher guessed was another hundred feet, then stopped.

Now Fisher heard something else: the gurgling rush of water.

A river. An underground river.

He loosened his grip slightly and let himself drop toward the ground until he could see under the bumper. The truck's headlights were still on, casting a white glare along the cave walls, but still it was too dim to see much. He flipped his goggles to NV.

The cavern was small, barely bigger than the average home's two-car garage. The ceiling dripped with stalactites and pale yellow mineral deposits that had formed into narrow hourglass-shaped columns. Down the gravel slope behind the bumper Fisher could see rushing water, black and roiling in the NV's washed-out color field. The river, moving from left to right, was about ten feet wide.

This was it, Fisher knew: endgame. Carmen Hayes would have done her job well. Wherever this subterranean river went, he had to assume it would eventually intersect with the Caspian Basin oil fields—and perhaps beyond even those. No more time. No time for stealth, no time to plan. If Manas got out . . .

He felt his mind go blank for a half second, felt it switch over to that primitive part that was fight-or-flight, do-or-die. *Don't think. Move. Whatever it costs, stop them here.*

From the driver and passenger sides of the truck he heard the cab doors open, then slam shut. Footsteps crunched on gravel.

Fisher lowered himself to the ground and rolled out.

— *49* —

HE came up in a crouch, plucked a pair of flashbang grenades from his web harness, pulled the pins, and tossed them through the truck's canvas flaps. Also known as M84s, flashbangs contained no shrapnel, but upon explosion gave off a million-candela flash of white light and overlapping 180-decibel crashes.

Even as the grenades *thunked* off the steel bed inside, Fisher drew the SC-20 from its back holster, crab-stepped left, and brought the barrel up.

The major, evidently having heard the thump of the grenades and recognizing the sound for what it was, had already turned and was sprinting back to the cab. The flashbangs detonated. A wave of blinding light and sound blasted out the back of the canvas flaps.

Fisher fired. The bullet caught the major high on the right shoulder blade, shoving him forward. Fisher adjusted his aim, curled his finger on the trigger—

"Bastard!"

To his right, out of the corner of his eye, he saw something rushing toward him: slight figure, pale oval face, short black hair. Fisher started to turn, but too late. Carmen Hayes, her face drawn back into a rictus, arms windmilling, and hands clutched into talons, dove onto his back, screaming and scratching and biting.

Fisher stumbled sideways. He dropped his right shoulder, cocked his elbow, and slammed it into the center of Carmen's face. Her nose shattered with a wet crunch. Blood gushed over her mouth and chin, but still she held on, fingernails clawing at his face. Fisher straightened up and ran backward, slamming her into the cave wall. Carmen grunted, held on.

The truck's engine roared to life.

Now shouting in Kyrgyz came from inside the truck.

Fisher thought absently, *Flashbangs wearing off*.

Again he slammed Carmen against the wall, then again, then once more. She went limp and slid off his back. He spun, thumbed the SC-20's selector to COTTONBALL. Afraid that with Carmen's shattered nose a full dose would jeopardize her, he punched the ball into the ground beside her waist, then thumbed the selector back to the 2-SHOT, and turned to the truck. The white backup lights were on.

The truck started moving, accelerating down the hill toward the river.

The truck's tailgate banged open, the canvas flaps flew back, followed by two, then three, then four soldiers leaping to the ground. Fisher took them as they came out and before they could get their guns up, double-tapping each one with a pair of bullets: torso . . . head . . . torso . . . head . . . torso . . . head. One by one they went down and rolled down the hill and into the water.

In his peripheral vision Fisher saw a hand appear out of the canvas flap and toss something toward him—baseball-size, oval-shaped. Fragmentation grenade. It landed with a *thud* in the gravel a few feet to his front and right. Shifting the SC-20 to his left hand and plucking a CS gas grenade from his harness with his right, he charged toward the grenade—a Russian RDG-5, he now saw—kicked it into the water, and side-armed the CS through the flaps.

Fwoomp!

The RDG-5 exploded. A geyser erupted from the river. A second later the CS grenade went off, and white gas gushed from the truck's canvas folds. Inside, the soldiers began coughing and shouting.

Fisher kept running toward the back of the truck. He adjusted his aim and fired a burst into the rear tire, shifted aim, fired another burst into the next tire forward. With a *whoosh-hiss*, the tires exploded. The truck kept rolling, half skidding toward the right, yawing on its deflated tires.

Fisher leapt onto the step bumper, threw the flap back. The remaining four soldiers were sprawled around the inside of the bed, retching. One of them saw Fisher, shouted something in Kyrgyz, and brought his AK up. Fisher shot him in the throat, then shifted, fired again, killing the second, then again.

The truck jolted to a stop. Fisher fired, but he was already falling backward, so the shot went high and right, missing the last man. Fisher landed flat on his back on the gravel, head underwater. He jerked upright and shook his head to clear it. As his vision returned, he saw a broad, white oval shape sliding toward him, thought, *Tank*, and rolled left as it screeched off the tailgate and crashed onto the ground. It bounced once on its runners, tipped sideways, then righted itself and started sliding into the water.

The truck's white backing lights went off. The truck ground up the hill a few feet, stopped. The backing lights came back on, and it rolled back down the slope. The bumper slammed into the tank, shoving the forward third of it into the water, the brownish fluid inside sloshing wildly. The truck's wheels started spinning, the shredded right rear tires churning up mud and gravel.

In the truck bed, the last soldier stumbled onto the tailgate. He raised his AK across his chest, glanced at Fisher, then turned his attention to the tank. He jerked the rifle to his shoulder, finger curling on the trigger.

Fisher lifted the SC-20 and snapped off three quick shots. One went wide; the second drilled into the man's ribs, the third into his forehead just above his eye. The man stumbled sideways and slumped back into the truck.

He rose to his knees and charged toward the cab, where he could see the major pounding the wheel, his teeth bared as he shouted what Fisher assumed were curses. Fisher glanced over his shoulder. The truck's wheels were spitting a rooster tail of muddy water and gravel that peppered the cavern's ceiling like hail. The tank was almost halfway into the water now, partially floating, rocking in the current.

Fisher took three bounding steps and skidded to a stop alongside the cab door. The major saw him in the corner of

his eye. He stopped moving. He glanced at Fisher, hesitated, then turned back to the wheel and gunned the engine. Fisher fired a two-round burst, both bullets slamming
into the man's ear. He toppled sideways and disappeared
from view.

Fisher sprinted forward, jerked the door open, shoved
the major's body across the seat onto the passenger-side
floorboards, and looked around. *Where is it, where is it?* He
gripped the parking brake handle, jerked it up into the
locked position. He turned off the ignition and climbed
down.

"Stop!" a female voice said.

Fisher froze. He swiveled his head right. Standing at the
rear of the truck, AK-47 raised and leveled with Fisher's
chest, was Carmen Hayes.

Not enough Cottonball, Fisher thought. "Carmen—"

"Shut up! Do you know what you've done? Do you
know?"

Her eyes glinted wildly in the dim light, but it was a vac-
uous intensity. Fisher had seen it before: the dead stare of a
conditioned prisoner. Conditioned or not, he had no doubt
she'd shoot him dead.

He lowered the SC-20 to his waist, the barrel slightly off
her center, and raised his left hand in surrender.

"Carmen, I found your message," Fisher said calmly.

She took a lurching step toward him. "Shut up! What?
What message?"

"From your shoe. The insole. The message to your parents. They've been looking for you."

Carmen stared at him for a long ten seconds. "No. I
don't know what—"

She started backing up, past the truck's bumper. Her right heel bumped into the tank, which was resting, half on the gravel, half in the water. She sidestepped to the left half a foot and started backing down the side of the tank.

"Carmen, don't—"

"I said, *shut up!*" she screeched.

One shove, Fisher thought. *One shove, and it goes in the river.*

"This is the only way," Carmen said. She jerked her chin toward the tank. "This is the only way to stop it."

I don't want to shoot you, Fisher thought. *Please don't make me—*

Suddenly she spun, backed up a step, and swung the AK toward the tank.

Fisher fired.

EPILOGUE

FISHER rolled to a stop beside the call box affixed to the brick pillar and pressed the call button. Through the twelve-foot-tall black wrought-iron gate, the gravel driveway took a sharp right into a tunnel of dogwood trees. Atop the pillar a camera swiveled around, the lens ring dilating to zoom in on his face.

A moment later a voice answered, "Yes?"

"I'm here to see Marsha Stanton," Fisher replied.

"What time is your appointment?"

"Mr. Flowers told me to drop by. I think I'm seven minutes early, though."

As had been his first, this was the right answer.

"Pull in."

The gates, set on hydraulic actuators, parted and swung open. Fisher pulled through and started down the drive. He got only twenty feet before he had to stop again, this time by a chain strung across the road between two barrel-size concrete pillars. A pair of men in civilian clothes walked up to his car, one at the driver's window, one at the passenger's. Strapped across each man's belly was what looked like a oversize fanny pack; it was in fact a fast pack, designed to hold some lethal variety of compact submachine gun.

"ID, please," the man at the driver's window said.

Fisher produced his general NSA identification card and handed it over. The man studied it for a moment, studied Fisher's face, then stepped back and muttered something in his lapel microphone. Whatever answer he got through the flesh-colored earpiece caused him to nod and hand the ID back to Fisher.

"Just stay on this road. It'll take you to the parking lot. You'll be met."

Fisher followed the directions, taking the tree-lined road another two hundred yards before emerging into an asphalt parking lot surrounded by azalea bushes thick with bright orange and red blooms. To his right stood a four-story antebellum plantation house with a wraparound porch. A man in a white lab coat stood on the porch; he raised a hand to Fisher. Fisher waved back.

AS he had on every other visit, Fisher found her on the rear lawn sitting in an Adirondack chair beneath a weeping willow. Beside her, a trio of ducks paddled across a pond, beaks poking water bugs on the surface. He walked across the carefully manicured grass and stopped beside her chair.

"Morning."

Daydreaming, she hadn't heard him come up. She turned her head and shielded her eyes against the sun. "Morning, Sam," replied Carmen Hayes. She gestured at the table before her, on which sat a chessboard; the black-and-white pieces were in various states of play on the board. "Been waiting for you."

"How's the hip?" he asked.

She smiled at him. "Fine. Better every day. You don't have to ask every time you come, you know."

Fisher shrugged, and smiled back. "The least I could do."

AS soon as he'd pulled the trigger on her in the cave, he'd immediately said a silent thanks to the thousands of hours he'd spent on firing ranges and combat courses. The SC-20's bullet had gone precisely where he'd wanted it to go: into Carmen's left hip, missing her pelvic girdle by a half inch. The impact had spun her around, causing her to lose her balance and stumble backward into the water. The AK-47's muzzle, which had only a second before been aimed at the fertilizer tank, twisted upward, flashing as she fell, bullets peppering the cave's ceiling.

Fisher had rushed forward, kicked the AK away, then dragged her up the incline, where he rolled her onto her belly and flex-cuffed her hands behind her back. Ignoring her screams, he dug a morphine syrette from his first aid pouch and jammed the needle into her thigh. After twenty seconds her moans faded to whimpering.

After a quick check to make sure all of Omurbai's men were in fact dead, he turned his attention to the tank, unreeling the Ural's winch cable and hooking it to the tank's runners. Next he climbed into the cab and slowly, carefully, dragged the tank from the river and up the incline, stopped, and set the winch brake.

He then jogged outside and made a quick OPSAT call to Grimsdottir and Lambert, who immediately contacted the Joint Chiefs, who, in turn, hearing that Fisher's goose chase had yielded results, detached a Chinook transport helicopter and a pair of Apache attack helos from the fight in Bishkek. Ninety minutes later, Fisher was joined by a trio of Ranger fire teams, who secured the tank and set up a defensive perimeter around the cave's entrance.

His job done, Fisher walked back into the cave and sat down with Carmen.

TWO hours after that, even as the tank itself was being secured for transport, a sample of the Manas fungus inside was already in the air and on its way back to Andrews Air Force Base, where it was handed over to Dr. Russo and her team from Lawrence Livermore National Laboratory's CMLS Directorate, who rushed it back to her laboratory for study.

As the chairman of the Joint Chiefs had predicted, the battle for Bishkek was a short one, lasting just under six hours. Even as the ousted former president and his cabinet were escorted back to the main government building, Omurbai and his core followers tried to escape the city and slip into the mountains to the north, but a platoon of Eighty-second Airborne soldiers was already ahead of him, orbiting in Chinooks above the roads leaving the city. Most of the soldiers accompanying Omurbai surrendered without a fight, but Omurbai and a handful of his most fanatical henchmen tried to fight their way through the roadblock. Outnumbered and outmaneuvered though they were, the Kyrgyz fought to the death until only Omurbai remained. As the U.S. soldiers approached, Omurbai used the last bullet in his AK-47 to kill himself.

SIX hours after the battle ended, the Romanian *Serviciul de Informații Externe*, which had helped spirit Fisher from North Korea, did the CIA one more favor, delivering to Kim Jong-il's foreign minister a letter from the president of the United States, in both English and North Korean. The letter's contents, while fully couched in the language of diplomatic protocol, was blunt in its message:

> *We're in possession of Omurbai's Chytridiomycota fungus; we've engineered a neutralizer; we know you helped Omurbai overthrow the government in Kyrgyzstan; we know you helped develop the fungus; we know you intended to use the fungus to destroy the Caspian Basin oil reserves.*
> *We're watching you, and if you don't behave, we're going to tell the whole world and then jerk your country out from under you.*

The response from the foreign minister was prompt and promising, if not agreeable:

*The government of North Korea denies any official involve-
ment in the events in Kyrgyzstan but is investigating certain rogue elements in its intelligence services who may have
been in unauthorized contact with Bolot Omurbai.*

The president's reference to the Chytridiomycota neutralizer, while not quite a lie, was in fact anticipatory. Four
days after Shirley Russo and her team began its reverse en-
gineering of Omurbai's Manas fungus, they created and began manufacturing in mass quantities an easily dispersible
agent that killed Chytridiomycota on contact.

FISHER took the chair opposite Carmen and studied the
board. He frowned and muttered, "You moved these."

She laughed. "No, I didn't. I'm just winning."

"Huh."

Fisher was glad to see her smile, something she'd been
doing more of in the month since she'd arrived at the CIA
safe house/private hospital. Designed to treat both the
physical and mental wounds suffered by case officers and
covert operatives in the field, the hospital had similarly
worked its magic on Carmen.

In the four months she was held by the North Koreans,
she'd been systematically broken down with both drug
therapy and stress conditioning. She still had frequent
nightmares, Fisher was told, but those were fading, and the
doctors expected her to make a full recovery. Carmen's parents had flown in from Houston a week after she was admitted and rented a house in Richmond so they could easily
make the daily drive to visit her.

Carmen's memories of her kidnapping and subsequent captivity were fuzzy, as was her recollection of what happened in the cave. To Fisher's chagrin, however, she vividly remembered him shooting her and relentlessly teased him about it.

THEY played chess for another hour until Fisher admitted defeat and laid down his king.

"You look mad," Carmen said.

"Don't like losing."

"Something tells me you don't lose very often. You're not going to shoot me, are you?"

Fisher sighed wearily.

"Sorry," Carmen replied. "Couldn't resist. Last time, I promise." Her smile faded, and she leaned forward and placed her hands over his. "I don't think I ever thanked you."

"For shooting you?" Fisher replied. "Happy to oblige."

"For saving me. For stopping me. For bringing me back home. Thank you, Sam."

Fisher smiled. "Happy to oblige."

They chatted for a few minutes more, then Fisher stood up. "Sorry, I have a plane to catch."

"Business?" Carmen asked.

"Not really."

"Where to?"

"Toronto."

The truth was, Fisher wasn't looking forward to the trip, but he owed Calvin Stewart as much. Of course, he wouldn't be able to tell the man's widow anything of value,

DON'T MISS
TOM CLANCY'S
NEW SERIES
END WAR
BASED ON THE
NEW VIDEO GAME.

COMING IN 2008

save the fact her husband was a genuine hero. What he could do, however, with the help of the CIA, was hand her a bank passbook that she would find contained enough money to see her safely through her golden years and the Stewart children through college.

"Travel safe, then."

"And you," Fisher replied. "They tell you when you can go home yet?"

"No. But when you come back, if I'm not here, you know where to find me."

"I do. Good-bye, Carmen." Fisher turned and started to walk away, then stopped and looked back. "Keep practicing. I'll want a rematch."

Carmen laughed. "Deal."

Tom Clancy's

SPLINTER CELL®

CREATED BY #1 *NEW YORK TIMES*
BESTSELLING AUTHOR TOM CLANCY,
WRITTEN BY DAVID MICHAELS

penguin.com
AD-01477 11